Christmas on My Mind

More Christmas romance from Janet Dailey

Long, Tall Christmas
Christmas in Cowboy Country
Merry Christmas, Cowboy
A Cowboy Under My Christmas Tree
Mistletoe and Molly
To Santa with Love
Let's Be Jolly
Maybe This Christmas
Happy Holidays
Scrooge Wore Spurs
Eve's Christmas
Searching for Santa
Santa in Montana

JANET DAILEY

Christmas on My Mind

KENSINGTON BOOKS
http://www.kensingtonbooks.com

KENSINGTON BOOKS are published by

Kensington Publishing Corp.
119 West 40th Street
New York, NY 10018

All Kensington titles, imprints, and distributed lines are available at special quantity discounts for bulk purchases for sales promotion, premiums, fund-raising, educational, or institutional use.

Special book excerpts or customized printings can also be created to fit specific needs. For details, write or phone the office of the Kensington Special Sales Manager: Attn. Special Sales Department. Kensington Publishing Corp, 119 West 40th Street, New York, NY 10018. Phone: 1-800-221-2647.

Kensington and the K logo Reg. U.S. Pat. & TM Off.

Library of Congress Card Catalog Number: 2015958948

ISBN-13: 978-1-4967-0197-8
ISBN-10: 1-4967-0197-6
First Kensington Hardcover Edition: June 2016

10 9 8 7 6 5 4 3 2 1

Printed in the United States of America

Christmas on My Mind

Chapter One

Branding Iron, Texas
Friday, November 26

Jessica Ramsey mouthed an unladylike curse as her aging Pontiac coughed, sputtered and stopped dead on the deserted two-lane road. Hoping for luck, she cranked the starter—again, then again. Nothing happened.

What now? She couldn't be out of gas. The gauge hadn't worked in months, but she'd filled up two hours ago in Amarillo. Maybe it was the fuel pump. Or worse, something like a blown head gasket, whatever that was.

She cranked the starter one last time. The engine didn't even try to turn over. Fighting tears, she slumped over the steering wheel. She'd trusted the old car to make it all the way from Kansas City to Branding Iron, Texas. It had come close, but not close enough. The green highway sign she'd just passed told her she had fourteen miles to go. It was too far to walk with her suitcase—let alone all her possessions stuffed in the trunk—and she had more sense than to hitchhike. She was stranded.

Glancing in the rearview mirror, she saw a battered-looking red pickup approaching. It was coming fast; and her stalled car, she realized with a lurch of panic, was right in its path. She punched the hazard light, praying it would work. But the truck didn't even slow down. The horn blared. Tires squealed as the pickup swung around her, missing the rear bumper by inches. Jess glimpsed two male teenagers in the front seat. Both of them gave her the finger before the truck roared on down the road. So much for chivalry.

Jess released the brake, shifted into neutral and wrenched the steering wheel hard to the right. She had to get the Pontiac off the road before another vehicle came along and crashed right into her. Since the car wouldn't start, her only option was to push it.

After glancing up and down the road, she opened the door, climbed out and walked back to the rear of the car. The sky was overcast. Empty fields of yellow-brown stubble spread on both sides of the road. The flat horizon was broken only by a distant barn and a silo. Jess was a city girl. It was as if she'd set foot on some alien planet, peopled only by distant farms and rude boys in pickups.

The cold November breeze whipped tendrils of her russet hair around her face. She clutched her light denim jacket around her ribs. The sooner she got the car off the road, the sooner she could get back inside. Without the engine to run the heater, the car wouldn't stay warm long, but at least she'd be out of the wind.

Bracing her arms above the rear bumper, she planted her sneaker-clad feet on the asphalt. At five-three and 119 pounds, Jess was no Wonder Woman. Determination—or more likely, desperation—would have to make up for her lack of muscle power.

The road's narrow, graveled shoulder sloped down to a grassy barrow pit. If she could push as much as one front wheel onto the incline, the car's momentum should do the rest. How hard could it be?

Steeling her resolve, she threw her whole weight against

the car. Her jaw clenched. Her muscles strained. Nothing moved.

Spent for the moment, she straightened to catch her breath. Maybe she was doing this wrong. It might work better to brace her back against the car and push with her legs. At least it was worth a try.

Jess turned around. Only then did she see the big, tan SUV that had pulled up a dozen yards behind her, the lights atop its cab flashing red and blue.

And only then did she see the big, tan person climbing out of it. He strode toward her, a take-charge expression on his face. Wearing a khaki uniform topped by a leather jacket with a sheepskin collar, along with a pistol holstered at one lean hip, he looked capable of lifting her car with one hand. He was also flat-out gorgeous, with dark brown hair, a square-jawed face and stern coppery eyes.

But she wasn't looking for gorgeous here, Jess reminded herself. In her roller-coaster life, the hot men she'd known had turned out to be nothing but bad news. Besides, there was no way a male as spectacular as this long, tall lawman wouldn't have some woman's brand on him.

"Having trouble, Miss?" His drawl was pure Texas honey.

Jess willed herself not to sound like a helpless whiner. "My car broke down. I was about to push it off the road, so nobody would hit it."

A faint smile deepened the dimple in his left cheek. "Could you use some help, or should I just leave you to it?"

"As long as you're here, I guess you might as well give me a hand." Jess spoke through chattering teeth.

"Here." He stripped off his leather jacket and laid it around her shoulders. It was toasty warm. Man warm. Now that he'd taken it off, she could see the badge on his khaki shirt and the name tag below it.

Sheriff Ben Marsden.

"What seems to be the trouble with the car?" he asked.

"I don't know. It just stopped dead, and now it won't start. It can't be out of gas. I filled the tank a couple of hours ago."

"Well, let's get it off the road. Then I'll take a quick look under the hood. Maybe it'll be an easy fix."

Ben Marsden was definitely a breed apart from the brusque city cops Jess had encountered. Following his directions, she climbed back into the driver's seat to steer while he pushed. The car rolled forward as if Superman were behind that bumper. No surprise there.

"That's far enough." She heard his voice through the open window. "Now pull the handbrake and pop the hood release."

By the time Jess climbed out of the car he had the hood up and was peering into the Pontiac's dim interior with the aid of a pocket flashlight. After a minute or two, he closed the hood and switched off the light. "I can't see anything wrong," he said. "But it smells like you might have a fuel leak—maybe a broken line. Nothing I can do here, but it shouldn't be too expensive to fix. There's a good, honest mechanic in town. Want me to call him for a tow?"

Jess thought a moment, then reluctantly nodded. She'd promised herself she wouldn't break into the fifty thousand dollars she'd inherited from her adoptive father— money she'd set aside for a new start. But the cash she'd saved from her waitressing job was almost gone, and she had to have a working car. For now, she'd put the tow and repair on her credit card and hope for the best.

The sheriff made a quick call on his cell phone, then turned back to her. "Silas is busy right now, but he says he can pick up the car in a couple of hours."

Jess suppressed a sigh. "I suppose I can wait here that long."

He gave her a scowl. "That's not a good idea. Get what you need out of the car and leave the keys under the floor mat. I'll drive you into town. At least we can find you a warm place to wait."

"Thanks." Jess retrieved her purse from the front seat and her suitcase from the trunk. All the way from Kansas City, she'd imagined driving into Branding Iron and carrying out her plan—a plan so audacious that, on the way here, she'd almost lost heart and turned back.

Now she was here. But getting around would have to wait until her car was fixed. She'd need a place to stay. But even a small town like this one should have a cheap motel or some sort of rooming house where she could crash until she found a job and an apartment—or left town, if things didn't turn out as she'd hoped.

Meanwhile it would be smart to get her hormones under control and stop ogling the hot Texas lawman who'd come to her rescue. The man was off limits—for more reasons than she even wanted to think about—starting with *hot* and *lawman*.

He opened the door of his SUV and took her suitcase while she climbed in and fastened her seat belt. The custom dashboard, complete with a police radio, a GPS, a dash cam and a computer, was impressive. The last time Jess had ridden in a police vehicle, she'd been handcuffed in the backseat. But those days were long behind her. After a few rough patches, she was starting a new life—and part of that new life, she hoped, was waiting right here in Branding Iron.

The engine purred as he pulled back onto the highway. "I don't suppose I should worry about anybody stealing my car," she said.

He chuckled, his dimple deepening. "No, I don't suppose you should."

"I'm not hearing much on your radio. Is it always this quiet around here?"

"Pretty much. We get an occasional drug bust, a few bar fights, some domestics and a runaway kid now and again. That's about it. It's a pretty easy place to be sheriff—most of the time." He glanced at her. His eyes reminded her of homemade root beer, just poured, with the bubbles still sparkling. "I don't believe I caught your name," he said.

"It's Jessica. Jessica Ramsey. But everybody calls me Jess."

"Well, welcome to Branding Iron, Texas, Miss Jess Ramsey. Where do you hail from?"

Here, Jess thought. But was she ready to tell him that? "I drove here from Kansas City," she said. "I was hoping my old beater would make it all the way, but no such luck."

"Were you planning a stopover in town, or just passing through when your car decided to take a vacation?"

Jess gazed out the window a moment. They were passing more fields, some dotted with black Angus cattle and framed by barbed-wire fences. Here and there, a windmill towered above the landscape, its vanes turning in the breeze. The clouds in the vast Texas sky were darkening.

"This isn't just a stopover," she said. "Branding Iron is where I was headed."

"Here?" His laugh was incredulous. "Nobody comes to Branding Iron—unless, maybe, they've got family here."

"Maybe that's what I have." Given that perfect lead-in, Jess decided to tell him her story—at least the important part. As sheriff, he probably knew the townspeople as well as anybody. Maybe he could help her.

"I was born right here in Branding Iron, at the old clinic," she said. "My mother put me up for adoption—I don't know her circumstances, but I'm guessing she was unmarried and in trouble. My adoptive parents were far from perfect. They divorced when I was nine. He disappeared, and she died when I was sixteen. It's been a long, rough road, but a few months ago I decided it was time for a new start." Jess took a breath before getting to the bottom line. "The first thing I wanted to do was find my birth mother."

The sheriff took his time, as if weighing what he'd heard. "That's quite a story," he said. "Did you find her?"

"I think so. I haven't met her, but I'm hoping that's about to change. The private investigator I hired found my mother's name and her address. She's still here in Branding Iron."

"Have you contacted her?" he asked. "Does she know you're coming?"

Jess's hands tightened on her beat-up leather purse. "I was afraid she wouldn't want to see me. That's why I decided to just show up and surprise her."

"Is that wise?"

"Maybe not. But that way, if she slams the door in my face, at least I'll get a look at her. It's important. She's the only real family I've got."

"What if she's married, with children? Maybe she won't want them to know about you."

"I've thought of that," Jess said. "And I wouldn't want to cause her any trouble. But she's still using her maiden name. That could mean she's single or divorced." She turned toward him, straining against the seat belt. "I'm only telling you this because you might know her. If you do, maybe you can tell me what her situation is and how to approach her—or even arrange a meeting if you think that would be best."

Saying nothing, he guided the SUV around a road-killed rabbit. Two ravens feeding on the carcass flapped skyward against the darkening clouds.

He was quiet for what seemed like a long time. Maybe

he suspected Jess of being some kind of con artist, out to win the poor woman over and fleece her of her savings. "I can't promise," he said. "But I'll try to do what's best for both of you. What's your mother's name?"

"Francine. Francine McFadden."

The SUV lurched slightly, crunching gravel on the shoulder of the road before he regained control of the steering wheel. Something about the name had clearly startled him.

"Do you know her?" Jess asked. "You do, don't you?"

"Yup."

"Then you must know where she lives. Can you at least drive me by her house?"

"No need for that. I know for a fact she isn't there."

"Well, where is she?" Jess demanded. "Is she out of town?"

"Nope." He shot her a narrow-eyed glance. "Francine is doing time in the county jail."

Chapter Two

Ben cast a sidelong glance at his intriguing passenger. Jessica Ramsey was huddled into his leather jacket, gazing out the windshield as she wrestled with what he'd just told her. She looked like a woman who'd reached the end of her rope—road-weary, cold and in a mild state of shock. Even so, she was a pretty thing—delicate features, with a sprinkle of cinnamon-hued freckles, framed by a mop of amber curls that fell to her shoulders. Her faded black tee, denim jacket and threadbare jeans looked good on her. But between her clothes and the car she was driving, he'd bet the lady was hard up for cash.

If she was looking for her birth mother to help her out, she was in for a big letdown.

Following protocol, he'd checked her car's license number when he pulled up behind her. The car was registered to Jessica Ramsey. No outstanding warrants, so she didn't appear to be running from the law. But the revelation that she was Francine's daughter had come as a shock. He'd known Francine a long time, but it had never occurred to him that she was a mother.

The lady didn't look much like Francine—except for her

striking violet blue eyes. Eyes like that were almost as good as a DNA test. Ben had dealt with his share of con artists claiming to be who they weren't. But he'd bet next Friday's paycheck she really was Francine's daughter.

Not that she'd have much to gain by it.

"Tell me about my mother, sheriff," she said. "Why's she in jail?"

"Drunk and disorderly. She punched a cowboy in the local bar, claimed he was feeling her up. The punch started a brawl in the place. And you can call me Ben, by the way."

"Does she have a lawyer?"

"No need. She pled guilty in exchange for dropping the assault and battery charge. The judge gave her three weeks plus six months' probation, with mandatory attendance at AA meetings. She's got about a week left of her sentence."

"I see."

"Sorry. I know this isn't what you were expecting," he said. "Francine's a good-hearted woman, the sort who'd give her last crust of bread to a stray dog. She just can't seem to stay out of trouble. She's been in and out of jail for as long as I've been sheriff. I'm guessing that, for her, being locked up might be warmer and more secure than being on the outside alone."

Jess gazed silently out the window. As he drove, Ben gave her a furtive side-glance. Maybe she was thinking that her long drive had been for nothing. Maybe she was about to change her mind, turn around and hightail it back to Kansas City as soon as her car was fixed. Knowing what she was about to face, he wouldn't blame her if she did.

They were nearing the outskirts of town when she finally spoke. "I want to see my mother. Will you take me to her?"

"Now?"

"Is there a better time?"

"I guess not, if that's what you want," Ben said. "There's no telling how Francine will take this. I'd be willing to talk to her first and tell her you've come."

"No. I'll tell her myself." She spoke with calm determination. "This won't be like I'd planned. But at least I've found her. It'll have to do."

The steel in her voice surprised Ben. When he'd first seen her trying to push her car, she'd appeared as fragile as a lost kitten. But now something told him Jess Ramsey was tougher than she looked.

The clouds had released a cold, misting rain, just enough to turn the dust on the sheriff's SUV to muddy streaks before it stopped. Gazing through the dirt-speckled windshield, Jess watched Branding Iron come into view. Since she'd warned herself not to expect much, she wasn't disappointed. Surrounded by smaller farms and modest ranches, it was right out of *Mayberry R.F.D.*, just large enough for the basic needs of the scattered community. There was a hardware and feed store with a Christmas tree lot on the outskirts of town, and a newer strip mall with what looked like a Super Shop Mart, the parking lot crowded with Black Friday bargain hunters. "That store's the biggest thing in the county," the sheriff said. "Until this past summer, when the company expanded it, it was just groceries. Now it's got clothes, housewares, electronics, you name it. It's brought in a lot of business—for the rest of the town as well. Hank's Hardware, where you saw the Christmas trees, used to be just a feed store. It's doubled in size in the past year."

He turned onto an old-fashioned main street where Christmas lights were being strung between the light poles. Branching off it were streets with schools, a bank, a couple of churches, and a low red-brick building that housed the library, the city and county offices and—her pulse quickened as she saw the sign outside—the jail.

"Isn't that where my mother is?" she asked as Ben Marsden drove past the place without even slowing down.

"It is. But I need to run a quick errand first. I promised Francine I'd stop by and feed her cat.

"Feed her cat?" She stared at him. "But you're the sheriff! She's in your jail!"

"I know. But her place isn't far, and Francine's right fond of that old cat. Somebody's got to look after him while she's doing her time."

"I can't believe this!" she said.

He chuckled. "Well, you're not in Kansas City anymore, Jess. As I said before, welcome to Branding Iron."

He drove to the end of the street and made a right turn onto a graveled lane. At the end of it was what looked like a run-down campground. As they drove in through the open gate, Jess could see rows of concrete pads with hookups for camp trailers. Most were empty, the spaces between overgrown with tall, dry weeds. The half-dozen scattered trailers that remained were small and dilapidated. Some showed signs of being lived-in. Most did not.

"My mother lives here?" Jess asked, dismayed.

"Right here." Ben pulled up to the nearest trailer, this one so small it looked as if a Volkswagen Beetle could pull it. Its aluminum sides were dented, and the screen door had a hole in it, low down, where someone might have kicked it in.

"You wanted me to see this, didn't you?" Jess said.

"Maybe you should. Come on." He opened the door of the SUV and climbed out. Jess opened her door and swung to the ground without waiting for him to come around and help her. Catching up with him at the trailer, she saw that he'd taken a set of keys out of his pocket and was unlocking the door.

"She gave you her keys?"

"She wanted me to check the place. Besides, I need to get the cat food. Take a look if you want." He stepped to one side, giving Jess a view through the door. Her heart sank but she forced herself to step inside.

The interior of the trailer wasn't dirty or smelly. But how could anyone live in such a cramped and cluttered space? One end was taken up by the bed, which was covered by a ragged quilt. The storage shelf below the ceiling was stuffed with clothes. The tiny bathroom had the toilet inside the shower. The only sink was in the kitchen, which had a microwave, a camper-sized fridge under the counter, and a couple of open shelves, cluttered with mismatched dishes and canned food. The rest of the trailer was taken up by an old-style TV and a sagging armchair. An electric space heater, unplugged, sat near the front, surrounded by stacks of magazines.

"This place could burn down in a heartbeat!" Jess said. "Nobody should have to live like this!"

"I know. Francine was renting a studio in somebody's basement before an old friend died and left her this trailer. She told me she needed to save money, but I'm not letting her come back here till the place is cleaned out and made safer. Not even then, if there's someplace else she can go. For now, she's better off in jail." Ben found a half-empty bag of cheap store-brand kibble behind the door. Stepping back from the trailer, he shook it, making a rattling sound.

Within seconds, a huge, scruffy-looking ginger tabby came bounding out of the weeds. Ben reached down to scratch its ears. "Come on, boy, it's chow time," he said, filling an old metal pan with kibble.

Jess liked cats. As the burly creature chomped down his food, she crouched to stroke his back. A rusty purr rumbled through his battle-scarred body. Glancing under the trailer, she could see a filled water bowl and a sturdy wooden box lined with a tattered blanket. Somebody cared about this cat.

"Does he have a name?" she asked Ben.

"He does. It's Sergeant Pepper."

"Like the Beatles?"

He answered with a shrug of his masculine shoulders. "I'm guessing your mother's a fan."

"So am I," Jess said. "At least we'll have something in common."

"You're sure you want to meet her, after seeing how she lives? Right now, you can walk away, and she'll never know the difference. Once you're in her life . . ." He let the words trail off.

Jess shook her head. "I've come too far not to do this."

"Then I have no right to stop you. But if it turns out badly, don't say I didn't warn you." He set the bag of kibble back in the trailer and locked the door. "Let's go," he said.

Silence hung in the cab on the short drive to the jail. Jess's hands twisted the handle on her leather purse. Ben was tempted to say more to her. Francine had a lot of baggage and a lot of needs. Taking on her problems could be an emotional drain. And, if it came to that, walking away could be a gut-wrenching ordeal. But no, Jess had already made up her mind. If the sight of that trailer hadn't deterred her, nothing would. It was time for him to back off.

He tried to imagine what it would be like, meeting a mother who was a total stranger. Ben's own mother had always been there for him, especially after his father died in a small plane crash. Ben had been nine then, his younger sister, Ellie, not much more than a toddler. His widowed mother had gone to work as the city librarian and managed to raise two children on her own. But now her health was failing. Last winter, after she'd suffered a bad fall, Ben had moved out of his apartment and back into the old family home to be with her. After all she'd sacrificed for him, it was the least he could do.

So far, things seemed to be working out. His mother was glad to have him, and not needing to rent made it easier to keep up the monthly child support he paid to his ex-wife, Cheryl.

It also gave his eight-year-old son, Ethan, a room of his own and a big yard to play in when he came to visit. In three weeks, when school was out, Ethan would be here for the holidays. For Ben, being with his boy was what made Christmas worth keeping.

Turning into the county lot, he pulled the SUV into his reserved parking place and turned to his passenger. "You're sure you want to do this." By now it was no longer a question.

"Let's go." Jess unfastened her seat belt, slipped his jacket off her shoulders and thrust it toward him. "I'm tempted to keep this lovely, warm thing, but you'd probably miss it. Thanks for the loan."

"Anytime." Ben took the jacket, swung out of the driver's seat and made it around the vehicle in time to help her out and escort her into the building. The double doors to the sheriff's office and jail were only a few steps from the curb. The check-in counter, where they stopped, was just inside.

"Sam." Ben spoke to the sixty-year-old deputy who had the shift. "This is Miss Ramsey. She's here to see Francine. Is the lady up for visitors?"

"I reckon so. She already ate her lunch and woke up from her nap." Sam slid a clipboard across the counter toward Jess. "You'll need to sign in and out, Miss. It's policy. And you'll have to leave your purse here."

"No problem." Jess picked up the attached ballpoint and wrote her name and the time. She seemed calm enough, but Ben couldn't help but notice how her hand shook.

"Have somebody bring Francine to the interrogation room," he said, knowing it would be easier on both women to meet there, rather than see each other for the first time through the iron bars of a cell. "Oh, and don't bother cuffing her," he added. "She'll be fine as she is."

"Sure thing." Sam pressed a button on the counter and relayed the request. Ben turned to Jess.

"I'll have to be there with you," he said. "I won't get involved unless you want me to, but I can't leave you two alone. It's policy."

Jess's nervous chuckle sounded forced. "What's the matter, are you afraid I'll slip her a weapon?"

"That's not funny, Jess. Come on. Let's go back."

He ushered Jess through a set of locking doors. A motherly looking woman wearing a khaki uniform and a deputy's badge waited for them in the hall. "Raise your arms, please, Miss," she said, and proceeded to pat Jess down for hidden weapons. Jess tried giving her a friendly smile. The woman didn't smile back.

Ben stood by, his expression unreadable. "Sorry, it's procedure," he said.

"I know. It's fine." Jess could've mentioned that this wasn't exactly her first rodeo. But the past was the past. She was a different person now.

"She's in here." The deputy nodded toward a closed door. "Buzz me when she's ready to go back." She disappeared down the hall.

Ben paused outside the door. "Ready?" he asked.

"How much time will I have with her?" Jess could feel her pulse galloping.

He shrugged. "That depends. For now, let's say you can be with her till one of you calls it quits. Okay?"

"Okay." Jess got his meaning. If, after learning who she was, her mother wanted nothing to do with her, the reunion would be over—at least for now.

"Then here goes." Ben opened the door, allowing Jess to step inside before he closed it behind them. The room was harsh and dim, with cement walls, a flickering fluorescent ceiling light, and a plain table with four wooden chairs. On the far side of the table sat a woman in a rumpled orange jumpsuit.

By Jess's calculation she should be in her midforties. She looked ten years older, but under these conditions, who wouldn't? The shapeless jumpsuit hung on her ample body. Her bleached platinum hair, slicked back and held with a pink plastic clip, was showing dark roots. Her face, bare of makeup, looked puffy and tired. Only her eyes—a striking violet blue, like Jess's own—held a spark of life.

"Francine," Ben spoke softly. "This is Miss Jessica Ramsey. She has something to say to you."

He moved a chair into place on the near side of the table and motioned Jess to take a seat. Heart drumming, Jess settled onto the edge of the chair. She wondered briefly if Ben was going to sit also. But he'd already moved back into a shadowed corner of the room.

Francine leaned forward a little. "Well, honey." She spoke in a friendly Texas drawl. "What's a pretty young thing like you got to say to an old bag like me? Are you here to tell me I've won the Publishers Clearing House giveaway? Lord knows I could use some good news."

"Sorry, it's not that." Jess found her voice. "But I hope you'll think this is good news. I can't believe I've finally found you."

Francine's eyes narrowed suspiciously. "If this is some kind of scam, sweetie—"

"No, it isn't." Jess swallowed the ache in her throat. "Francine, I'm your daughter."

The woman's guarded expression froze as if she'd been blasted by a stun gun. Her mouth worked before she managed to get words out. "You're . . . you're *Annie?*"

"Is that what you named me?" Jess's eyes were misting.

Francine shook her head. Tears were welling in her eyes. "I wasn't allowed to name you for real. But it's what I called you whenever I thought about my little red-haired baby, living a happy life somewhere, because I loved her enough to let her go." Trembling, she pressed her hands to her face. "Oh, Lordy, I always wanted to see you again. But not here in this shameful place. Not with me like this. . . ."

She broke off. Sobs racked her body. Her shoulders shook as she slumped over the table. Torn, Jess glanced back at Ben. "Can I . . . ?"

He nodded.

Jess pushed off her chair, walked around the table and wrapped her arms around her mother. For a long moment they clung together, both of them weeping. Jess hadn't known what to expect today. On her way from Kansas City she'd imagined a dozen different scenarios—some awkward, some cold, some even funny. But she could never have imagined so much emotion, or such a deep, immediate connection to the woman who'd given birth to her.

Somehow, she had to make something good come of this—for both of them.

Jess straightened as they drew apart. Wiping her eyes, Francine looked up at her. "Are you gonna be around when I get out of this calaboose, or are you just passin' through?"

"You're all the family I have," Jess said. "I came here to find you, and I have no plans to leave."

Francine managed a tearful smile. "That's dandy, hon. We'll have a lot of catchin' up to do once I'm sprung. But for now you look like you could blow away on a strong wind. Ben—" She motioned to the sheriff. "Get some food in my girl and find her a place to stay. I'll owe you one."

Jess had to smile. "Do you always give orders to the sheriff?"

"She does," Ben said. "But I don't always follow them."

"Well, go on then, you two," she said. " 'Scuse me, but after this big news, I'm feelin' like I got hit by a ten-ton truck. I need some time to take it all in. But you come back soon, sugar. Hear? Winnin' the Publishers Clearing House is nothin' compared to what you just gave me."

After Jess promised to come back the next day, Ben buzzed for the deputy to escort Francine back to her cell. Jess's legs felt as wobbly as rubber bands as she signed out at the counter and collected her purse. Given the circumstances, the reunion with her mother couldn't have gone better; but now that it was over, it was as if every ounce of strength had been sucked out of her body.

"Are you okay?" Ben took her arm and walked her outside. Heaven save her, the man was a rock.

"I'm fine. Just overwhelmed, that's all. But you don't have to babysit me. Just give me my suitcase and point me toward the garage. I'll walk over there and see if my car's been towed in. I'm sure they'll have a place to wait."

"Not so fast, lady. Francine ordered me to see that you ate something. Branding Iron isn't known for fine dining, but Buckaroo's, a couple blocks down Main Street, makes pretty good pizza. How about I split one with you and we can talk? My treat."

"You don't have to do that."

"Yes, I do. Just ask your mother. Come on." He swept her toward his SUV. Jess didn't resist. She hadn't bothered with breakfast this morning. By now she was so hungry that the very suggestion of hot pizza triggered a stomach growl. And she wouldn't turn down the company of the hot sheriff either, even if it was just for a quick lunch. Ben Marsden was great eye candy, but the last thing she needed was some lawman checking her out and looking into her past—a past she'd done her best to leave behind.

Ben was glad he'd ordered the extra-large supreme pizza. For a little thing, Jess Ramsey had a trooper's appetite. Casting a side glance at her slender figure, he couldn't imagine where she'd put the four big slices she'd downed in the past fifteen minutes. But he'd always liked being with a woman who enjoyed good food. He'd read somewhere that it was a sign she'd enjoy other sensual activities as well. But he had no plans to go down that path.

With the pan between them empty, she leaned back in the booth seat, sipped from her mug of root beer and regarded him with her stunning eyes. Road-worn and emotional as she was, she still looked damned good. Gussied up and ready for a nice date, she'd be a real traffic-stopper.

"Thanks, I didn't realize how hungry I was," she said. "And thanks for easing things with Francine. It would've been a lot harder without you there."

"Part of my job," he said.

"Like feeding Francine's cat? Tell me, sheriff, do you have a mean side?"

"I do. But don't worry, I save it for the bad guys." Ben squared himself for the serious conversation he needed to have with her. "Jess, I'm glad you got off to a good start with your mother. But if you don't understand what you're getting into with her, things could turn sour in a hurry."

"Okay. So tell me about her." Jess put down her mug and leaned toward him. "I get it that she's troubled. But she's so sweet and funny. Surely, with someone here to care about her—"

"So you're really planning to stay?"

"If I can find a place to live and some kind of job, yes. My mother needs help, and I want to be here for her."

"Then listen to me, Jess. Francine's a delightful woman—all my deputies like her. I do too. But she's an alcoholic mess. When she drinks—and she will—she's over the top. Today, when you met her, she was cold sober. But when she's on the bottle, she swears like a drunken sailor, gets in fights and usually ends up passed out in some alley. Get in her way, and she can be meaner than a skunk."

"But what about Alcoholics Anonymous? Didn't you tell me that she'd be going to their meetings as part of her probation? Won't that help her?"

"It could, if Francine wanted help. But we've been down that road with her before. She'll come up with every excuse in the book not to show up at those meetings—she's sick, it's too cold, it's raining, or she's just too passed-out drunk to go. If you get her there, she'll sit in the back and sleep, or pretend to. There's a good group in the county, but the last sponsor she had finally threw up his hands and quit. If you're not prepared to handle that kind of behavior, the kindest thing you can do is say good-bye now and find a reason to walk away. Otherwise you could both end up with your hearts broken."

Emotions flickered across Jess's pretty face—shock, dismay and finally determination. "You've given me a lot to think about. But she's my mother, my own flesh and blood. I can't walk away until I've done everything I can to help her."

And what about you, Jess? You look like you could use some help yourself. Who's going to help you?

Ben kept that thought to himself. Jess had already shown herself to be fiercely independent. Telling her she needed help wouldn't set well with her. And as sheriff, Ben knew better than to get personally involved in situations like this. The sooner he could back off and get back to work, the better for all concerned.

"Right now, I need to see about my car," Jess said. "If you'll leave me at the garage, with my suitcase, I can manage from there."

"Let me give them a call." Ben whipped out his cell phone. "Even if they've got your car, they can't fix it till you give them the okay." He scrolled down and punched in the call. "Silas? It's me, Ben. Did you get time to tow in that old green Pontiac? . . . Yeah? . . . Sure, she's right here. I'll put her on."

Jess took the phone. "Hello? Have you got my car?"

"Yup," a nasal voice answered. "Looks like the fuel line. Good news is, it won't cost much to fix—maybe a couple hundred with the tow. Bad news is, we ain't got the part. We can order it in, but it'll take a couple of days. You want us to go ahead?"

Jess hesitated. For a beat-up old car, even two hundred dollars was a lot of money. But she didn't have much choice. "Sure," she said. "Go ahead. I'll give you my cell number. You can call me when it's done."

She gave him her number, ended the call and returned the phone to Ben. "It looks like I'm stuck on foot for a couple of days. But that's not your problem. Just drop me off at the nearest cheap motel."

He looked bemused. "Sorry, but the nearest motel,

cheap or not, is forty miles up the road in Cottonwood Springs. There's nothing here in Branding Iron."

Her heart sank. "No boarding house? No bed-and-breakfast?"

"That's what I said. Nothing."

"I suppose I could crash in Francine's trailer . . ." Even saying the words made her cringe.

"Not on your life," he said. "My mother has a spare room in her house. She'll be happy to put you up for a few days. You're coming home with me."

Chapter Three

As Ben drove across town to his mother's house, Jess took in the quiet streets, the modest homes and yards. Most were neatly tended, a few cluttered with weeds, old appliances and junk cars. Here and there a sign advertised a home business—a backyard welding shop, a beauty salon, a cake decorator. If anybody in Branding Iron had money, they didn't appear to flaunt it.

Ben hadn't tried to get her talking again. He seemed to know that she had a lot to think about, and she did.

She'd told him she was determined to stay. But she'd be foolish to ignore his warning about Francine's behavior—and even more foolish to assume that, just by being here, she could heal her mother's addiction. Alcoholism was a disease, and the only known cure had to spring from a deep motivation to change. Could she foster that motivation in her mother? Did she have the patience to try, fail and try again? If not, maybe Ben was right. Maybe the kindest thing she could do was walk away now, before it was too late.

"Here we are." Ben slowed down in front of a two-story frame house with white siding and dark green shutters. Gingerbread trim shadowed the wide covered porch. A bare wisteria vine, promising springtime beauty, spiraled up a corner post to creep across the edge of the roof. Set on a quiet street, with a stately sycamore in the well-groomed front yard, the home was the picture of graciousness, respectability and security—all the things that, if she'd ever known them, were missing from Jess's memory.

"This is where you grew up?" Jess asked as Ben pulled into the driveway.

"It is. My great-grandfather built the place after World War One. It's been in the family ever since."

"And your mother won't mind having me stay for a couple of nights? I hate to impose on someone who doesn't even know me."

"Relax." Ben gave her a boyish grin. "I called her while you were in the restroom at Buckaroo's. She said she'd enjoy the company. Knowing her, she'll treat you like family."

"But does she know who I am? Does she know about . . . ?"

"About Francine? Sure, I mentioned it to her. You can expect a few questions, but my mother's never been one to judge. Come on, you'll be fine." He climbed out of the vehicle, retrieved her suitcase from the back and strode on around to open her door. A tall, silver-haired woman dressed in gray slacks and a cheery red cardigan came down the steps, one hand gripping the wrought-iron rail for support. She appeared to be in her late sixties at least, maybe older. She must not have been young when Ben was born.

"Welcome, Jessica. I'm Clara." She was thin and slightly stooped, clearly not strong, but her smile and her sparkling brown eyes lit her face. "Come on inside. My daughter's old room is set up for guests, so it's all ready for you. Ben,

be a dear and take that suitcase upstairs. I've got fresh carrot cake and hot tea in the kitchen. If that sounds good to
you, we can sit at the table and visit a little."

Jess had just filled up on pizza, but she wanted a chance
to know her hostess better. "It sounds wonderful," she
said. "I'll even serve if you'll let me."

"Hey, save some cake for me. Then I've got to get back
to work." Ben headed up the narrow staircase with Jess's
suitcase. She heard the thump as he set it on the floor. By
the time he reappeared in the doorway of the cozy, old-fashioned kitchen, Jess and Clara were seated at the kitchen
table with small slices of carrot cake and cups of steaming
ginger tea. He grabbed a paper towel and wrapped it
around the generous wedge of cake Jess had cut for him.
"I'll take this on the run," he said. "Just got a call about a
drug bust. Couple of middle school girls smoking weed in
the Shop Mart parking lot. They need me to show up, give
them a good scare and talk to their parents. Thanks for the
cake, Mom."

He vanished out the front door. A moment later Jess
heard the SUV roar out of the driveway, siren wailing.

Jess shook her head. "Good grief, is all that fuss necessary? It's just a couple of kids—and they're girls!"

Clara gave her a knowing smile. "The siren and lights
are just theater. Ben's way with lawbreaking kids is to
make a big deal of it, put the fear of God into them so,
hopefully, they'll never do it again. Most of the time, it
works."

"I can tell you're proud of him," Jess said.

"I am. Ben's been through some rough times—losing his
chance at the NFL when he blew out his knee in college,
going to work for his father-in-law, and then having his
marriage break up. But he's done all right for himself since
he came home. He's a good sheriff and a good son."

"You mentioned something about a daughter."

"Yes. Ellie would be about your age. She's married to a lawyer and lives in San Francisco. I get a call from her every few weeks, but I don't see as much of her as I'd like." For a moment she looked wistful. Then she smiled again. "Ben tells me you plan to settle here in Branding Iron."

"Yes, if I can find a job and a place to live—and if things work out with my . . ." Could she say the word? "My mother."

"Ben told me you came to find her," Clara said. "I think you're very brave. You're going to have your hands full, trying to help Francine."

Clara's acceptance was like the opening of a door into a warm place. Only now did Jess realize how much she'd needed a sympathetic ear—and how much she needed to learn about her mother.

"Ben tried to talk me out of getting involved with her," she said. "But now that I'm here, how can I just turn my back and walk away?" Still nervous, she took a bite of cake, then another. "This cake is delicious. I hope you won't mind sharing the recipe."

"Not at all. I actually made it for the little group I'm hosting here later today—the committee for planning this year's Cowboy Christmas Ball. You're welcome to join us—it would give you a chance to make some friends here. Heaven knows, if you stay and take on Francine, you're going to need some support."

"Thanks. Let me think about it." The thought of meeting the respectable ladies of the town was enough to make Jess cringe with dread. But Clara was right. If she stayed in Branding Iron, she was going to need friends. And she might never have a better chance at making some than today.

"What can you tell me about the Cowboy Christmas Ball?" she asked. "It sounds like a lot of fun."

"Oh, it is—although it's also a lot of work behind the

scenes. The idea for a Cowboy Christmas Ball started over in Anson. It's still a huge thing there. But a few years after that, folks in Branding Iron decided they wanted their own. Our first Christmas ball was held here after the boys came back from World War One. It's become a tradition. Everybody dresses for an old-fashioned western dance— even the children. There's a barbecue, plenty of food and dancing. And we usually sign a big-name country band for the music. It's the biggest event of the year. Most of the planning's already been done. This meeting is mostly just to go down the checklist and make sure everything's covered."

"It does sound like fun," Jess said. "And it would be a great chance to meet people. I want to learn more about the town and especially about Francine. How well do you know her?"

"We were never close friends—she's quite a bit younger than I am. But we both grew up here in Branding Iron." Clara gazed out the window, as if looking into the past. "I remember what a beautiful young girl she was—wild, to be sure, but so full of life. Then it all changed. . . ." Her voice trailed off.

"What happened?" Jess leaned toward her. "Did it have something to do with me—or with my father, whoever he was?" She'd seen the name and the note on her birth certificate—*Denver Jackson, deceased.* But that was all she knew.

"Francine didn't tell you?"

"We only had a few minutes together. She said we could talk more when she got out of jail. But if you know what happened, I'd like to hear your version."

"I can only tell you what I saw and heard." Clara stirred a sugar cube into her tea. "She was about seventeen, as I remember, and the prettiest girl in town. He was a rodeo cowboy, a bull rider, passing through to earn a little prize money at the county rodeo—handsome as the devil's own, with flame-red hair—" She glanced up at Jess. "Hair the same color as yours.

"When the rodeo money wasn't enough, he signed on to help with the haying season. All the girls were crazy for him, but it was Francine he chose. When her father, who owned the bank at the time, ordered him to stay away from her, he left and went back on the rodeo circuit. She went with him."

"That must've been a hard life for her," Jess said.

Clara nodded. "I don't know the details. Francine claimed later that they'd gotten married, but I don't know if that was true. Nobody ever saw a ring or a license. A few weeks after they left town, he was killed by a bull in the arena—the story was in the paper, so we knew about it here."

"And Francine?"

"She was right there and saw it happen. You can imagine what that must've done to her. When she finally came home, pregnant and half out of her mind, her father had disowned her. He wouldn't even let her in the house to get her things. Heaven knows where she found shelter or how she lived, but she had her baby and gave it up. After that she left town and disappeared. Nobody knew where she'd gone, but about eight years ago she came back. And now . . ." She gave Jess a reassuring smile. "Here you are, my dear."

Jess blinked back tears. After Ben's warning, she'd questioned her decision to stay in Branding Iron. Now that she knew Francine's story, those questions were fading. As Clara had said, here she was—and it had to be for a reason. No one else could provide the love and support it would take to save her mother. She was the poor woman's only chance.

"Are you all right?" Clara laid a gentle hand on her arm.

With effort, Jess found her voice. "Yes, just emotional. I

had no idea . . ." She swallowed the lump in her throat. "Thank you for telling me about my mother, and especially for taking me in. Now, I hope you'll let me clear the table and take care of these dishes." Standing, she began collecting the cups and saucers.

"I can do that." Clara rose. "Since I've taken a couple of falls, Ben treats me like an invalid. But that's far from true. I just need to be careful. Why don't you get some rest before my friends show up? The upstairs bath is right across the hall from your room. Feel free to take a shower. Run along now." She shooed Jess out of the kitchen and up the stairs.

The room in which Ben had left Jess's suitcase looked much the same as it must have when his sister was in high school—the pink-checked ruffled coverlet; the bed piled with pillows and stuffed animals; the bedside lamps with lace doilies under their bases; and the dresser with its tall mirror and little round stool, covered with fabric that matched the bed cover and the window curtains.

On the wall was a framed photo of a pretty, dark-haired girl in a cheerleading costume. This had to be Ben's sister, Ellie. Even in the picture, she looked strong-willed. Jess couldn't help wondering about the wistful tone in Clara's voice as she spoke of her. Maybe something had gone wrong between them. Or maybe Ellie was just too involved in her California lifestyle to spare much time for her mother.

After stacking the stuffed animals in the corner, Jess hefted her suitcase onto the bed and opened it flat. She'd packed hastily, and most of her clothes were wrinkled. But she found black leggings, a tunic-length tweed sweater and black slippers that would look presentable enough for company. Clara's friends on the Christmas Ball committee would probably look like they'd stepped out of *Good Housekeeping*. But they would just have to take her as she was.

A quick shower would feel heavenly before she put on clean clothes. In the old-style bathroom, with the shower-head mounted above the footed tub, she stripped naked. She'd turned on the water and was about to climb in when she noticed the steel razor lying next to the sink—and the single toothbrush in the porcelain holder.

Her heart went *thud*. Of course, this would be Ben's bathroom. And his bedroom would be on this floor too. It shouldn't be a big deal. But as she stepped into the warm shower, she couldn't help imagining him standing in this very spot, the water sluicing over his drool-worthy super-hero body.

She willed the image away. Any notion of romance with the handsome sheriff was a dead-end road. He might be unattached, as his mother had let her know. There might even be some sizzle between them. But all he'd have to do was enter her name into the FBI's National Instant Criminal Background Check System, and she'd be history. It wouldn't matter that she'd paid her dues or that her testimony had put the real criminal—her former husband—behind bars. To a square-jawed Sir Galahad like Ben Marsden, she'd be tainted goods. End of story.

After turning off the water, she climbed out of the tub and dried herself with an oversized white bath towel, which she then wrapped around her body, tucking it at the top like a sarong. Clutching her discarded clothes, she stepped out into the hall.

She would have gone back into the guest bedroom to get dressed, but something caught her eye—a door on the far side of the bathroom. Was that the door to Ben's room?

Overcome by curiosity, she walked closer. If the door

had been tightly closed, there was no way she would have opened it. But it stood slightly ajar, almost beckoning her to steal a look inside.

Feeling vaguely naughty, she peered through the narrow opening. Ben's mother had mentioned that he'd been an NFL hopeful. Would the room be lined with high-school and college football trophies, maybe framed news articles and photos of his teams? Jess hoped not. There was something juvenile about men who never moved on past their athletic glory days.

She used her bare toe to nudge the door open a few more inches. She saw no trophies. Just a rumpled bed, hastily made with a faded quilt on top, and a blue terry robe flung across the foot. A basket of laundry sat on the floor. There were venetian blinds on the windows and a chest of drawers standing next to a half-open closet. On the nightstand, next to the bed, were three things—a digital alarm clock, a book and a framed school picture of a young boy.

Against her better judgment, Jess took a step inside the room. She could see the photo better now. The boy, a dark-haired, bright-eyed little fellow, looked enough like Ben to be his son. His grin, which showed a missing front tooth, was so infectious that Jess caught herself smiling back.

"Jess? What are you doing in here?"

The deep voice came from right behind her. Clutching her clothes to her chest, she forced herself to turn around. Ben loomed above her, his black eyebrows drawn into a scowl.

There was no way out but the truth.

"I'm sorry. I'd just come out of the bathroom. Your door was partway open and I was curious. If I'm out of line, please forgive me."

His scowl deepened. "Out of line? I'd say it was more like plain old snooping," he said. "Whatever you were up to, I wouldn't recommend walking into a man's bedroom dressed in nothing but a towel. You could put the wrong ideas into his head."

Jess could feel the heat rising in her face, but she chose to brazen it out. "Even if the man's mother is right downstairs?"

"My mother hasn't been strong enough to climb these stairs for the past year. Nobody comes up here but the cleaning lady—and Ethan, when he's around." Moving past her, he strode to the foot of the bed, took his terry bathrobe and laid it over her shoulders. It was so roomy that even with her arms full of her clothes, it covered Jess all the way around. "There. I could say that's better, but it would be a lie."

The twinkle in his eyes left little doubt that he was joking.

"Is Ethan the boy in the picture? I take it he's your son."

"He is." Pride resonated in Ben's voice. "His mother has him during the school year, but he'll be here in a couple of weeks for Christmas vacation. The closed door on your side of the hall is his room. You're more than welcome to look inside."

"Never mind." If he wanted to make her feel silly, he was doing a good job.

"If you're still around, you'll get to meet him."

Jess got the message—he still wasn't counting on her to stay. For now she chose to ignore it. "He looks a lot like you," she said. "How old is he?"

"Eight. That's last year's picture. By now he should have both his front teeth."

"Handsome boy." She turned to go, then paused, glancing back. "How did it go with the weed-smoking girls?"

"Their folks came and picked them up at the jail. By then they were bawling their eyes out. I don't think they'll try that again for a while."

"So what are you doing back here so soon?" Jess asked.

"My mother needed some things for her committee meeting. Since she doesn't drive anymore, I picked them up for her. And I thought that, as long as I was here, I might as well see if you needed anything."

"Uh . . . thanks, I guess. And for what it's worth, no, I'm fine."

"Mom said she invited you to come to the meeting."

"Yes. It sounded like a good idea—although I'm always nervous with new people."

"You'll be fine." He gave her a roguish glance. "But I'd suggest you put some clothes on first."

"Oh—please, just pretend this didn't happen!" Taking her cue, Jess fled back to the guest room. It hadn't been the smartest move, wandering half-undressed into Ben's room. True, she hadn't expected him to show up. But if she wanted to make a good impression on the sheriff, on his mother and on the townspeople, she would have to mind her manners. Being Francine's daughter was already a strike against her. The last thing she needed was to be tarred with the same brush.

Ben whistled his way down the stairs. His encounter with Jess had been . . . interesting? Was that the word for it? Wrapped in nothing but a towel, with that shower-fresh face and those big, innocent eyes, she was part seductress, part curious child. Under different conditions, he wouldn't have minded finding out more. But out of respect, if nothing else, his mother's house was no place for flirtation. Maybe later, if Jess stuck around and got a place of her own. . . .

Holding that thought, Ben gave his mother a farewell wave, went out to his vehicle and headed back to work.

*   *   *

As Jess helped set up for the committee meeting, she could feel her nerves tightening. "Are you sure you want me here?" she asked Clara as she unfolded extra chairs around the coffee table. "Maybe I'll just be a distraction."

"It'll be fine, dear." Clara cut the cake and arranged the saucers and forks on a tray. "I'll introduce you, and you can tell us whatever you like about yourself. Then we'll get down to business. You can listen and learn, or feel free to add your own ideas."

"But will they know who I am and why I'm here?"

Clara smiled. "Word does travel fast around this town, but not quite that fast. I haven't told anybody about your reason for coming, and I'm sure Ben wouldn't either. But if you don't mind a word of advice, being open and up-front about your mother will win you friends in the long run and could prevent some misunderstandings."

"Thank you, that's very wise," Jess said. But before she could think it over, the front doorbell rang. Jess moved out of the way as Clara hurried to answer it. Two figures, briefly silhouetted by the afternoon sunlight, stepped into the living room.

"Come in and have a chair," Clara said. "I'd like you to meet my houseguest, Jessica. Jessica, this is Connie Parker, and her daughter Katy."

"Pleased to meet you, Jessica." The woman who took Jess's hand was in her forties, her graying hair slicked back from a careworn face that would have been plain except for the sparkle in her gray eyes. "Say hello, Katy."

"Hullo." As Katy extended her hand, Jess realized the young woman had Down syndrome. Dressed in light blue sweatpants and a pink shirt with a kitten on the front, she gave Jess a sweet smile. "Katy goes everywhere I go," Connie said. "So when they asked me to be on the planning committee, of course they invited her too."

Jess gave the small hand a warm squeeze. What a self-absorbed jerk she'd been, to feel as if her own concerns were the center of the universe. Compared to what others were dealing with, they were nothing. "Hello, Katy," she said. "I'm happy to meet you."

"Connie's husband, Silas, runs the garage in town," Clara said.

"Then I've spoken with him on the phone," Jess said. "He's waiting for a part so he can fix my car. Come sit down. Maybe you can tell me more about the Cowboy Christmas Ball."

They were taking their seats when the doorbell rang again. The next arrival was an older woman named Maybelle Ferguson. Stout and matronly, with a no-nonsense air about her, she greeted Jess with cool reserve, casting a disapproving glance at her black leggings. *Well, I can't win them all*, Jess told herself.

With everyone seated, one chair remained empty. Clara glanced out the front window, then at the mantel clock. "It's about time to start," she said. "Has anybody heard from Kylie?"

Maybelle opened her folder of notes. "You know Kylie. She's always a Last-Minute-Lucy. Once she has that baby, she'll be even worse. Let's just start without her."

"How about we give her another five minutes?" Clara suggested. "Meanwhile, I'd like to formally introduce Jessica and let her tell you a little about herself."

Jess cringed inwardly. Clara had put her on the spot. But the gesture was well meant, like forcing bitter medicine down her throat.

With all eyes on her, Jess told the briefest possible version of her story—how she'd been adopted as a baby and, after losing her legal parents, decided to find her birth mother, who turned out to be Francine.

Connie was wide-eyed. "Wow!" she said. "This should be a movie! I can't wait to find out what happens next!"

Maybelle had drawn back into her chair, looking as if Jess had just broken out with some exotic disease. "Well!" she huffed. "*Well!*"

Katy smiled her angelic smile. "Hey, you found your mom. That's really nice."

The doorbell chimed twice. Before the end of the second ring, the door flew open. "Don't get up, anybody," a cheery voice called. "Sorry I'm late!"

The woman who burst into the room looked a little older than Jess. She was blond, pretty and late in her pregnancy. As she took her seat, Clara made the introductions.

"Jess, this is Kylie Taggart. Her husband, Shane, is Ben's best friend. Kylie, Jess is Francine's birth daughter. She came here to find her mother."

"Oh, my stars!" Kylie beamed in delight. "So you're Annie!"

Jess's jaw dropped. "You knew about me?"

Kylie nodded. "I spent a little time with Francine last year. She told me about you. She said you had red hair and that she'd never stopped thinking about you. I can't believe you're really here! You could be just what that poor woman needs!"

"So, are you here to stay?" Connie asked.

"I hope so," Jess replied. "But first I'll need to find a place to rent. Clara was kind enough to take me in for a couple of days, but I don't want to impose on her any longer than I have to. As soon as I get my car back, I can start looking."

"You know, it's a shame Branding Iron doesn't have any place for people coming into town to stay," Kylie said. "We'd get an even better turnout for the Christmas Ball if folks from out of town could get a room here and not have to drive home."

"Opening a place like that would cost money," Connie said. "And who's got money around here?"

"We're wasting time," Maybelle interrupted. "We've got a lot of decisions to make. Let's get started."

"Cake now or later?" Clara asked.

"Later," Maybelle said. "We can't talk with our mouths full, can we?"

Jess settled back in her chair to listen. She had a lot to learn about the town and the people in it, and she was just getting started.

Chapter Four

Maybelle, who chaired the planning committee and insisted on following parliamentary procedure, called the meeting to order. As Clara read the minutes from the last session, Jess sat back to listen.

The Cowboy Christmas Ball would be held in the high school gym, the only place with enough room for the townspeople who'd already bought tickets and extra guests who would pay at the door. Since the menu was traditional, and the Nashville band had been booked over a year ago, there were few decisions to be made. This meeting was mostly for the purpose of making sure everything was covered down to the last detail.

As they went down the list—ticket sales, decorations, plates and utensils for the buffet, security, cleanup and even a pre-party dance instruction class, Jess paid as much attention to the women as to the business at hand. She reflected on how each had responded differently to the news that she was Francine's daughter—Clara with graciousness, Connie with curiosity, Katy with sweet acceptance, and Kylie with warm enthusiasm.

Only Maybelle had seemed put off. But that shouldn't

be surprising. There were bound to be people in Branding Iron who'd judged Francine harshly and would view her daughter the same way. Until she could change their minds, she would just have to live with that.

Still, she couldn't deny that it hurt.

Forcing the thought aside, Jess focused her attention on the plans for the ball.

The local firemen would dig the barbecue pit and cook the prime beef. The rest of the food for the buffet table would be donated by people in the town, who'd already signed up for their dishes. The proceeds would go to pay the band and fund next year's ball, with any leftover cash going to the schools for supplies, field trips and other activities.

"Are all the food assignments filled?" Maybelle asked Connie, who was in charge of the buffet.

"Plenty of folks have signed up to bring food," Connie said. "We've got more than sixty people on the list. But they're all going to need confirmation and reminder calls to make sure they don't forget. With so much to do, I could sure use somebody to do the calling. Any volunteers?"

The women glanced at each other. This was clearly a job nobody wanted.

"How about you, Jessica?" Clara offered. "We could give you a list, and you could make the calls from here, since I know you don't have a landline phone."

"Oh, but I don't—" Jess scrambled for an excuse. Once, out of desperation, she'd taken a job at a phone center, making sales calls to strangers. She'd hated it. This wouldn't be the same, but the thought of calling all those people she didn't know made her want to cringe.

"Oh, please, Jessica," Connie said. "I could really use your help, and it would be a great way for you to get to know people here."

"Please, Jessica." Katy echoed her mother.

Jess knew when she was outgunned. "All right, I'll do my best," she hedged. "But I may need some help."

"Yay!" Katy clapped her hands.

Kylie raised her hand and spoke. "I move that we accept Jessica as a member of the Christmas Ball committee."

"Seconded." Katy had been in enough meetings to know the rules.

Maybelle raised an eyebrow. "This is highly irregular."

"It's been moved and seconded, Maybelle," Connie said.

"Oh, very well," Maybelle said with a disdainful sniff. "All in favor?"

"Aye!" chorused the rest of the committee. Maybelle didn't bother to ask who was opposed.

Jess sensed that she'd been railroaded, but Connie was right. If she wanted to be welcomed and accepted in the town, this thankless job was a gift. "Thank you," she said. "And please call me Jess."

Ben was nearing the end of a long day—one that showed no sign of ending anytime soon. A rear-ender on the highway into town had become a drug bust after the smashed Corolla turned out to be stolen. Fortunately his deputy had run the plates and called for backup before trying to arrest the armed driver, who'd suffered a nasty head gash and surrendered without a fight. With the man in custody, Ben and the deputy had found a large stash of meth and marijuana in the smashed trunk.

The seventy-six-year-old farmer whose pickup had hit the Corolla was unhurt, but he was so jittery that Ben had called his daughter to calm him down and drive him home. The smuggler had been stitched up at the clinic. Now, dosed with pain meds, he was sleeping it off in a holding cell. Ben hoped he'd be out until the state troopers came to pick him up in the morning. But the man couldn't be left here alone. Tired and hungry, Ben had sent his deputies home to their families and stayed to write up a report of the incident and wait for the night shift to come in.

Walking back down the corridor to the cells, he looked in at the sleeping prisoner and thought of all the things that could've gone wrong out there on the highway—gunfire, with somebody getting shot, maybe killed; or a dangerous chase through town, putting more folks in danger. He could only be thankful that none of those things had come to pass. Life was too precious for such tragedies—and the burden of his job was to try to keep them from happening.

He was about to go back to his office, and maybe order a pizza, when he heard a sound coming from farther down the hall. It was the sound of deep, heartfelt weeping.

Besides the drug smuggler, only one other person was locked up tonight—Francine.

A few strides carried him down the hall to her cell. Through the bars, he could see her huddling on the edge of her bunk with her face buried in her hands. Her shoulders shook with sobs.

"Francine, are you all right?" he asked.

She raised her head, her eyes bloodshot, her hair disheveled, her face blotched with tears. "Lord, look at me, sheriff! Look at what a mess I am! My little girl comes all this way to find her mother, and this is what she gets—a broken-down old wreck in jail! I wouldn't blame her if she left and never looked back!"

Tears would likely be good for the woman's soul, Ben thought. But he couldn't just walk away and leave her like this. She probably wanted sympathy. But what she needed right now was tough talk.

"Your daughter cares about you, Francine," he said. "Now that she's met you, she's determined to stay and help you change your life."

"She'd do that for me?" Francine wiped her nose on the sleeve of her orange jumpsuit. "Even after I gave her away?"

"I've no reason to believe she holds that against you," Ben said. "Jess means well. But I don't think she knows what she's getting into. I've seen you in and out of here over the years. I've seen you go to AA and then quit, sober up and then fall off the wagon again. I've picked you up off the street and hauled you out of bar fights. If your daughter thinks she can change you, she's got an uphill battle ahead of her."

"Oh, I know that." Francine sounded like a little girl who'd just been scolded for getting her shoes muddy. "But now I've got my baby back. With her bein' there for me, things are bound to turn the corner."

"Are they?" Ben shook his head. "Nobody can change you—not even your own daughter. You have to change yourself." Ben leaned closer to the bars. "Think about this, Francine. What if Jess puts her faith in you, gives you her all, and you let her down? You'll break her heart. Is that what you want?"

Francine looked down at her hands. "You sure do know how to stick the knife in and twist it, Ben Marsden."

"Somebody has to say this. You've got less than half of your sentence left. Don't lead her on. If you can't change— or if you don't want to—tell her up front and let her go. If you love her, that would be the kindest thing you could do."

"I'll think on it, but it's not what I want." Francine was silent for a moment. When she looked up at him, her expression had changed to a sly smile. "My girl's a lovely little thing, isn't she? I get the idea you kind of like her. Am I right?"

Like her? The words caught Ben off guard. Sure, he liked Jess. She was pretty, intelligent and fiercely compassionate. But he'd barely had time to get to know her. And even if he was attracted to her, his life was complicated enough without a new woman in it.

The sound of his two night shift deputies arriving gave

him an excuse to leave without responding to Francine's question. "Sleep on what I said," he told her. "Ask yourself how badly you want to change, and what you're willing to do."

She nodded. "Will you be bringin' my girl around?"

"That depends on her, and on how much time I have. See you tomorrow, Francine."

By the time he'd briefed the deputies and made it out the door, it was dark. Ben was still hungry, but his mother usually left something to warm up when he worked late. He would wait and eat when he got home.

The night was chilly, the air around the jail tinged with cigarette smoke and diesel fumes. The security lights mounted under the edge of the roof elongated Ben's shadow, casting it ahead of him as he walked to his SUV. He was just climbing inside when his cell phone rang. He took the call.

"Hi, Dad!"

Ben's spirit lightened. There was no voice he'd rather hear than his eight-year-old son's.

"Hi, Ethan. Isn't it about your bedtime? You've got school in the morning."

"Yeah. I'm in my bed, talking to you under the covers."

"What's up? Some big secret?"

"Sort of. I wanted to ask you something, and I don't want Mom to know."

"Will she be mad if she finds out?" The last thing Ben needed was to get crossways with his ex. Cheryl could fight dirty, and she wasn't above using her control of Ethan as a weapon.

"Maybe. I think Mom's getting married again."

"Oh?" Questions flooded Ben's mind. He was fine with Cheryl getting remarried, but how would it affect Ethan? And how would it affect their current custody arrangement? "Are you happy about that?"

He could hear the sound of Ethan shifting in the bed.

"Maybe not," he said. "Mom's boyfriend is from Boston. His name is Nigel. I think he's rich."

"Nothing wrong with that." But this didn't sound good, Ben thought. "Do you like him?"

"Not much. He's kind of snooty. He's got a big house by the ocean. Mom showed me pictures of it. He wants Mom to move there, and he wants to send me to the boarding school where he went. He says it's to make a gentleman out of me. But I think he just wants me out of the way."

"It sounds like I need to talk with your mother."

"Not yet. She'll know I told you." He paused. Ben could hear him breathing into the phone. "Here's the thing, Dad. If Mom gets married, can I come and live with you?"

In a heartbeat! Ben wanted to say. But Cheryl had a way of throwing up roadblocks. He would fight her in court, if need be, for more access to his son. But that would take time and money. Meanwhile, he didn't want to get Ethan's hopes up only to have them crushed.

"I'd like that more than anything," he said. "But it's something I'll need to work out with your mother."

In the silence on the other end of the phone, Ben could sense his son's disappointment. "Hey, when are you coming for the holidays?" he asked.

"School lets out in three weeks. But Mom says I can get out early because she wants to go to Boston with Nigel and meet his family. Can we go sledding, like we did last year?"

"You bet, if there's snow. If not, maybe we can ride my friend Shane's horses. And we'll have a big Christmas tree at Grandma's house. Do you know what you want yet?"

"I'm thinking about it."

"Well, let me know. And let me know when I can plan to drive to Dallas and pick you up."

"Gotta go! Mom's coming upstairs!" Ethan ended the call.

Ben pocketed his phone, wondering what changes lay ahead. Cheryl's remarriage to a wealthy easterner, if it really happened, could be a real game changer—for better or for worse. Nothing would make him happier than to have his son live with him. But would Cheryl let Ethan go, or would she hang on to the boy out of pure meanness? No matter how it played out, he'd be damned if anybody was going to subject his precious boy to the horrors of boarding school.

Driving down Main Street, he saw that the Christmas lights were up—colored twinkle-bulbs strung on wires between the streetlights and across the intersections. The display, which went up right after Thanksgiving, was nothing spectacular, but it was Branding Iron's way of signaling the start of a holiday season rich in tradition. Ethan loved the Christmas parade with Santa in an antique sleigh drawn by a team of massive gray Percherons. And that night, there'd be the annual Cowboy Christmas Ball.

If Ben attended the ball, it would only be as part of his job. Most years he volunteered to work security that night so his deputies could attend with their dates and families. No reason for this year to be any different. If Ethan wanted to go and enjoy the food and kids' games, and maybe meet up with some friends, the boy could go with his grandmother or with one of the neighbor families.

As he turned up the street to home, he could see that the lights were on in the living room and kitchen. His mother, always tired by the end of the day, was usually in bed by nine. A glance at the dashboard clock told Ben it was nine-thirty. Maybe she'd stayed up to talk to him, or—the thought gave him an unexpected tingle—he might find Jess waiting for him when he walked in.

He'd tried to block today's upstairs incident from his thoughts. But seeing her with her curvy little body wrapped in nothing but a large towel, with beads of water glowing on her creamy shoulders and on her long golden eyelashes, had done some naughty things to his libido. His self-control had been worthy of a medal—and would continue to be. Cute, sexy and sassy as Jess might be, he was no candidate for romance—especially under his mother's roof.

He parked the SUV, crossed the porch and opened the front door. Jess was snuggled on the sofa with a book. The reading lamp made a halo around her, its soft light dancing on her fiery curls. She looked up at him and smiled.

"Hi," she said. "Your mother's already gone to bed. I told her I'd stay up to welcome you home." She closed the book and held it up to show him the cover. "I haven't read Jane Austen in years. Your mother has quite a collection."

"She gave a home to a lot of the worn-out books from the library," Ben said. "Did she leave me some supper? I'm starved."

Jess rose, uncurling her body with the grace of a cat. She looked like a cute teenager, Ben thought, with her black tights and long, baggy sweater. "There's lasagna in the fridge," she said. "I'll put some in the microwave for you."

"You mean I won't have to warm up my own supper? Hey, I could get used to this," he teased.

"Don't. As soon as my car's ready tomorrow, I'm done with mooching off your mom. I plan to start hunting for a place to live—and a job."

He followed her into the kitchen, where a place was already set for him. Jess scooped a generous square of lasagna onto his plate, put it in the microwave, took a covered salad out of the fridge and filled two glasses with cold apple juice.

"Join me?" he asked, hoping she planned to stay.

"I ate with your mother. But I'll keep you company." She set the heated lasagna on the place mat in front of him, then took a seat at the opposite side of the table.

Ben heaped some salad on his plate and took a taste of lasagna. "This is delicious, but I can tell it's not my mother's recipe," he said. "Did you make it?"

"Yes. I wanted to give Clara a break. Sorry you weren't here to share it with us—and to celebrate my becoming a member of Branding Iron's Cowboy Christmas Ball committee."

"That didn't take long," Ben said between bites. "You must've charmed those ladies. I'm impressed."

"Don't be. They needed somebody to telephone people, and I was there. I suspect charm had nothing to do with it." She sipped her juice, her silence working up to a question. "Did you talk to my mother again? How is she?"

"She's doing some heavy-duty soul-searching—a good thing, if you ask me. Having you show up out of the blue has been a lot for her to take in."

"Are you saying she's sorry that I'm here?" Jess's expression reminded Ben of a little slapped kitten.

"No, nothing like that. But she's ashamed of where you found her and what she's become. Francine wants to change, Jess, but I'm not sure she knows how. You've got a long, tough road ahead of you."

"I know that but, for better or for worse, she's all the family I have. Can you tell me more?"

"She's desperately afraid of disappointing you—and she seems to be worried that you've never forgiven her for putting you up for adoption."

"I forgave her early on. But I didn't know her story till your mother told me—how she ran away with my father, and he was killed by a rodeo bull. She was in no condition to care for a baby. I can't blame her for wanting to give me a chance at a better life."

"And did you have a better life?"

She lowered her gaze, but not before he caught the flash

of buried hurt in her eyes. In his job, Ben had learned to read people. This fragile-looking woman was holding something back.

"Did you have a better life, Jess?"

She hesitated a moment, then shook her head. "Not every adoption has a happy ending. My adoptive parents passed all the screenings. My dad had a good job. My mom was a full-time homemaker in a pretty suburban house. White picket fence, the whole package. The first few years were fine, what little I remember of them. Then my dad lost his job, had an affair, and left us. Mom had no supportive family and no job skills. We lost the house, of course, and ended up living in a cheap motel where she cleaned rooms to pay for the rent. When I got old enough to carry a mop, I helped her. There were a few men in her life—no, none of them touched me. She'd have killed them if they had. But they never stayed long. By the time the last one left, she was sick—leukemia."

Ben studied her across the table, aching to cross the distance between them, wrap her in his arms and cradle her like a child. Even after the loss of his father, his own childhood had been a picnic compared to hers. That she'd survived— courageous, emotionally strong and capable of loving—was a miracle.

"I was sixteen when she died," Jess said. "Somehow, working nights, I managed to finish high school. I was even taking a couple of college classes when I got married. I was just nineteen. It was a mistake. Don't ask me to go there."

It surprised Ben to hear that she'd been married But, as he reminded himself, there was plenty he didn't know about Jess Ramsey.

"Believe me, you're not the only one who's made that kind of mistake," he said.

"As the old saying goes, it's water under the bridge. I

was divorced and hanging on by the skin of my teeth when I got a call from a lawyer in Los Angeles. My long-lost adoptive father had died. I was his only legal heir. The money wasn't a fortune, but it was enough to put in the bank for a new start. You know the rest of the story."

Ben finished the last forkful of his lasagna. "You're one tough lady, Jess. I had no idea you'd been through such hard times."

Jess stood and began clearing away the dishes. "I'm not asking for sympathy," she said. "But now that I've told you, I'd like to ask a favor."

"Name it." Ben rose to help put the leftovers in the fridge.

"I don't want Francine to know about my past," she said. "She put me up for adoption so I could have a happy life. I'd like her to go on believing that's what she gave me."

Her compassion stunned him for an instant. "I understand. My lips are sealed."

"That means I don't want the word to get back to her by way of anybody else. You mustn't tell a soul, not even your mother." Her eyes narrowed. "I probably shouldn't even have told you."

"Then why did you?" He stood facing her, his gaze probing hers.

"Because you opened the door," she said. "I needed somebody on my side who understood the truth. Somebody I could trust. Was I wrong?" Her skin was luminous, her lips as full and ripe as June strawberries. Ben had to check himself to keep from leaning down and kissing her, not because of her story but because she was an extraordinary person—and because he could imagine how she would taste.

"You're not wrong, Jess," he said. "As sheriff, I've learned to keep a confidence. Your secret is safe with me."

"I appreciate that." She finished loading the dishwasher,

added detergent and started the cycle. "Now if you'll excuse me, I'll be going up to bed. It's been a long day."

"You're sure you don't want to keep me company and watch the ten o'clock news? It helps me unwind." He imagined sitting on the couch with her in the darkened living room, not quite touching, but maybe slipping an arm behind her shoulders, feeling the warmth that emanated from her sweet woman's body.

On second thought, it might not be a good idea.

"Thanks for the invitation, but I'd fall asleep for sure. You'd have to drag me up those stairs. I'd better go while I'm still on my feet."

"Sleep tight, then. I'll check on your car tomorrow and let you know when it'll be done. Silas can deliver it, if you don't mind driving him back to the garage. Oh, and thanks for supper."

"Like I said, don't get used to it." The stairs creaked lightly as she vanished from sight. Ben wandered into the living room, found the remote and switched on the antiquated TV between his mother's corner bookshelves. As he sank into the sofa, Ben heard soft footsteps overhead and the sound of water running in the bathroom. By the time he went upstairs to bed, Jess would probably be asleep.

As the commercials played onscreen, he went back over the details of her story. Everything she'd said had made sense and fit her reason for coming here. But he'd spent too many years as a lawman not to have questions.

Was Jess telling the truth? He had no reason to disbelieve her. But he'd bet good money she wasn't telling him everything. She'd married at nineteen. By now he'd guess her age at—what? Twenty-six or so? She'd glossed over those missing years. But then, why should it matter? She had shown herself to be a good person, kind, forgiving, and honest. Wasn't that enough?

He yawned, willing himself to stay awake until he could

go upstairs without running into Jess again. She was an attractive little thing. He liked her—liked her a lot. But the suspicious side of his nature refused to lie down and be still. The woman was hiding something—and his gut instinct told him it wasn't good. Until he knew more about her, he'd be smart to keep his guard up—and his male impulses in check.

Chapter Five

Jess had always been an early riser, but last night she'd gone to bed exhausted. By the time she'd opened her eyes to morning, brushed her teeth, splashed her face, and pulled on her fleece jogging suit, it was nearly eight o'clock. She pattered barefoot down the stairs to find Clara seated at the kitchen table, sipping coffee and doing the newspaper's crossword puzzle.

Clara glanced up with a smile as Jess walked in. "Good morning," she said. "How about some coffee?"

"That sounds great. No, please don't bother getting up. I can get it." Jess filled a cup from the coffeepot, then took a seat. "I didn't mean to sleep this late, but that bed was heavenly. Thank you again for putting me up."

"No trouble at all, dear. Know that you're welcome to stay as long as you like. I'd have fixed you some bacon and eggs but I wasn't sure you'd want a big breakfast."

"Coffee's fine for now, thanks. I'm guessing Ben's left for work."

"He has. And he wanted me to tell you that Silas will be bringing your car around this afternoon."

"Great. Maybe after I take Silas back to the garage, I'll

drop by the jail and see my mother. Meanwhile, after lunch, I'll see what I can do about whittling down your phone call list." She glanced at Clara's newspaper. "Does that paper have a classified section?"

"Here you are." Clara picked up the paper, peeled off the back page and passed it to Jess. "Not much to it, as you'll see. Branding Iron's a pretty small place."

"One apartment and one job. That's all I need." Jess spread the single page on the table, scanning the columns. Many of the ads featured items for sale—cars, appliances, food supplements, a business or two and a house with grazing land. The Help Wanted section was no more encouraging. Besides the usual "make money at home" schemes, which Jess had never trusted, there were a couple of ads for farm workers, one for a truck driver and one for a dishwasher at Buckaroo's—that might at least be someplace to start. She certainly knew how to wash dishes.

In the For Rent section there were a couple of possibilities—a small, affordable studio in the basement of a home, and a free room in exchange for taking care of someone's elderly parents. But neither of these would do if she had her mother with her, Jess realized. For herself and Francine, she'd need a two-bedroom place, and there was nothing like that in the paper.

Nothing for a struggling single woman and her misbehaving mother.

The enormity of what she was about to do hit Jess like a rolling two-ton boulder. Taking an emotionally fragile alcoholic under her wing was going to be a huge responsibility. Whatever Francine was surviving on now, probably welfare, couldn't be much. And even with an adequate place to live, if she had nothing meaningful to do, she could easily go right back to her old habits.

Ben's blunt advice had been spot-on. If things didn't

work out with Francine, there'd be nothing left of this well-meant undertaking but two broken hearts. She had just one chance to help her mother. She had to do this right.

"Are you okay, Jess?" Clara was watching her with a worried expression.

"I'm fine." Jess rose, carried her cup to the sink and began unloading last night's clean dishes from the dishwasher. "But what I'm about to take on is sinking in. I'll be dealing with a lot of responsibilities in the time ahead. What I need right now, I think, is a good long walk to clear my head."

"That might be just the ticket," Clara said. "It's a nice, sunny morning. Go on, I can finish up in here. But wear something warm. Have you got a coat?"

"I left it in the trunk of my car. But I can layer. I'll be fine." Jess hurried upstairs to put on her sneakers, warm socks and a merino sweater under her track suit. With a quilted vest to top it off, she felt almost cozy.

"Take your phone," Clara called up the stairs. "I'll give you my number, so you can call if you get lost."

"Got it!" Clara was a dear, Jess thought. But it was as if the woman had missed having someone to fuss over. Ben probably wouldn't stand for it. Maybe her daughter, Ellie, had resisted being mothered as well. That could be the reason for the seeming distance between them.

Five minutes later she was out the door, striding along the sidewalk, filling her lungs with the crisp, wintery air. Even as a girl, Jess had relied on walking to calm her nerves and help her think. She could feel how much she needed it today.

The Marsden home was in a neighborhood of vintage houses, set along a winding street. The oaks and sycamores that overhung the walks were bare of their leaves, but the area would be an oasis of pleasant shade in summertime. It was clearly the nicest part of town. How lucky Ben was to have grown up in a setting like this.

Clara had worried about her getting lost, but Jess knew enough to keep track of where she'd been. Taking note of the street signs and the direction she was walking, she was confident she'd have no trouble finding her way back.

Coming to a stop sign, she took a right turn in the direction of Main Street. The houses in this neighborhood were more modest. Scattered here and there were signs advertising small home businesses—lawnmower repair, custom sewing, dog grooming, and more. There didn't appear to be a problem with zoning laws here, if Branding Iron even had such regulations.

She reached another corner and paused, debating which way to turn. Flipping a mental coin, she went left. This time she found herself on a short one-way backstreet, not much wider than an alley. A single block in length, its far end merged with Main Street, coming out between the post office and Merle's Craft and Yarn Shoppe. The half-dozen houses here had an old-fashioned look, with broad front porches and gingerbread trim. But they were smaller than the homes in Clara's neighborhood, with faded siding, sagging steps and weedy yards. It was as if the people who lived in these places had been here for decades and grown too old to care for their properties. Still, this little street, so close to downtown, must've been charming in its day.

The shabbiest home of all had an overgrown yard, boarded up windows and a No Trespassing sign on the rickety metal gate. Intrigued, Jess stopped to look at it.

Judging from the untrampled weeds growing up through the wooden steps, the place had been vacant for months, at least.

It looked as if it might have a second floor, if the windowed gables were any indication, but it was hard to tell from outside. The exterior, gray asbestos siding with faded blue shutters, looked as if it hadn't been painted in fifty years. Leafless vines of Virginia creeper had grown over the porch to hang like tangled brown curtains from the eave.

Nailed to one of the porch supports was a hand-lettered sign: FOR SALE BY OWNER. POSSIBLE CONTRACT WITH DOWN-PAYMENT.

A phone number was written at the bottom. Almost before she had time to think, Jess had her cell phone in her hand and was keying in the number. One of the ladies in yesterday's committee meeting had mentioned the need for a place to stay in Branding Iron. Could this old house, so close to the center of town, be fixed up as a bed-and-breakfast?

Questions flew through her mind as the phone rang on the other end. Was the place even livable? Could she afford to buy it? Would the bank give her a loan if she needed it, to make the necessary repairs?

A woman answered. Yes, the house was still for sale. It had belonged to her grandfather, who'd passed away last winter. The family had hoped to find a buyer to fix it up, but no one had expressed any interest until now. Yes, she lived just a few minutes away and would be happy to come over and show it.

As she waited, Jess's head spun with ideas. From the street, she could see an overgrown driveway leading back to a closed garage behind the house. That would mean, Jess hoped, extra storage space and room for guest parking. If the house has only one bathroom, she would need to add another, a major expense. That could be a problem.

But she was getting ahead of herself. It wouldn't do to get excited about the place until she'd had a look inside.

A twenty-year-old Cadillac—Jess guessed it must have belonged to the grandfather—pulled to the curb and stopped. The woman who climbed out appeared to be in her forties. She was nicely dressed in slacks and a down jacket, but her manner seemed harried, as if she'd rushed away from something important.

"Come on, I've got the key," she said, leading Jess up the walk and onto the porch. "We'd really like to get this place off our hands. Last summer some high school kids broke in through a window and had a wild party. They were even smoking weed. The sheriff said it was lucky they didn't set the place on fire. We figure it's only a matter of time before something like that happens again."

There was a hasp with a padlock on the front door. The woman, who hadn't bothered to give her name, fumbled for the key in her purse. "Grandpa was ninety-three when he died. For the last few years he wouldn't let anybody in here. After he passed away, we had to hire a man to haul out the junk so we could put the place up for sale." She found the key and thrust it into the lock. "It needs a lot of fixing up, but the house is solid. My husband replaced the furnace and water heater ten years ago, and paid for a new roof when the old one started leaking. The plumbing and wiring are okay as far as I know, but the rest . . . well, you'll see."

The door creaked open into a dim space. Shafts of sunlight filtered through the openings between the window boards, making it possible to see, though not well. Jess stifled a groan as she looked around.

The teens who'd partied in the house had spray-painted graffiti on the walls and left burned spots, empty beer cans and joint stubs on the moldering carpet. The air still reeked of marijuana smoke, an odor Jess remembered all too well from her days of cleaning motel rooms. As Jess walked into the kitchen, something ran across her foot—a mouse, most likely. And one mouse would be sure to have brothers, sisters, aunts, uncles and cousins. Francine's cat, Sergeant Pepper, would have a field day here.

The kitchen space was functional, complete with cupboards and counters, a dirty stove, and an even dirtier fridge. The bathroom, with a shower over the tub and a moldy plastic curtain, would need a thorough disinfecting before it could be used. The two bedrooms off the hall were empty.

"What's upstairs?" she asked, noticing the stairway off the dining area.

"When Grandpa had his family here, the kids' rooms were up there—and there's a second bathroom with a tub. This was a nice house once. I wish I'd brought a flashlight so you could see it better."

Bedrooms upstairs and a second bathroom. That would almost make the project possible. But the work and expense it would take to make the place appealing—good grief, was she really crazy enough to take this on?

Francine had another nine days left on her sentence. If Jess could get the kitchen, bathroom and downstairs bedrooms livable by then, her mother could help her fix up the rest. But would Francine be willing, or even interested?

"I'll need a day or so to think about it," she said. "Do you feel all right about lending me the key? I'd like to come back for a second look with a flashlight."

The woman twisted the key off her key ring. "Here. I've got a spare at home. If you decide you don't want the place, you can drop it off at my house. Here's my address and phone number." She handed Jess a card.

"Thanks. I guess I'd better ask your ballpark price and the kind of contract terms you're expecting."

The figure the woman quoted was surprisingly low, but then Branding Iron wasn't Kansas City. "We were thinking ten percent down and the rest on contract with a balloon payment in five years. If that doesn't suit you, feel free to make an offer and I'll discuss it with my husband. He's the businessman of the family."

"I'll think about it and get back to you by the end of tomorrow." Jess's pulse was racing. With the fifty-thousand dollar inheritance she had stashed away, the down payment was doable, and there would be enough money left over for some basic refurbishing. It wouldn't be a slam-dunk, she reminded herself. She'd need to get the bed-and-breakfast up and running and make enough money for the monthly payments. If she didn't get enough business, she'd have to get a job. Otherwise, she could go belly-up and lose her whole investment.

The prospect was scary—more than scary, it was terrifying. But what would she have if she didn't take a chance and do this?

With the key in her pocket, she stood at the gate and watched the Cadillac drive away. Questions flocked into her mind—all the questions she'd forgotten to ask. Where were the washer and dryer hookups? Where was the furnace? What was stored in the garage?

She would have to go back to find the answers. Maybe Ben would have a flashlight she could borrow. Or maybe she should buy her own. She was already becoming too dependent on the handsome sheriff.

The sheriff who, if he chose, could strip her secrets bare with a few clicks of his computer mouse.

But never mind that. Right now she had other things on her mind. Excitement gave her feet wings as she retraced her steps back up the gently sloping streets to the Marsden home. She could hardly wait to tell Clara about the house.

She found the front door unlocked, but nobody was home. Clara had left a note on the kitchen table.

Jess—I've gone to an early lunch and a matinee with some friends. Make yourself comfortable. If you want to start calling, the list is by the phone. Just tell folks that you want to confirm what they're bringing and remind them to have the food at the gym by 6:30 on December 18. Thanks. C.

Jess changed out of her track suit, into jeans and a turtleneck, then warmed some leftover lasagna and washed it down with a can of Diet Coke. Hunger satisfied, she settled herself next to the phone on Clara's small desk, braced herself for an onerous task and began calling the people on the list.

Everyone who answered was nice. But after the first few calls, Jess came to anticipate the moment when, after hearing her name, they'd ask who she was. "I'm new in town and right now I'm staying with Clara," became her stock answer. Explaining that she was Francine's daughter would only complicate things. Word would get around soon enough. More than likely, it already had.

She was a third of the way down the list and taking a break to stand up and stretch when the phone rang. It was Silas, letting her know her car was ready. He'd be by to pick her up and take her back to the garage, where he could print out the paperwork and run her credit card.

True to his word, he showed up a few minutes later, a lanky, plain-spoken man dressed in grease-stained coveralls. "I met your wife and daughter yesterday," Jess told him as they drove away. "I liked them both."

"Yeah, they're a good pair." He spoke with a slow drawl. "I guess you noticed how Katy is. We prayed for a baby for years. When God finally answered, he sent us

Katy. We figured we must've deserved something special to get one of his sweetest angels."

"That's what she is, all right." Jess swallowed the lump that had risen in her throat. "She's lucky to have such loving parents. Thanks for getting my car done so fast, by the way, and for picking me up."

"No trouble at all," he said. "Connie tells me you're Francine's daughter."

He would know, of course. "That's right," Jess said. "Since she's all the family I have, I plan to stay around and try to help her."

"Well, good luck with that. Francine's got a kind heart. But she can be a handful when she's liquored up."

"So I'm told. I'm hoping to change that."

"Well, if you can, it'll be more than a passel of preachers and social worker types have been able to do."

"I know it won't be easy," Jess said. "But she's my mother. All I can do is try."

"Here we are." Silas pulled up in front of the garage. Jess followed him inside and paid for the repairs and the tow, which totaled out to the exact, reasonable amount of his estimate. Opening the trunk, she found the quilted coat she'd left there and slipped into its warmth.

The Pontiac started up fine. Jess pulled away from the garage and headed for the jail to see Francine. With luck, Ben would be there too. Maybe he'd have time later to look at the house with her. She could certainly use a second pair of eyes and a cooler head than her own.

But what was she thinking? Ben was responsible for the safety of the whole county. Just because he'd come to her rescue and taken her under his roof didn't mean she could ask for his help whenever she needed it.

As she pulled into the parking lot on the jail side of the county building she noticed the sheriff's big, tan SUV

parked in its reserved spot along the curb. Jess willed herself to ignore her quickening pulse. Of course Ben would
be here. He worked here. And he'd probably be too busy
to pay her much attention. Anyway, she hadn't come to
see him. She'd come to see her mother.

Should she mention the house to Francine or wait till it
was a sure decision? Preoccupied with the thought, she
opened the outer door and pressed the buzzer to be admitted through the second door into the jail.

"Yes?" The intercom crackled. She recognized the no-
nonsense voice of the female deputy she'd met the day before.

"Jessica Ramsey. I'm here to see Francine."

"One moment please."

Jess was preparing herself to be frisked again when the
door opened and Ben stood there, as big as a barn door
and as gorgeous as a Roman god. His dimple deepened as
he gave her a smile. "Hey, I see your car's fixed," he said.

"It is. And the fix was even affordable."

"I told you Silas was a good guy. Come on in." He held
the door for her.

"Do I need to be patted down again?" Was she secretly
wishing he'd do the job?

"You're fine," he said, handing her purse to the woman
at the counter. "Francine's the only one in lockup today,
and nobody in their right mind would break her out of
here before her time's up."

"About that," Jess said. "Can we talk for a minute before I see her again?"

"Sure." He opened the door to his office, ushered her
inside and offered her a chair across from his desk. "If
you've had a change of heart, I wouldn't blame you. Yesterday had to be pretty rough."

"Nothing's changed," Jess said. "In fact, I've come up

with a plan. I hadn't meant to talk to you about it, but as long as you're here, I could use some cool-headed advice."

"I'm listening." *Sarsaparilla—that was the name of the old-fashioned root beer that matched his eyes.*

"Here's the thing," she said. "I'll be needing a place to live and a way to make money. Once she's out of jail, so will Francine. And she'll have a better chance at recovery if she's got something to do."

Ben frowned. "Sounds like a pretty tall order. What've you got in mind?"

"I've found an old house!" As she spoke, Jess could feel her enthusiasm mounting. "I've already talked with the owner. With the money my father left me, I can make the down payment and fix the place up into a bed-and-breakfast! Francine can help me!"

"Whoa there." He was shaking his head, half laughing.

"What's the matter? Don't you think I can do it?"

"Judging by what I've seen of you so far, there's nothing you can't do if you put your mind to it. But you could be getting in over your head."

"Don't you think I know that?" Heaven help her, she was convincing herself. The more Ben cautioned her against the venture, the more determined she became to go ahead.

"Think about it," he said. "It won't be a simple matter of buying the place and fixing it up. You'll need insurance, a business license, and deposits for the power and water. Once you're open, you'll need to advertise. Those things all cost money. As for the labor—you're such a little thing. How much can you do on your own? And who knows how much help Francine will be. Are you sure you want to jump into this?"

She met his gaze with determination. "I'm getting more sure by the minute."

He exhaled, as if mentally counting to ten. "All right, where is this project of yours?"

She told him.

He muffled a curse. "I know that old place. I arrested a bunch of kids in there last summer. They'd made a real mess. I'd be surprised if it was ever cleaned up."

"Cleaning up would take some work, all right. But I'm not afraid of getting my hands dirty. And the location is perfect, right off Main Street. Once the driveway's cleared of weeds, there'll be room for off-street parking. I've got a key to the place. I can show it to you if you have time to look."

He stood, with an air of impatience. "I've got time now if you want."

"Don't you have to be here?" Jess asked.

"I'll have my phone. If anybody needs me, they can call. Give me a few minutes to square things away here and we can go."

"Fine, and thanks." She stood and moved to the door. "Is it all right if I go say hi to my mother?"

"Go ahead. She's in her cell, at the end of the hall. For now, she's the only one in here. Are you going to tell her about the house?"

"Not until it's certain." Jess made the decision as she spoke. "And not until we've had more time to talk. Call me when you're ready to go. Oh—and we'll need a flashlight."

"There's one in the vehicle. I won't be long."

She left his office and walked down the hall where a half-dozen cells were lined up along one side. The walls between them were solid, but there were bars on the side facing the hall. The first cells Jess passed were empty, sad little spaces, not much bigger than walk-in closets. Everything was white inside, with a single bunk attached to the wall and an exposed toilet and basin in one corner. Jess couldn't imagine which would be worse—the boredom, the lack of privacy or the plain humiliation of having to be there.

Francine's cell was like the others, except that a plywood screen had been put up to give her some privacy on the toilet. Some tattered celebrity gossip magazines lay scattered on the rumpled blanket that covered her bunk. Francine looked up from the one she was reading.

"Why, hello, sweetie! Have you come to spring me out of here?"

"Not quite." Jess smiled at what she hoped had been a joke. "But when you do get out, I've got plans for us."

"Plans, you say? How's about a trip to Vegas? Now, that would be a treat, honey! We could get us some sexy new outfits and burn up the town! Ever play blackjack? I could teach you a thing or two."

Once more, Jess felt the tug of doubt. What if Francine wasn't interested in the bed-and-breakfast? What if all she wanted was to get out and enjoy her idea of a good time—which could get her right back to where she was now?

"I'll tell you more later," she said. "I'm afraid my plan doesn't include a trip, just a lot of hard work. But it's something that could change both our lives."

Francine didn't look pleased. "Well, as long as it starts with a trip to the beauty parlor to pretty me up, I'll give it a listen. At least it'll be somethin' to look forward to."

Jess suppressed a sigh. She'd hoped her mother would be eager to hear about the plan. But Ben had been spot-on about Francine. Changing her would be impossible if she didn't want to change herself.

"While you're here, is there anything you need?" she asked. "Anything I can get you that they'll let you have?"

"Some new magazines would be great. The one I just finished came out while Kim Kardashian was still married to that ball player."

"If it's okay with the sheriff, I'll get you a whole stack of them." Jess glanced back up the hallway to see Ben waiting for her. "I've got to go now, but I'll be back tomorrow."

"I'll be right here, honey." Francine picked up another magazine and started reading again.

Spirits sagging, Jess hurried after Ben, who'd retrieved her purse and was already headed for the front door. At least she knew what she was up against. But something told her the real challenge wasn't going to be fixing up the bed-and-breakfast. It was going to be motivating Francine.

Chapter Six

Jess sat lost in thought as Ben drove down Main Street. Strings of Christmas lights twinkled from the lampposts. Tinsel garlands draped the shop windows. Ben had left the SUV's radio on. The local station was playing Elvis Presley's husky rendition of "Silent Night."

It had been a long time since Jess had felt like celebrating Christmas. Maybe this year would be different.

Or maybe it wouldn't.

Ben turned the radio down before he spoke. "For a lady who was bubbling over twenty minutes ago, you're mighty quiet. How did the visit with your mother go? Did you tell her about the house?"

"I told her I had a plan. She asked me if it included a trip to Vegas."

Ben made a sound like a strangled laugh. "Why am I not surprised?"

"It's like she thinks I'm Santa Claus and everything's going to be fun and games when she gets out. What if she doesn't care about the house? What if she doesn't want any part of the work involved? You told me this wouldn't be easy. I'm just beginning to understand how right you were."

"Let me give you one piece of advice." Ben rounded the corner, pulled up in front of the old house and turned in the seat to face her. "Ask yourself this question. What if you were on your own and Francine wasn't in the picture? Would you still take on this project, or any other? Would you do it for yourself?"

"I . . ." She hesitated. "I don't know. I hadn't thought about it that way."

"If you really don't know, or if your answer is anything short of a *yes*, then you might want to step back and think it over. Francine's a good-hearted woman, but she's as flighty as a grasshopper. If you can involve her and help her, fine. But you can't count on her sticking it out, not even with you."

"So I should just take her to Vegas, blow my inheritance and call it good?" There was an edge to her question.

"That's not what I meant." Ben switched off the engine and reached for the big flashlight that was mounted on a bracket under the dash. "Come on, let's go have a look at the house."

Jess found the key in her purse and led the way through the gate and onto the porch. It was late afternoon, still light enough to see, but the sun was low. The house would be even darker than when she'd been there this morning.

Ben switched on his flashlight as Jess opened the door. "Phew! That weed smell's almost as strong as when I was here last summer," he said. "It doesn't look like anybody's touched the place since then. If you take this on, you'll need to give it a good airing out." He shook his head. "Kids!"

"Getting rid of the carpet should help with the smell," Jess said. "Help me pull up a corner. I want to see what's underneath."

Ben found a loose corner and yanked it up. The carpet was so old, it came apart in his hands.

"Shine the light under there," Jess said. "I'm hoping there'll be—yes! Hardwood! With luck it'll just need a good waxing."

"And you'll kill your back doing it," Ben muttered. "Shall we have a look at the kitchen?"

They made their way to the back of the house. "Hold the light." He crouched next to the sink and opened the cabinet doors underneath. A mouse darted out of a hole in the back and scurried away.

"I'm thinking Sergeant Pepper will make short work of the rodent population," Jess said.

"You're not afraid of those little pests?" He glanced up at her. "My ex was terrified of them."

"I'm scared of criminals and terrorists and drunk drivers. Mice and spiders I can deal with—and have."

"Good. If you take this place on, you'll do a lot of dealing. You may want to just call an exterminator. More expense. And you'd better hope the place doesn't have termites. Come in closer. Shine the light under here." He peered into the dark space. His side pressed against hers, warm and man-solid. The contact triggered a tingle of awareness that flowed like warm honey through Jess's body.

Was Ben feeling it too? But that couldn't be allowed to matter, Jess told herself. She had a long, sad history of getting involved with the wrong men. She wasn't about to let it happen again—especially since *this* wrong man was the law in Branding Iron, Texas.

"The pipes look okay," he said. "No rust or spots where they might've leaked. But you won't know for sure till the water's turned on. In case you wind up with a flood on your hands, you'll want somebody here who can turn off the main line and fix the problem—that is, if you're fool enough to buy this place."

"I'll keep that in mind," Jess said.

Standing, he stepped back from the sink. "Where are the furnace and water heater?"

"I forgot to ask. But the woman did tell me they were replaced ten years ago."

"Fine, if it's true. But let's have a look. I'm betting this place has a half-basement. Most of these old houses do." He led the way through an open doorway at the rear of the kitchen, down a single step into a small area that could have served as a mudroom. Off to the left, the flashlight revealed a worn wooden stairway descending into murky darkness.

"You can stay up here if you want," he said, starting down.

"No, I've got to see it sometime." Jess followed him, keeping close behind his broad, protecting back. She was doing her best to appear brave, but the prospect of going down into that dark hole was downright spooky.

Spiderwebs festooned the doorway into the lower room. Ben used the flashlight to brush them away. Jess knew the spiders wouldn't likely harm her. Even so, despite her brave words to Ben, the thought made her skin crawl. She stuck to him like a cocklebur as he stepped into the lower room.

The flashlight's beam shone on cement walls and a ceiling of sturdy joists that supported the main floor, along with the pipes and wires that served the house. Fingers of dim light filtered through one tiny, dirt-encrusted window. An electrical breaker box was mounted on one wall. A single wire clothesline was strung overhead.

"No termites, as far as I can see. And everything else looks shipshape," Ben said. "Of course there's no way to know for sure till the water, gas and electricity are turned on."

Jess's gaze followed the clothesline to something in the shadows. "Over there!" she exclaimed, pointing. "Shine your light!"

In the far corner, the beam revealed a hooked-up twin washer and dryer. Their olive-green color suggested they'd been bought in the 1970s. "Dare I hope they're still working?" Jess mused, thinking aloud.

"I wouldn't be surprised. Those old machines were built like Sherman tanks. They were made to last."

She glanced up to catch him studying her, his expression unreadable. "Goodness, sheriff, you surely aren't encouraging me, are you?" she teased.

"Don't bet on it. I still think you'd be crazy to buy this place." His brown eyes warmed. A faint smile tugged at the corners of his mouth. "All I say is, if you're going to take this on, along with Francine, you'd better be one tough little woman."

Something in his voice quickened Jess's pulse. The forbidden tingle she'd felt earlier, when they'd knelt in the kitchen, awakened and stirred.

That was the moment when a gumdrop-sized brown spider dropped from the ceiling on a strand of silk to dangle eight inches in front of Jess's face.

With a startled yelp, she jumped backward. Ben caught her as she stumbled against him. She shuddered, cowering against his chest as his arms closed around her. He felt as solid as a fortress and powerful enough to fight off an army of giant horror-movie spiders. For a few breaths she closed her eyes and let him hold her, savoring the rare sense of being safe and protected. *I could stay like this for a very long time,* Jess thought. But she'd learned the hard way not to want things she couldn't have. And getting too close to Ben Marsden would be a sure recipe for heartbreak.

When she dared to glance up again, the spider had retreated into the shadows of the ceiling. Ben's arms tightened an instant before he let her go and stepped back. "I thought you weren't afraid of spiders," he said.

"That wasn't a spider. That was a monster."

He chuckled. "For what it's worth, I've seen that kind before, though not as big. They look scary enough, but they won't hurt you."

"Not unless you count giving me a heart attack."

"Hey, why not adopt him as a pet? You could even give him a name. That's a secret my dad taught me when I was little—when something scares you, give it a name. Most of the time it worked—especially with the evil monsters under the bed. Try it."

Jess decided to play along. "Okay, how about Oscar? He can guard the basement, sort of like a watch-spider." She paused. "You know, I think it's really working."

Ben laughed, steering her toward the stairs with a hand at the small of her back. "That's the spirit. Let's leave Oscar to keep an eye on things and take a look at the top floor."

As they climbed, shimmers radiated from the light pressure of his hand through her coat. The chemistry was there, all right. If she were to cast aside all common sense, it would be easy to fall for this man. But once he learned about her past—and as a lawman, he was bound to— she'd be just another lowlife, no better than the brawlers and con artists who passed through his jail every day. So much for making a clean break with her past.

"You say you haven't seen what's up there?" They were in the living room again, standing at the foot of the stairs.

"The woman who showed me the place said there were bedrooms and a second bath. That would be perfect for the bed-and-breakfast. But neither of us wanted to go up there in the dark."

Ben stepped ahead of her. "Let me lead the way then, in case Oscar has some even bigger kinfolk living up there."

Jess suppressed a shudder. "I'll be thinking of names."

He directed the flashlight beam up the stairs and began

to climb. Jess followed a few feet behind, one hand clinging to the bannister. The stairs were covered with worn, gritty carpet that would need to be torn out. It would be nice, she mused, if she were to discover more hardwood underneath. But she was getting ahead of herself. For now, that could wait.

Ben stopped on the landing and gave her a moment to catch up. The narrow hallway ran to the far side of the house, ending in a small window that had been boarded from the inside. On either side of the hallway there were two rooms—a tiny bathroom with antiquated plumbing, which looked like a converted storage closet, and three children's rooms with slanted ceilings, faded wallpaper and little dormer windows.

These rooms had a different feel to them than the larger, empty bedrooms downstairs, as if they'd been abandoned long ago. In one room, the wallpaper was covered with childish crayon drawings. In another, an old-fashioned crib had been left behind, its mattress gone. What had happened to the children who'd lived in these rooms? Had they grown up? Maybe even passed on by now?

Ben was quiet, as if he too felt the silent ghosts of the past. At last he spoke. "Seen enough?"

"I think so, thanks," Jess said. "I won't keep you any longer. Let's go."

Ben led the way downstairs with the flashlight. By the time they stepped out onto the porch, the sun was going down in a crimson blaze, painting the town and the bare fields beyond with amber gold. Jess was just locking the door when Ben's cell phone rang.

He turned partway to answer it. "Hey, Ethan. What's up?" He paused; then a grin lit his face. "You're kidding! That's great news. . . . You bet. I'll be there by tomorrow night. We'll have a great road trip back. . . . What's that? . . . Absolutely. Don't we always have it up when you come?"

Another pause. "No snow yet, but pack warm. We'll cross our fingers for a white Christmas. See you."

Pocketing the phone, he turned back to Jess. "Good news! I'm getting my son early. I'll be leaving tomorrow afternoon to drive to Dallas and pick him up. We'll be back here the next day. But right now ..." He grinned down at Jess, his eyes twinkling like a schoolboy's. "How would you like to help me put up a Christmas tree?"

The question caught Jess off guard. She stared up at him in surprise.

"We always have the tree up at my mother's house when Ethan gets here. He looks forward to it every year, so it's got to be done tonight, before I leave. Mom and I have always done it together, but she's not strong enough anymore, especially at the end of the day. The work will wear her out. So I'm recruiting you." Ben paused. "If you don't say no right now, I'm going to assume it's a yes."

Recovering, she laughed at his excitement. "Sure, I'll help. It just took a minute to sink in. Lead the way."

Without the sun, the breeze was chilly. Ben helped Jess into the SUV, then called to let his deputies know his plans. "I'll be in for the first hour in the morning to take care of any last-minute business," he said. "Then I'll be gone for the rest of the day, and the next day as well. Ruth, you're in charge till I get back."

"So what's next?" Jess asked as he ended the call.

"Next we go home, change vehicles, get me out of uniform, and go tree shopping."

Twenty minutes later they were driving back toward the main road in Ben's well-used pickup truck. Ben had switched his khaki uniform for blue jeans, cowboy boots and a warm woolen shirt with a fleece-lined denim jacket.

As they drove, he glanced her way and caught Jess looking him over. "What?" he asked, "Have I grown an extra pair of ears?"

Jess was grateful for the dim interior of the truck cab, which hid the rush of heat to her face. "It's just that this is the first time I've seen you out of uniform."

"Oh? And which way do you like me better?" he teased.

"No comment." He was mouth-wateringly gorgeous either way, but something told her the wretched man was well aware of that. "Where are we going to get the tree?" she asked, changing the subject.

"Only one place. Hank's Feed and Hardware on the road out of town opens a Christmas tree lot every year. Since we're early, there should be plenty of nice trees to choose from."

A moment later he braked at the stop sign and swung the truck onto a familiar-looking road. After an instant's puzzling, Jess recognized the two-lane highway where her car had quit. A quarter mile ahead was a low, wooden building with Christmas lights strung in front and off to the side. Cars and trucks were clustered along the shoulder of the road.

"Looks like Hank's already busy. Glad we didn't get here any later." Ben pulled the truck behind the line of cars and switched off the engine. A makeshift chicken wire fence surrounded the Christmas tree lot, which was filled with fresh, bushy pines and firs. Couples and families wandered among them, inspecting the trees and listening to the Christmas music that blared from a speaker mounted on the side of the hardware store. All that was missing was snow.

"Let's get looking. The best trees will go fast. They won't last long." Ben climbed out of the truck and strode around to open the door for Jess. The pickup was high, with oversized tires. When Jess hesitated to climb down, he reached up, clasped her waist and swung her to the ground, leaving her slightly breathless. "Come on," he said, guiding her with a hand at her elbow.

"I must've gone tree shopping when I was little." Jess stretched her legs to match his eager strides. "But I know my mother and I never got a tree after my father left us. We couldn't spare the money. I haven't had one since—there just didn't seem to be much point."

Her words stopped him midstride. He turned to face her. His eyes reflected the glow of the Christmas lights strung above them. "You're kidding, right?"

"Would I kid about something so pathetic?"

"I don't suppose you would. But never mind, because we're going to change that. This year you're getting the full Christmas tree experience, starting now!"

Circling her shoulders with his arm, he ushered her into the Christmas tree lot. Several people turned to stare. Maybe they weren't used to seeing their sheriff with his arm around a strange woman. But Ben seemed oblivious to the gossip he was likely causing. Jess found herself liking him for that.

A familiar figure waved and beckoned them over. Kylie Taggart was tree shopping with two cute middle-school-aged children and a tall, dark, strikingly handsome cowboy who was holding a tree up for her approval. He had to be her husband, Shane, who was Ben's best friend.

"Hi, Jess!" Kylie's coat was buttoned tight over her burgeoning belly. "I was hoping I'd run into you. I see Ben's taken you in hand." She introduced her husband and her children, Hunter and Amy.

"I commandeered Jess to help me get the tree up," Ben said. "Ethan is coming early, and I worry about Mom not being strong enough to take it on."

Shane grinned down at Jess. "Ask Ben to tell you about Kylie's Christmas tree hunt last year. It was quite an adventure."

"Yes!" Kylie laughed. "I ended up in jail for trying to cut down a tree on city property. That's how I met your mother, Jess. She was there, too, a friend when I needed one. I came to like Francine. I still do."

"Thank you for that," Jess said. "I can only hope more people feel the way you do."

Kylie reached out mittened fingers and gave Jess's hand a squeeze. "I know you might not have an easy time ahead. If you ever need to talk, I'm here."

"That means more to me than you can imagine." Jess gave her a smile as Kylie's family pulled her away to look at more trees.

Ben was already checking out a nearby tree, inspecting all sides, then putting it back in the row. Since they needed to get the tree set up and decorated tonight, Jess knew they didn't have much time. But she held her tongue as Ben inspected, then rejected, the next dozen trees he saw. None of them, it seemed, were good enough for Ethan's Christmas.

"Over there!" Maybe the thirteenth tree would be the charm. Ben headed for a row of the most expensive trees on the lot. There were only a few of these, probably because few people in Branding Iron could—or would—pay out that kind of money for a tree. But they were beautiful—tall, straight, lushly green, and perfectly shaped.

"This one!" He stood the tree on the end of its sawed trunk and turned it slowly. "What do you think?"

"It's beautiful. But do you really want to pay that much for something you'll be throwing out in a few weeks?"

"Hey, it's for Christmas!" He motioned the husky teenage lot boy over. "Take this out to the black pickup. I'll pay up front—careful now, don't break any branches."

"Don't worry, I won't, sheriff," the boy responded as he shouldered the tree and headed out of the lot.

Jess walked with him to the checkout line, where they waited their turn behind the other customers Anxious to get going now, Ben fished his credit card out of his wallet to have it ready. Standing beside him, Jess felt an odd, prickling sensation at the back of her neck, as if someone was staring intently at her from behind. She'd never credited herself with psychic powers, but the feeling was too strong to ignore.

She wheeled around, abruptly enough to catch the disapproving glare on Maybelle Ferguson's face before the woman turned and walked away.

"I'm afraid we may have triggered some gossip," she told Ben as they drove home with the tree in the back of the pickup.

Ben had been humming along with "Blue Christmas." He stopped. "Gossip? What gossip?"

"You know—the county sheriff hanging out with the new scarlet woman in town."

His laugh was warm and belly-deep. "Scarlet woman! Hey, I kind of like that."

"I'm serious. When we were in line, I caught Maybelle Ferguson giving me this *look*. It was like being stabbed in the back."

He turned the truck off the main road and back onto the street they'd taken from the house. "This is a small town, Jess. As a newcomer, you can expect some of that. But as long as we're both single and not doing anything more scandalous than buying a Christmas tree, I say, let them gossip. They'll soon get tired of it, or find something juicier to talk about."

"But—" Jess bit back the rest of her argument. Ben wouldn't understand how much she needed the friendship and approval of the people in Branding Iron. He'd grown up here, in a respected family. Everybody seemed to look up to him. He'd have no idea how it felt to be an outsider, branded before she even had a chance to prove herself.

Ben parked the pickup in the driveway and helped Jess to the ground. They crossed the porch and opened the front door to be greeted by the smell of savory beef-and-bean chili. Clara, wearing an old-fashioned apron over her sweater and slacks, greeted them from the entrance to the kitchen.

"Come on in, you two. Supper's on the table. And I've already cleared out a corner for the tree."

Ben gave her thin shoulders a hug. "I told you not to overdo, Mom. You'll wear yourself out. But that chili does smell good."

"Just the thing for a cold night," Jess said. "Don't worry about cleaning up. I'll do that. And then you can supervise from your rocking chair while we decorate the tree. We're depending on you to tell us exactly what to do."

While they sat at the kitchen table, feasting on chili, green salad and skillet corn bread, Jess told Clara about the house and her idea for making it into a bed-and-breakfast.

"That's a wonderful idea!" Clara exclaimed. "The town needs a place for people to stay over. But such a risk, dear. Doesn't it worry you, the idea of all the things that could go wrong?"

"Of course it does," Jess said. "That's why I haven't made a final decision yet."

"Don't think you can talk her out of it, Mom," Ben said. "I already tried that. The more I argued against her taking on that house, the deeper she dug in her heels."

"I'm sure Jess has the wisdom to make the right choice," Clara said. "I know that old house. One of my grade-school friends lived there. We used to play dolls in her upstairs room. Then her mother left and took the three children with her. I never saw my friend again."

"So the old man who lived there alone was your friend's father?"

"That's right. He never remarried after his family left. I've heard that he became quite strange in his old age—but who am I to judge the poor man?"

"And the woman who sold me the house?"

"His granddaughter. She moved back to town with her husband about ten years ago. I've never gotten to know her, or had a chance to ask her about my friend. People move on." Clara's voice had taken on a wistful note.

"Hey!" Ben broke into the conversation. "If we're finished eating, what do you say we get that tree in?"

"Let's do it," Jess said. "Do go in the living room and sit down, Clara. I'll finish up here while Ben does the muscle work. Then I'll come in and help."

As Ben charged out of the kitchen, Clara gave Jess a knowing smile. "Ben insists that he only does the tree for Ethan. But he's loved Christmas all his life. When it comes to getting that tree up and decorated, he's as eager as a little boy!"

"I'll keep that in mind. Now please go relax and enjoy the show." Jess guided Ben's mother gently but firmly to the living room and saw her seated in her favorite chair.

While she was clearing the table, Jess heard the bump and rustle of Ben hauling the tree into the house. She was loading the dishwasher when he came into the kitchen, his hair mussed, his eyes dancing, his skin and clothes giving off the spicy scent of fresh pine. "Water for the tree stand," he explained, as he found a two-quart pitcher in the cupboard and filled it from the tap. "Are you about finished in here? I just need to get the decorations out of the closet upstairs. Then we'll be ready to hang them on the tree. That's when I'll need your help."

Jess couldn't help smiling as he rushed out of the kitchen with the water. Moments later she heard his footsteps on the stairs and the intermittent rummaging in the overhead storage closet. Clara was right. When it came to Christmas, Branding Iron's steely-eyed lawman was like an enthusiastic boy.

Jess shook her head as she rinsed the dishes. How could any man be so adorable—as well as chivalrous, brave and equipped to handle anything?

Heaven save her, was she falling for a blasted Boy Scout?

Chapter Seven

Jess added detergent to the dishwasher and switched it on. By the time she'd finished wiping off the counter, she could hear music from the living room. Someone must've put a CD in the boom box that sat on one of the shelves. A soft Christmas melody, a jazz piano version, drifted to her ears.

Drying her hands on her jeans, she crossed the open hallway. The stately tree stood in front of the window—lush, emerald green, and almost as tall as the old house's nine-foot ceiling. Ben had made the right choice. It was perfect.

Ben stood next to the tree, surrounded by a fortress of boxes. With a glance at Jess, he opened the nearest one. "This might take a while. These lights go on first—but not until after we've untangled them. Here, take the end and back up while I try to unravel this mess."

As he passed Jess the string of lights, Clara rose, yawning. "Just thinking about you doing all that work wears me out," she said. "If you'll excuse me, I believe I'll toddle off to bed and leave the decorating to you youngsters. Good night—and have a good time."

With that she made her way down the hall to her bedroom and closed the door.

"Do you think she's all right?" Jess asked.

"I'm guessing she's just tired and wants to curl up in bed with a good book," Ben said. "I'll check on her before I turn in. I always do."

"She's lucky to have you."

"I was lucky to have her growing up. I could say it's payback time, but I could never repay her for all she did."

"You mentioned your father when we were in the old house. What happened to him?" Jess straightened the cord he fed her, leaving the untangled part lying loose on the floor.

"My dad died when I was nine," Ben said. "He taught science during the school year. In the summer, he raised hay on some farmland he owned south of town. But his real dream was to fly. He got his license, bought a used plane and started a crop-dusting business to pay for it."

"And . . . he crashed?"

"That's right." Ben finished unsnarling the light cord and plugged the end into an outlet behind the tree. The long string lit like magic, bathing the room in a soft glow of color.

"I don't think Mom ever forgave him for flying and getting himself killed," he said. "But she never stopped loving him. She was a pretty woman, and smart. She had chances to get married again, and maybe make life easier for us. She never did."

"But you must've managed all right."

"We were lucky. Dad had a little insurance, and we sold the farmland. The house was already in Mom's family, so there was no mortgage to pay. And she managed to get a job at the library." He studied the tree with a thoughtful frown. "Mostly we did fine. But I never stopped missing my dad. That's why I do my best to be there for Ethan, even if it's by long distance a lot of the time."

He shrugged, dismissing the conversation. "Stand over

there, on the opposite side of the tree. We'll wrap the lights from my side to yours and back again."

"You're in charge." Jess took her place. "Tell me what to do. I don't remember decorating a Christmas tree before."

He laughed, with that belly-deep resonance that tickled her to her toes. "Trust me, there's nothing to it. By the time we're finished, you'll be an expert."

The string of lights was long, the tree very tall, but Ben knew exactly where the lights should go. By the time they reached the last of them, he was standing on the kitchen step stool to twine the end of the cord around the topmost part of the trunk.

"Oh—" Jess stepped back to admire the lit tree. "It's so pretty this way. We could stop now."

"No, you don't. We're just getting started."

He climbed down from the stool and opened another box, this one stuffed with glittering garlands of gold tinsel. They shook them out to fluff the metallic strands and draped them over the branches.

"Now for the ornaments." He began opening box after box, all of them lovingly packed with tissue or bubble wrap to protect their contents. There were shiny glass balls, and small figures of angels, Santas, reindeer, birds, and other animals. Some of these looked very old, as if they'd been passed down in the family for years. As Ben told her the story of one, then another and another, Jess couldn't help thinking of how different her own life had been from his—with no family history, no holiday traditions, nothing but the unending struggle to survive.

When the last ornament had been hung, Ben went to the dimmer switch on the wall and turned the overhead light down to a faint glow. "How does it look to you?" he asked, stepping behind her. His hands lingered on her shoulders as he turned her to face the tree.

"It's . . . magical," she whispered, and it was. The shimmer of colored lights on tinsel, reflecting in the shiny glass balls, cast a halo around the tree. The small, traditional ornaments appeared as silhouettes, softly lit from behind. The fragrance of pine and the tinkling piano music made Jess feel as if she'd stepped into a fairy-tale setting.

Releasing her shoulders, Ben reached into the last box. "One more thing," he said, lifting out a glistening gold star. "This always goes on last, right at the top of the tree. Since this is your first time, you can do the honors."

He handed her the star. Crafted of thin metal, faceted to reflect light like a jewel. It looked old, well used, and very precious.

Jess gazed up at the top of the tree. Even from the step stool, she wouldn't be able to reach high enough. "Unless you have a handy ladder, you'd better take this." She thrust the star back toward him.

"No, we can do it. Hang on." He positioned the step stool about eighteen inches from the tree. "Okay, climb all the way up. If you get shaky, I'm right here."

Jess mounted the three steps. Even standing on the highest one, the top of the tree was almost an arm's length beyond her reach.

"All right, I'm going to lift you higher," he said. "Ready, on the count of three. One . . . two . . . three!"

Crouching slightly, he wrapped his arms around her legs below the knees and heaved her upward. Jess had seen more graceful versions of the lift in Olympic pairs skating. But what Ben's move lacked in elegance, it made up in power, raising her high enough to stretch for the treetop with her hands.

As she struggled to position the star, a vision flashed through her mind of the whole decorated tree toppling over and crashing to the floor. But Ben was holding her steady—for the moment. "Got it?" He grunted with effort.

"Almost . . ." Holding her breath, Jess maneuvered the hollow base of the star over the top of the tree. "Got it!" she breathed as the star settled into place.

With a mutter that sounded like *Thank God!* he began easing her down toward the step stool. He was making an effort not to drop her, but a shift in her weight threw him off balance. He stumbled backward toward the tree. Twisting himself to one side just in time, he fell to the carpet with Jess on top of him.

For the space of a few heartbeats, they lay still. As the shock of the fall wore off, Jess became aware of his warm, solid bulk beneath her and his arms wrapping her to cushion her against the tumble. That devilish tingle she always seemed to feel when he was physically close surged through her body like a warm spring flood.

He stirred against her. "Are you all right?"

She pushed onto her forearms, looking down into his concerned brown eyes. "Yes, and so is the tree. How about you?"

"Right now I feel like I've been tackled by a three-hundred-pound halfback. But nothing's broken. I'll live. Wow, that tumble was spectacular."

"I can't believe you didn't crash into the tree." She looked down at him, a giggle rising in her throat. She knew it would be smart to get up, but something made her want to stay.

Was it because she really, really wanted him to kiss her?

He must have wanted the same thing, because in the next instant, he did.

His hand moved to cradle the back of her head and pull her down to him. His firm mouth was like warm velvet, his kiss sensual and lingering, setting off fever waves of response. She parted her lips, deepening the contact, tasting his faint, sweet saltiness, filling her nostrils with the clean aroma of pine. From the moment he'd rescued her on the road, some secret part of her had wanted this man to kiss her. Now it was happening, and all she could think of was wanting more.

But no—this was the first step down the road to getting her heart trampled. Ben Marsden didn't know who she was, or *what* she was. Once he learned the truth, the upright lawman would turn his back and walk away. If she wanted to make a life for herself in Branding Iron, she couldn't afford to give him that chance.

Pulling back, she sat up. "Something tells me this isn't a good idea," she said.

"Maybe not." His eyes twinkled. "But you can't say it wasn't a helluva lot of fun."

The man was incorrigible—and appealing enough to melt a heart of granite. But she couldn't let him get to her. Jess forced herself to stand, cross the room to the boom box and switch off the Christmas music.

"You've got a long drive ahead of you tomorrow," she said. "Now that the tree's finished, maybe we should call it a night."

"Spoilsport." Still teasing, he rose to his feet. "Go ahead. Since we're sharing a bathroom, the rule is ladies first. I'll unplug the tree lights and check on my mother."

Jess retreated up the stairs. Ben gave her plenty of lead time. By the time she heard his footsteps in the hall and the sound of water running, she was in bed.

In bed but not asleep. Her churning emotions were liable to keep her awake for the rest of the night.

Kissing Ben had been a dream, but Jess knew she'd crossed a forbidden line. And the longer she remained in this house, imposing on Clara's hospitality, the greater the danger of it happening again. Tomorrow Ben would be driving to Dallas to pick up his son. By the time he returned, she would need to be out of here.

As things stood, she had two days—and two choices. She could buy the house and move in, or she could pack her car, say good-bye to Francine and leave town.

She considered that she could come back and get Francine when her jail time was up. But being on the road with her unpredictable mother was a scary prospect. Francine needed stability and support. The best way to provide that support would be to buy the house and stay in Branding Iron.

For what seemed like hours she tossed and turned, weighing one option, then the other. She heard the shower running in the bathroom, heard the creak of Ben's footsteps in the hallway as he passed her door on the way to his room. If things were different, she could fall in love with the man. Maybe she already had. But there was no happy ending written into this story.

She had to get Ben Marsden out of her head and out of her heart. For that she was going to need some distance from him. But running away would be nothing more than a temporary fix—worse, her disappearance could prompt him to check on her past. She'd made a few friends in Branding Iron and found the prospect of a future here. If she didn't take a stand and put down roots now, when and where would she find a better chance?

The night hours crawled past. By the time the first dim fingers of dawn filtered through the ruffled curtains, Jess had made her decision. Now was the time for the bigger challenge—carrying it out.

After stopping by Francine's trailer to feed Sergeant Pepper, Ben had arrived early at work. He'd spent the first hour catching up on messages and reports, mostly routine. Then he'd spoken with his deputies and checked the jail roster. The mayor's twenty-year-old son was in holding again, picked up by the deputies on a DUI charge. Despite his father's influence, the kid would undoubtedly lose his license and do some serious jail time. Maybe that punishment would straighten him out, but that remained to be seen, and right now Ben had other things on his mind.

He'd planned to look in on Francine, but she was taking her morning shower, and he was anxious to get on the road. Reminding himself that Jess would probably stop by and see her later, he made one last check of things and left.

He'd hoped to see Jess at the house that morning, but her bedroom door had been closed, and there'd been no sign of her downstairs. Now, as he drove out of town toward the freeway, Ben savored the memory of kissing her last night. Nice, he thought as he recalled those soft, willing lips. Better than nice. Too bad he couldn't have kept her there all night.

True, he'd broken his own rule against romancing a woman in his mother's house. But Jess had been so alluringly close, and he could tell she'd wanted that kiss as much as he did. Their bodies had fit together as if each had been molded to the other; and when their lips met and clung, that single kiss had felt so right, so perfect. . . .

Guilt? No way. He wasn't feeling as much as a twinge of regret for what had happened. He was a red-blooded male, damn it, and it had been far too long since he'd held a sweet, sexy woman like Jess in his arms. The only issue facing him now was finding the right time and place for it to happen again.

Maybe next time he could take her out on an actual date—dinner, not at Buckaroo's but somewhere nice, out of town, with a long drive home in the dark. . . .

Turning up the radio in his pickup, he sang along with the Chipmunks, not caring that he couldn't match the pitch of their silly voices. Christmas was coming, he was on his way to pick up his boy, and he'd met a woman who looked like an angel and kissed like . . . well, never mind. His life wasn't perfect, and probably never would be. But right now he had no complaints.

By eight-thirty that morning, Jess had telephoned the woman who owned the house, made a verbal offer and gotten an acceptance. The price, a little lower than what she'd been quoted, was within the range of fairness, and the terms would leave her enough cash to make at least the basic improvements on the house.

The process was eased by the woman's husband, who happened to be the loan officer at the bank. Jess hadn't been sure she could finalize the contract on a Sunday, but he'd had copies of the necessary forms on his home computer. He'd helped draw up the contract and set up the transfer of Jess's funds from her Kansas City bank for first thing Monday morning. He'd even phoned the utility companies and arranged to have the weekend crew turn on the lights and water by the end of the day. The gas would be on tomorrow.

He'd also taken Jess's application for a line of credit she could use in the remodeling—the loan to be secured as a second mortgage on the house.

Jess walked out of his home on shaky legs and feet that could barely feel the sidewalk. She was a homeowner—or at least a house owner. When she thought of the hard work and possible pitfalls ahead, it almost made her nauseated. But she felt pleasantly giddy as well. She'd done it. She'd taken the first step toward having her own bed-and-breakfast.

The next step would be telling Francine. She hoped her mother would be enthusiastic about the project. But knowing Francine, there was no telling how she'd take the news.

Last night as she'd wrestled with the decision to buy the house, Jess had remembered Ben's wise advice: *Ask your-*

self this question. What if you were on your own and Francine wasn't in the picture? Would you still take on this project? Would you do it for yourself?

Jess had asked and answered that question in the night. She really did want this for herself—something of her own that would be part of the community, something she could grow and take pride in. If Francine wanted to be involved, so much the better. If not, Jess would have to find other ways to help her mother.

With the plan in place and moving forward, it was time to tell Francine.

She arrived at the jail, parked her car and went inside. By now, Ben's staff knew her. After leaving her purse at the front counter, she was admitted without the customary pat down. She found Francine in her cell, eating breakfast off a plastic tray.

"Well, hello, honey." Francine looked up with a grin. She was dressed in fresh clothes, her hair newly washed and combed. "I was starting to wonder if you'd come to your senses and given up on me."

"No way am I giving up on you," Jess said. "I told you I had a plan, and now that it's under way, I want to tell you about it."

Francine listened, shoveling down her scrambled eggs and pancakes as Jess described the house. "I know that place," she said. "Some of the kids think it's haunted. For all I know, they may be right."

"Well, whoever's haunting the place, they'd better move over and make room for the new owner," Jess said. "I plan to clean it up from attic to cellar, get it looking spiffy and open it as a bed-and-breakfast."

"And you're expecting me to help you." Francine sounded less than enthusiastic. "And here I was hoping for a beauty makeover and a trip to Vegas."

"I can't force you to help me," Jess said. "But it would

give you a better place to live than that old trailer. And you could share the income once we open the place up and start making a profit."

Francine's eyebrows knotted in a thoughtful frown. "Sounds a lot like work to me. And I've never been big on scrubbin' floors and swabbin' toilets. I'll have to think on it."

Jess's spirits plummeted. She'd tried to prepare herself for this kind of response, but she hadn't realized how much the letdown would hurt.

"You've got five days to make up your mind, Francine," she said, knowing she wasn't ready to call the woman *mother*. "If you don't want to be part of this, you can go back to your trailer and do whatever it is you'd rather do than be with me. It's up to you. Now, if you'll excuse me, I've got a house to clean."

Blinking back tears, Jess turned away from the cell. She didn't like herself right now, but maybe tough love was the only way to deal with an impractical, overgrown child like Francine.

She'd gone a half-dozen steps when she heard her name called. She turned back to see that Francine had put her tray aside and was standing at the bars.

"You'll come back and see me again, won't you?" She looked like a sad-eyed puppy in the pound.

"Of course." Jess reached through the bars and squeezed her mother's plump shoulder. "I'll try to come every day. If I don't make it, you'll know I'm just busy with the house. But I hope you'll think about my offer. If you're willing to come on board, we could make a great team, the two of us."

Had she meant what she'd said? Jess wondered as she collected her purse and went out to her car. Would she and Francine really make a great team, or would the woman prove to be nothing but a millstone around her neck?

Never mind, she told herself. She'd come to Branding

Iron in search of her birth mother. Now that she'd found her, and made a commitment to stay, she had little choice except to play out this drama, wherever it led.

Now what? Jess started the car. She couldn't do much in the house until she had lights and water, which wouldn't be turned on until later in the day. She was also going to need tools, work clothes, and some basic supplies.

Also, she hadn't forgotten her promise to Clara and the Christmas Ball committee. More than half the numbers on the list still needed calling. She would go back to Clara's and get that done now, Jess resolved. With luck, she'd be able to start on the house by late afternoon.

Her tentative plan was to begin with the bathroom and one bedroom. That way she'd at least have a place to clean up and a place to sleep. The sleeping bag she'd brought in the car would have to do for a bed until she could find some furniture. After that would come the kitchen—a huge job. Once it was done, she'd be able to get some pans and a few dishes and cook her own meals. Next on her list would be the second bedroom for her mother—if Francine decided to move in.

Once the downstairs was cleaned, furnished and decorated, she and Francine could move upstairs and leave the two bigger bedrooms for their paying guests. The plan seemed like a sensible one, but the thought of the time and work involved left Jess weak in the knees.

If she was to make the payments on the house, she'd need to be open for business by Christmas week. In view of all there was to do, that seemed impossible. But she'd taken this project on. She would make it work or go down fighting.

Jess parked the car in front of Clara's house and went inside. She found Ben's mother standing at the stove, warming up the chili for lunch.

"Hi, you're just in time." Clara stirred the chili and lifted the pot off the burner. Only then did she turn around.

"Good heavens, Jess!" she exclaimed. "You look like you just climbed on a bucking bronco about to go out of the chute! Are you all right?"

With a nervous laugh, Jess pulled out a kitchen chair and sank onto the edge. "Never better. I just bought myself a house."

"So you did it!" Clara clapped her hands. "Good for you! But my, you're one brave girl!"

"Maybe too brave. It's just sinking in how much there is to be done, and how easily I could lose the place."

"Have you told Francine about it?"

Jess sighed. Her shoulders sagged. "I did. I asked her to move in and help me, but she wasn't the least bit excited. She said that it sounded like a lot of work and that she'd think on it. All she really seems to want from me is a trip to Las Vegas—and now that I've bought a house, I certainly can't afford that. I don't understand her. This is a chance to rebuild her life. It's almost as if she's too lazy and indifferent to care."

Clara ladled chili into two bowls. "I'm sorry things didn't go better. You're probably too worked up to be hungry, but you'll feel better if you eat something." She set one bowl of steaming chili in front of Jess, along with a glass of milk and a slice of buttered corn bread. With the other bowl, she sat down at the place she'd set across the table.

"Your mother isn't a bad person," she said. "But after your father died, she went to pieces. She was such a wreck that she didn't even feel capable of caring for her own baby. After all these years, nothing much has changed. She's lived on welfare, hung out in bars, been in and out of jail, again and again. . . ." Clara reached across the table and laid a cool, thin hand on Jess's arm. "Nobody, least of all Francine herself, has expected her to be responsible for anything—not until today, when you asked for her help." Clara's warm brown eyes, so like Ben's, met Jess's. "I don't think your mother's lazy and indifferent, dear. I think what she really is, is scared."

"I'll remind myself of that next time I see her." Jess blinked away the tears she'd been holding back since leaving the jail. She'd come to Branding Iron hoping to find a mother like the woman sitting across from her—someone cultured, understanding and kind. Instead she'd found Francine, and a whole new set of challenges. But the reality was what it was. All she could do was buckle down and try to make the best of it.

"You look exhausted," Clara said. "I'll bet you didn't sleep a wink last night. Maybe you should go upstairs and take a nap."

"Not yet." Jess finished the last of her chili and rose to help clear the table. "I promised myself I'd finish calling the people on the list you gave me."

"Oh, heavens, don't worry about that," Clara said. "I can do it. I've got plenty of time—and you're worn out."

"Thanks, but what would the ladies on the committee think of me if I dropped the ball as soon as something came up? I need to make the calls."

"Oh, I suppose you're right. But after that, dear, you really do need to get some rest."

"After that, I'll need to go shopping for some tools and cleaning supplies. As soon as the utilities are turned on, I want to start on the house."

"But there's no need for that!" Clara pointed to a door at the back of the kitchen, one Jess had scarcely noticed before now. "I have all kinds of tools and mops and cleaners in the basement. Please feel free to take them to your house. You can bring them back when you're finished."

"You're sure? I hate imposing on you, but that would be great." *And it would save me so much money over having to buy new supplies,* Jess thought.

"No trouble at all," Clara said. "I have a cleaning lady who comes every two weeks. She brings her own things, so my old brooms and mops and buckets are just sitting in the basement, along with my husband's old tools. Once in a while Ben uses them to fix something, but he won't miss them for a few weeks, especially now, with Ethan here. Feel free to take anything you need."

"You just saved my life!" Jess gave her a careful hug— Clara felt so fragile. "I promise to keep track of what I take and to replace everything when I'm finished."

"I'm happy to help," Clara said. "Now run along and make your phone calls. I can finish here in the kitchen."

Jess sat down at the small desk in the living room and found the list in the drawer. Her finger shook as she punched in the first number and waited for the ring. This was really happening. She'd bought a house, and in a few hours she'd be walking through the door as the new owner.

She was scared to death.

Chapter Eight

By the time the pickup swung off I-20 and onto the exit ramp, Ben's hands were cramped on the steering wheel and his knee was throbbing. He never looked forward to the daylong drive from Branding Iron to Dallas, but it was the price he gladly paid for time with his son.

Through the murky twilight, the lights of Dallas sprawled to the horizon. Ben had spent the most miserable years of his life here, after the shattered left knee, which still pained him sometimes, had ended his hopes of playing in the NFL. In the long run, the accident had ended his marriage as well. Cheryl had wed him with the dream of being married to a pro-football superstar and enjoying the glamorous lifestyle that went along with it. Instead she'd ended up tied to a broken man who worked for her father's insurance company and hated every minute of it.

Ben had never blamed her for the affair that had put an end to their doomed marriage and sent him home to Branding Iron. But that didn't mean he enjoyed dealing with her on these visits to pick up Ethan. Tomorrow when he arrived at her fancy gated condo, she'd be waiting, as always, to twist in the knife and collect her pound of flesh. By now he'd grown to expect it.

Taking the familiar street, he pulled up to the Holiday Inn that was twenty minutes away from Cheryl's place and checked into the room he'd reserved earlier. He was ready for a decent meal, a shower and a good night's rest, but his first priority would be to let Ethan know he was here and planning to pick him up for breakfast in the morning.

He made the call and waited four rings before Cheryl picked up. "Hi, Ben." Her voice was flat, neutral. She had company, he surmised.

"Hi." He tried to sound upbeat. "I just wanted to let you and Ethan know I'm in town. Could you put him on?"

There was a beat of silence. "Oh, I'm sorry. He's at a sleepover."

Why was this not surprising? "Didn't you know I was coming to get him in the morning—and that I wanted him packed and ready to go?"

"Yes, I did. But it was his cousin's birthday. How could I not let him go, especially when he begged me? I was hoping you'd understand, but I should've known better. All you ever think of is your own agenda."

Ben fought the urge to grind his teeth. In the background he could hear a man's voice. The accent, even over the phone, sounded Bostonian. If Cheryl's new love was in town, it made sense that she'd welcome the chance to have Ethan gone for the night. Ben was annoyed, but he wouldn't give her the satisfaction of knowing it.

"I'd be happy to pick him up at his cousin's in the morning," he said. "Just give me the address and let them know I'm coming."

"That won't be necessary," she said. "My sister-in-law will be dropping Ethan off here around ten. I'll call you when he's ready to go."

"Fine." Ben ended the call before his temper could boil

over. He'd learned from sad experience that losing his cool with Cheryl would just backfire on him When it came to Ethan, she was holding the strings and she knew how to pull them.

At the time of the divorce, Ethan had been a baby who needed his mother full time. Ben had agreed to give her custody with visitation rights for him. Now that his son was growing up, he wanted more time with the boy. But good lawyers cost money, and Cheryl's wealthy family had the best. Maybe if she was serious about marrying Nigel, he could talk her into letting him have Ethan for the school year. He already knew it was what his son wanted.

If he intended to negotiate with Cheryl, he'd be smart to keep the peace between them.

In the motel coffee shop, he ordered a hot beef sandwich and forced himself to eat it. Back in the room, he showered, crawled into bed, switched on the TV and clicked through the channels. There was nothing on worth watching, but at least some mind-numbing entertainment might relax him enough for sleep.

As his eyes glazed over a silly sitcom rerun, Ben's thoughts wandered back to last night and that stolen kiss at the foot of the Christmas tree. He hadn't planned it, hadn't even meant for it to happen. But in that brief moment when Jess's soft lips pressed his, he'd felt magic swirling through his body—as sweet as Christmas and as sensual as sin.

Jess was a special woman. She might not make it as a supermodel, or even a college homecoming queen like Cheryl had been. But her spunky nature and caring concern for other people lent her an inner beauty that stunned him at odd moments. He barely knew her, Ben reminded himself. But if he wasn't careful, he could find himself falling for the woman.

Not that he was about to let it happen. Right now, he had too many complications in his life to even think about a relationship—his job, his mother, his son, his ex-wife—all demanding his attention. Adding a girlfriend to the mix would be unfair to everyone involved, especially to the girlfriend.

As for marriage . . . That wasn't even in the picture. He was in no condition, emotionally or financially, to start a new family. Jess would make some lucky man a great wife, just not him.

But, damn it, he could really use more of those kisses.

Holding that thought, Ben switched off the TV, rolled over and went to sleep.

Jess stripped off her rubber gloves and massaged her aching back. She had spent most of the last two hours on her hands and knees, scrubbing away layers of unspeakable grime and grit. But she'd done it. The bathroom was actually clean and usable.

Reaching for the handle, she flushed the toilet just to hear it work. The sound was music to her ears.

The floor, which had been covered by a layer of dirt, had turned out to be blue ceramic tile—a nice surprise. The walls would need fresh paint. The naked lightbulb in the ceiling and the cracked mirror above the vanity would need to be replaced. But all the fixtures worked, the water was running clear and the whole room, from floor to ceiling, had been scrubbed with disinfectant. Jess ached in every bone and muscle, but the thrill of accomplishment was worth the pain. This was her house, and little by little she was going to make it into something charming, if not beautiful.

The electricity and water hadn't come on until the end

of the day. Before starting on the bathroom, Jess had taken time to gather the needed supplies and check out the rest of the house with the lights on. By now it had to be almost ten o'clock.

Spending the night here was out of the question. The gas company wouldn't be sending a man to turn on the furnace till tomorrow, so the house was cold—to say nothing of what could be crawling around in the dark. But by tomorrow night she'd at least have one bedroom ship-shape, even if she had to sleep on the floor. She wanted to be out of Clara's house before Ben returned with his son. After that sizzling kiss, there was no way she'd feel right about staying under the same roof.

Sooner or later, she was going to need a bed for herself, and, she hoped, one for Francine, to say nothing of tables, chairs and other things, once the house was ready. Maybe in one of the bigger towns she could find a secondhand furniture store and pay them to deliver. There was no guarantee she'd get the line of credit she'd applied for at the bank. She would need to make every cent of her own money go as far as possible.

Giving the place a last-minute lookover, Jess turned on the front porch light, locked the door and went out to her car. Early tomorrow she'd be back, ready to start on the rest of the house. A mountain of work awaited her, but the most vital task of all was the one she dreaded most—convincing her mother to come and help.

"Let's hit the road, buddy." Ben tossed Ethan's duffel bag into the backseat of the truck cab and helped his son buckle the seat belt. After the usual grilling Cheryl had given him, all he wanted was to be out of Dallas and heading home.

"So how was the sleepover?" he asked as he started the truck.

"Okay, if you like baby stuff," Ethan said. "My cousin is six. I was the only kid my age at the party. I didn't want to go, but Mom made me."

"Well, it doesn't matter now. We're on our way, and we're going to have a great time." Ben kept his reaction to himself as they headed up the on-ramp onto the freeway. Cheryl had made a point of mentioning that their son had begged to go to the party. But it would serve nothing to tell Ethan his mother had lied.

With the late morning hour and the need to get on the road, Ben hadn't had a chance to talk with Cheryl about taking their son for the school year. But he'd met Nigel, a pale, lanky fellow with an affected accent and a formal manner that reeked of old money. The fact that he was wearing designer sweats and a slightly rumpled look confirmed that he had, indeed, spent the night in the condo with Cheryl.

As for Cheryl, she'd changed little from the honey-blond homecoming queen he'd married—except that she was nastier. "Ben is sheriff of Podunk, Texas, or whatever they call the place," she'd told Nigel when she introduced them. "He might've been another Peyton Manning, but after his knee went out, he couldn't make a go of it anyplace but his hometown. I don't suppose he ever will. He's even living with his mother these days."

Ben had returned Nigel's cold handshake, bitten back a snarky retort and left with his son. Cheryl always did her best to make him feel like a failure. Mostly he tried to ignore her jabs, but sometimes, like today, she got to him.

In high school he'd been voted most likely to succeed. In college he'd been a hero on the football field—until the last game of his senior year, when he'd gone down under a three-hundred-pound tackle and ripped out the ligaments and tendons in his knee. After that it was all over.

He and Cheryl had married the summer before, when they discovered she was pregnant. Their dreams of NFL glory had lasted less than six months. After Cheryl's miscarriage and Ben's accident, they'd struggled on for four more years while he finished his degree in sociology and went to work as a claims adjustor for his father-in-law's big insurance company. Between his own discontent and Cheryl's, even having Ethan hadn't been enough to save their crumbling marriage.

After the divorce, Ben had returned to Branding Iron, mostly because his mother was alone and unwell. He'd tried to tell himself his law enforcement career was making a difference, even if it didn't pay much, and even if hauling drunks off the street, scaring a few misbehaving kids and making the occasional drug bust weren't exactly big-city crime drama material. By now he'd put down roots. But in staying, he'd given up hope of ever becoming more than what he was—a small-town lawman with no bragging rights except the respect of his community.

"Is the Christmas tree up?" Ethan's voice broke into Ben's thoughts.

"You bet it is!" Ben said. "We got it in and decorated it last night."

"You and Grandma?"

"No. Grandma needs to rest these days."

"Who, then? You said 'we.' "

"A friend. You'll meet her. She's staying at your grandma's house for a few days while she finds a place to live. I think you'll like her." *Now why had he said all that? It wasn't as if Jess was going to be a long-term part of his son's life.*

"You won't find any presents under the tree yet," he said. "For one thing, it's still early, and for another, you haven't told me what you want."

"I'm still thinking about that," Ethan said. "I guess I'm waiting to see if I get to stay with you."

That would be the best Christmas present ever, Ben thought. But he still hadn't talked to Cheryl about it, and he didn't want to get the boy's hopes up. "I guess we'll have to see what happens with your mother and Nigel," he said. "But I promise you one thing—I won't sit still for your being packed off to some fancy eastern boarding school."

"Thanks." Ethan gazed out the window as the city thinned to suburbs, then to open fields and farms. "Hey, can we stop at the reptile showplace for lunch?"

The off-freeway roadside exhibit, a relic left over from the 1950s, served greasy hamburgers and hot dogs on stale buns, but Ethan had loved the place since he was old enough to make the drive to Branding Iron with Ben. Stopping there had become a tradition.

"Sure," Ben said. "Meanwhile, you'll find a couple of chocolate nut bars in the glove box. Pass me one and take the other one for yourself. Then let's think about some things you'd like to do when we get home."

Jess braced herself for frustration as she walked into the jail. What kind of mood would she find her mother in today? Would she be willing to help with the house, or had she already closed her mind to it? As Jess walked down the row of cells, she tried to remember Clara's wise advice— Francine wasn't dragging her heels because she was lazy. If she was holding back, it was most likely out of fear.

Jess had started her day early, making coffee at Clara's, then leaving for the house before dawn. In the first hour, she'd pried the boards off two windows, then managed to sweep out the main floor, raising dust and a few spiders, but at least no cockroaches. Tearing up the carpet would be a backbreaking job. Maybe Clara would know a couple of husky local boys who could use a few hours of work to earn Christmas money.

Deciding to take a break, she'd walked out back to the garage and used one of her keys to unlock the door. Wonder of wonders, the garage was crammed full of *furniture!* The pieces were old and dusty, some of them broken; but much of what was here could be salvaged. She could even see some bed frames against one wall.

The find was a godsend. But she would need help hauling things out of the garage and into the house—a job that couldn't be done until the place was clean.

She'd known all along this was going to be a big job, but the true enormity of it all was just dawning on her— One reality stood out like a blazing banner.

She couldn't do this alone—not if she wanted to have the place ready by the Christmas ball.

"Hi, sweetie!" Francine, who must've heard her coming, was standing at the bars, a smile on her face. "My goodness, aren't you a sight!"

Her eyes took in Jess's oversized sweatshirt, scrounged from Clara's donation box, her scraggly ponytail and dust-smeared face. "What on earth have you been doing, honey, Dumpster diving?"

"I've been cleaning house," Jess said. "The bathroom's usable, and now I'm working on the downstairs bedrooms. The place should at least be fit for roughing it by the time you get out of here."

"About that," Francine said. Jess's heart dropped. She'd just begun to realize how much she was going to need her mother's help.

Francine leaned closer to the bars. "I've been thinking

over your proposition, and I'm willing to come—but it's got to be on my own terms. There are three things I want."

"Tell me." Jess was ready to grant her anything within reason—short of a trip to Las Vegas.

"First, I want to bring my cat, Sergeant Pepper."

"No problem at all. I like cats, and we could use him to get rid of the mice. In fact, I was going to ask if I could bring him over early."

"That would be fine, dear. But you'd better wait till that cute Sheriff Ben is around to help you. The Sergeant won't take kindly to being hauled off by somebody he doesn't know, and he's got claws like a damned Bengal tiger."

"So what's your second condition?" Jess asked, hoping it would be as easy.

"I want to bring my boom box and play my music anytime I want to—and I want my TV in my room."

"Again, no problem." Whatever music Francine liked, Jess could put up with it. And the TV should be fine. "And the third condition?" she asked.

"This'll cost you a few dollars, but I figure if you can buy a house, you can spare it. When I get out of here, I want to go to the beauty parlor and get the full treatment—the works! I want my daughter to see her old lady all fixed up!"

The request was a bit startling but not unreasonable. "Fine," she said. "I can even make you an appointment if you'll tell me who to call."

"Sure." Francine was all smiles now. "I'll give you the number, honey. We're going to make a great team, me and you."

As Jess left the jail and started her car, vague misgivings crept over her. Was she being played? Could she really trust Francine to keep her part of the bargain? But what choice did she have? If she wanted to help her mother, the only way was to take this chance.

On the way back to the house, she stopped at Shop Mart and bought a few necessities—hand soap, toilet paper, a couple of towels and a few snacks to tide her over lunch. She got back to the house to find a van from the gas company pulling up to the curb. Hooray! With luck, she'd be able to work in warmth, and even ease her sore muscles with a hot bath at the end of the day.

It took the gas technician a little less than an hour to inspect the line and the connections, turn on the gas and light the furnace and water heater. Since the stove and clothes dryer were electric, it remained to be seen whether they would work.

After showing her how to adjust the thermostat and briefing her on what could go wrong and what to do, he gave her his card and drove away, leaving Jess to enjoy the warmth that was filling the house—*her* house, which would soon become a cozy home, ready to welcome paying guests.

At least that was what she had to keep believing.

The floor in what, for now, would be her bedroom was covered with a threadbare rag rug. Since the rug was lighter than a carpet and not fastened down, Jess was able to roll it lengthwise and drag it into the living room. That done, she swept away the dust underneath, filled a bucket with sudsy water and began scrubbing the hardwood floor on her knees. Later she would have to refinish the wood, or at least oil it. And the walls would need to be stripped of their dingy paper and painted as well. But for now her only goal was to get the room clean.

After wiping down the walls and sweeping cobwebs off the ceiling with a rag wrapped around the broom, she went outside, collected her suitcase, coat and blankets from the trunk of the car and piled everything in a corner. Then she started on the kitchen.

The hours flew by. By the time she'd finished the fridge, the countertops and the outside of the stove, the inside of the house had grown so dark that she had to turn on the lights. Pausing to wolf down a stick of string cheese and guzzle a can of guava nectar, she leaned against the counter to survey her work. She'd done so much scrubbing that her fingers were raw inside her rubber gloves. But she still had the drawers and cabinets to finish, as well as the dreaded inside of the stove, which would have to wait until tomorrow after she bought some oven cleaner.

She thought about taking a break, maybe running to Buckaroo's for a burger and a shake. The idea of real food was enough to make her stomach growl. But right now she looked like an extra in a zombie apocalypse movie. Besides, if she stopped to rest, she'd be too tired to start working again.

After filling a fresh bucket of soapy water and unwrapping a clean sponge, she started on the drawers below the counter.

Minutes, then what seemed like hours, crawled past. Jess wondered what time it was. She hadn't brought a watch, but she guessed it must be past ten. She'd carried in the blankets from the trunk of her car, planning to make them into a bed on the floor. Would she be all right spending the night here alone?

But why worry? This was Branding Iron, Texas, not her old neighborhood in Kansas City. Nobody was going to—

The click and squeak of the opening front door scattered her thoughts. Jess's heart slammed. Why hadn't she thought to lock the door behind her when she came in? And where was her purse, with her cell phone in it? She couldn't even remember where she'd put it down.

Frantic, she glanced around for a weapon. There was

nothing within reach but the broom. It wouldn't fight off any intruder bigger than a twelve-year-old, but it would have to do.

She was getting a grip on the broom handle, holding it like a baseball bat, when she heard the door closing, followed by a footstep and a deep, familiar voice.

"Jess?"

She almost fainted with relief. Stepping into the kitchen doorway, she saw Ben in the living room with a pizza box in his hands. "Hey, put down that broom," he said, laughing. "I come in peace, bringing food."

The aroma of cheese and pepperoni made Jess's knees weak. And the sight of a tired-looking Ben gave wings to her drooping spirit. She pulled off her rubber gloves, and they sat side by side on the rolled-up rug from the bedroom with the open pizza box between them and a couple of cold, canned sodas that had emerged from the pockets of his leather jacket.

"Thank you," she breathed between ravenous bites. "I was famished."

"I figured you might be." He grinned as she devoured her second slice. "Feeding you is like feeding a starving bobcat."

"When did you get back?"

"We got in about nine-thirty. Ethan had gone to sleep in the truck. I hauled him upstairs, tucked him in bed and looked for you. That was when Mom told me you'd bought the house, taken all your things and moved in." He glanced around, looking past her, into the kitchen. "I can tell you've already made some headway. But this is a huge job for one little lady."

"I'm just finding that out," she said. "Francine's coming on board when she gets out of jail. I figure she can help me paint and decorate. But meanwhile, I'm going to need help hauling out the carpets and moving the furniture I found in the garage. I was hoping you'd know a couple of strong boys I could hire for a few hours at a time, preferably with a truck, to haul things away—oh, and I'll need your help catching Sergeant Pepper and bringing him over here. Francine said I mustn't try it alone."

"Sure, I can handle him—with a carrier box from Animal Control and a heavy-duty pair of gloves. Sergeant Pepper won't go gently to his new home. You'll want to keep him inside till he gets used to the place, or he's liable to run back to the trailer park."

"Is he . . . uh, housebroken?"

Ben shrugged. "Francine kept him in the trailer when the weather was bad, so I'm guessing there's a litter box somewhere. If I find it, I'll bring it, along with his kibble and bowl."

"Thanks. I've never had a cat, or any other kind of pet. I've got a lot to learn about animals."

"You'll be fine. The Sergeant will teach you everything you need to know." Ben glanced down at the half-empty pizza box and closed the lid. "Francine's got a camper-sized microwave in her trailer. I'm sure she wouldn't mind my bringing it over here for you. Then you can warm up the rest of this pizza tomorrow."

"That would be great, especially since I still need to clean the oven. But please ask her first. I've already learned that I can't second-guess what Francine will think or say." Jess rose, picked up the closed pizza box and carried it to the fridge. Returning from the kitchen, she found Ben standing by the door. He waited while she crossed the room to face him.

"Thank you for coming by, and for the pizza," she said. "You've been a lifesaver, and not just tonight."

His eyes were laced with weariness. "Come back home with me, Jess. You're worn to a frazzle, and you need a decent night's rest. You can't stay here tonight."

Jess shook her head. "Don't worry about me. The heat's on now, and I've got blankets. Believe me, I've crashed in worse places than this."

"Stop being so stubborn. After a miserable night on the hard floor, you'll be too sore to move."

"I'll be fine. Your mother's been wonderfully kind to me, but I've imposed on her hospitality long enough. It's time I was on my own, even if it means roughing it for a few days."

"You weren't imposing. My mother was glad for the company." His darkening gaze took her in. "Is that the only reason you're running away, Jess? Or is it me you're running from?"

Her pulse warmed and quickened as his fierce, gentle eyes held hers. Now was the time to back away with a clumsy excuse and end the moment, Jess told herself. But her feet were rooted to the floor. "You don't even know me," she whispered. "You don't know anything about me."

"And right now I don't give a damn."

His kiss swept her up like a storm, powerful and possessing, and yet so tender that she could have wept. What little was left of her resistance melted in his arms. Clasping his neck, she pressed upward against him, her toes leaving the floor as their mouths and bodies clung . . . and clung.

When they finally broke apart they were both breathing hard. She looked up at him, her lips damp and swollen from the kiss that had left her aching for more. "I think you'd better leave," she said.

"So do I, or we'll both be in trouble." He held her at arms' length, his big hands cupping her face. "Good night, Jess. Lock the door," he said, and then he was gone.

Jess slid the bolt home and sagged against the locked door, her knees barely holding her. . . . *Or we'll both be in trouble*, Ben had said. But for her, the warning had come too late. She was already in more trouble than she could handle. In the face of all caution and common sense, she'd fallen for the man who was the law in Branding Iron, Texas.

Chapter Nine

Jess had told herself she was tired enough to sleep anywhere. But Ben had been right about the hard floor. At the crack of dawn, with the long, miserable night behind her, she stumbled to her feet, aching in every joint and muscle. After pulling away the rag she'd stuffed under the bedroom door to keep out the mice, she tottered into the bathroom and turned on the shower. The hot water was pure bliss. She stood in the spray, letting it ease her soreness as she shampooed her dust-coated hair.

She should have swallowed her pride and gone home with Ben last night. At least she could have slept in a soft bed, awakening to coffee and breakfast. And last night's blistering kiss would probably never have happened.

She had wanted that kiss—ached for it. And when his cool, firm lips captured hers, she wouldn't have cared if it had never ended. But what an all-fired mess she'd made of the situation. She could hardly avoid Ben when she needed his help. But until she could reset the boundary between them, things were going to be awkward, to say the least.

She'd moved out of Clara's house, in part, to avoid the complication of sharing a roof with Ben. Now here she was, in complications up to her ears. Whatever it took, she needed to get the situation—and her churning hormones— under control.

By the time she'd dried off, put on clean clothes and blasted her hair with the blow dryer, she felt almost like a new woman. As she drove to the convenience store for a jolt of caffeine, she made a mental list of things she absolutely needed before tonight. At the top of the list was a foam pad or air mattress to sleep on, and a pillow. Then there was oven cleaner, instant coffee, a saucepan and skillet for the stove, a few dishes and utensils, milk, sugar, sandwich ingredients, dish and laundry soap . . . The list was getting longer and longer, and everything she bought would make one more dent in her precious funds. She had to get her place making a profit, or she wouldn't last more than a couple of months.

After buying coffee and a doughnut at the convenience store, she headed back to the house. It was too early to shop, and she wouldn't be visiting Francine till later in the day. But she could finish scrubbing the kitchen for starters, then maybe pry more boards off the windows to let in the light. Jess added window cleaner and paper towels to her mental list.

After pulling up to the curb in front of the house, Jess switched off the engine and took a moment to sip her coffee. The sunrise was a pearlescent glow in the eastern sky, the weather chilly but clear. If she wanted off-street parking for guests, she would need to clear the weeds off the driveway before the snowstorms moved in. For that, she was going to need a Weedwacker. Maybe Hank's Hardware would rent her one. While she was there, she could pick up some paint samples to show Francine.

Overwhelmed for the moment, she slumped forward, her forehead resting on the steering wheel. Heaven help her, with everything screaming to be done at once, she scarcely knew where to begin. But begin she would. And by the time she was finished, her bed-and-breakfast would be the warmest, most welcoming place in Branding Iron!

Inside the house, she sat on her suitcase, found a pen in her purse and made a rough to-do list on the back of yesterday's grocery receipt. Next to the items that had to be done right away, she drew a star. There were far too many stars. But at least the list was a step forward on her way to getting organized.

After deciding to work through the morning and break for shopping later, she took up where she'd left off last night, washing out the kitchen cabinets and drawers. It was slow work, involving countless nooks and corners, but at last she finished that job and started on the kitchen floor. The worn, aging linoleum would need replacing, and the cabinets could use a fresh coat of paint, but those projects would have to wait. The areas her guests would see—the living and dining areas, the bathroom and the bedrooms— would need to be prettied up first.

She'd just finished the floor when she heard a rap on the front door. She opened it to find Ben standing there, with a dark-haired young boy at his side.

"You must be Ethan," she said, relieved that Ben hadn't shown up alone. After last night, that could have been awkward for them both. As it was, she could barely look at the man without drowning in the memory of that kiss.

When Ben introduced them, Ethan, who looked like a miniature version of his father, grinned and shook her hand. "We brought you some presents," he said.

"Here you are, as ordered." Ben picked up the heavy-duty plastic pet carrier he'd set on the porch behind him. The yowls coming from inside made Jess hesitate to take it from his hand.

"The Sergeant wasn't too happy in the truck." Ben set the carrier down on the floor. "And he doesn't like this cage much either. You'll want to turn him loose in the basement till he calms down and decides to make friends."

"Here's his food and his water bowl." Ethan handed her a weighted paper bag. "His litter box is in the truck. I'll get it. But you'll need to buy more litter and a scoop."

A scoop. Yes, that little chore would be part of keeping the cat in the house. Never mind, she'd get used to it.

"I'll get the litter box," Ben said. "Ethan, you bring the jar and that piece of cardboard. Okay?"

As the two hurried out to the truck, Ethan double-stepping to match his father's long strides, Jess couldn't help but wonder what they were up to. Why would they need a jar?

Dropping to a crouch, she peered through the sturdy wire door of the pet carrier. Two angry yellow eyes glared back at her. "Hi, Sergeant," she said. "Remember me? I petted you back at the trailer. We're going to be friends, aren't we?" She stuck a tentative finger between the wires.

"Yikes!" She jerked backward as the cat hissed and lunged at her. Shaken, she examined her fingertip—no blood, but Sergeant Pepper had let her know he wasn't in a petting mood. Ben had said the cat would teach her. She'd just had lesson one.

When they came back from outside, Ben had the plastic litter pan, half filled with something that looked like coarse sand. Ethan was holding an empty glass peanut butter jar and a piece of cardboard.

Jess waited with the meowing cat while they went downstairs. Sooner or later, she'd have to brave the basement to try out the washer and dryer. But she wasn't anxious to run into Oscar again.

A few minutes later they were back. Ethan clutched the glass jar, which now had the lid on. "Look!" He held it up for Jess to see the huge spider trapped inside. "Isn't he cool?"

In spite of feeling weak-kneed, Jess managed to smile. "What are you going to do with him? Keep him for a pet? He looks big enough to walk on a leash."

"He wouldn't like being a pet," Ethan said. "I'm going to look on the Internet to see what kind he is. Then I'll take him out and turn him loose in Grandma's old wood shed. He can catch bugs out there and find a safe place to sleep."

"You must really like spiders."

"Yup. The only thing I like better is snakes." Ethan took a moment to study his prize. "I want to be a biologist when I grow up. I'm already learning lots of stuff."

Glancing up at Ben, Jess caught the glow of fatherly pride in his eyes. "I'm impressed," she said, meaning it.

From inside the pet carrier, a discontented yowl gave notice that Sergeant Pepper wanted out. "You can get his bed out of the truck, Ethan," Ben said. "Once the Sergeant is settled downstairs with his food and water, we can start bringing in the other things."

"Other things?" Jess gave Ben a puzzled glance.

His gaze warmed as he looked down at her. "You'll see."

"That's quite a boy you've got," she said, filling the silence that teetered on the edge of becoming awkward once Ethan had left.

"He's something, isn't he?" Ben said. "I don't remember being that smart at his age. All I cared about was sports—and later on, girls." He shook his head. "Look at me now. I don't have anything to show for either one except an ex-wife and a banged-up knee."

"You have Ethan."

"That I do. And he's worth more to me than the Heisman Trophy, a half-dozen MVP awards and all the money I might've made in the NFL. I guess that makes me a rich man."

Ethan came back in, lugging the box Jess had seen under the trailer. Ben took the carrier, with the Sergeant vocalizing his displeasure. After a moment's hesitation, Jess followed them to the basement with the cat's food dish and the water bowl, which she'd filled.

With everything set up next to the stairs, Ben opened the door of the carrier. The cat streaked out and disappeared into the darkest corner of the room, behind the furnace. "He'll be fine," Ben said. "You'll want to leave him down here for a couple of days. Then you can crack the door open to the kitchen and give him a chance to explore."

"Don't forget to scoop out his litter box," Ethan reminded her.

"I'm pretty sure my nose will remind me," Jess said, forcing a laugh.

Jess followed Ben and Ethan out to the truck, then helped them bring in more treasures. Francine had allowed them to take her tiny microwave, her portable boom box and her TV, which was going to need some kind of service connection to get it working. And Ben had broken into his camping gear for a folding cot and self-inflating pad, a couple of lightweight camp pans and a box of plastic dishes and utensils. There was also a battered but solid wooden chair, sturdy enough to climb on.

"I figure these will do you till you find something better," he said. "Meanwhile, at least you won't be sleeping on the floor. How was last night, by the way?"

She pulled a face at him. "How do you think it was?"

His dimple deepened as he gave her the belly-deep laugh she'd come to love. "Ethan and I are going to Buckaroo's for lunch. We'd be pleased if you'd join us."

Jess hesitated—she didn't need to get any closer to this man and his appealing son. But how could she refuse? "I'd love to," she said. "While I'm thinking about it, do you know a couple of local boys I could pay to roll up the living room carpet and haul it away?"

"I might," he said. "But if you don't mind a suggestion, you'll want to paint the walls before you take the old carpet out. That way you won't need to protect the floor from paint spills."

"Oh—duh!" Jess gave the side of her head a mocking poke. "Good idea. I should've thought of that myself. Sometimes I feel like such an idiot."

"You're learning, and you're doing great," he said. "Most women I know wouldn't be brave enough to take on a project like this one."

"Maybe most women you know are smarter than I am."

He chuckled. His hand reached out, then stopped, as if he'd meant to give her a playful slap on the butt, then thought better of it. "Come on," he said, shooing Ethan out the door ahead of them. "Let's go get some lunch."

Buckaroo's was decorated for Christmas in the usual way, with a grubby-looking string of lights and tinsel hanging above the counter. The country songs that blared from the speakers the rest of the year had been replaced by twangy cowboy versions of Christmas music. What the place lacked in class, it made up for in down-home holiday comfort.

Ben found a corner booth and ordered cheeseburgers, fries, and shakes for himself, his son, and Jess. "I'm expecting you to eat us both under the table." He teased the woman who was fast capturing his heart. Even after a bad night, and dressed in her baggy work clothes, Jess managed to look fresh and pretty. And that kiss last night had almost melted his toenails.

"Maybe I could eat *you* under the table." She gave Ben a mischievous glance, then nodded toward Ethan. "But I wouldn't bet against this growing boy here."

Ethan grinned back at her. The two of them had clearly hit it off.

"What do you want to find under that big Christmas tree at your grandma's house?" she asked Ethan.

"I'm still deciding," Ethan said. "What I'd really like would be for my mom to let me stay here and go to school."

"That's the present I'd like too," Ben said. "But you can't put that under the Christmas tree. So you'd better think of something you can open, Ethan."

"Like a boa constrictor?" Ethan's brown eyes danced with mischief.

"Nope. Your grandma wouldn't like that. Neither would your mother."

Ethan sighed. "Mom won't even let me have a dog, or a cat."

"So no pets for now," Ben said. "Nothing you can't take home." It was a shame, he thought, that a boy who loved animals as much as Ethan did wasn't allowed to have one. He'd change that if Ethan was allowed to stay with him. No snakes, but Clara could be talked into a dog. And even a horse wouldn't be out of the question if he could pay his friend Shane to board it at his ranch. But any future plans for Ethan were on hold until Cheryl returned from her holiday in Boston.

Cheryl had a vindictive streak. He wouldn't put it past her to take Ethan back east just because she could, forcing Ben to fight her in court for joint custody. But he had to believe she'd ultimately do what would make their son happiest. Meanwhile, he didn't want to get Ethan's hopes up, only to see them crushed.

The teen waitress brought their order to the table. The food was hot, fresh and good, and they were all hungry. Ben took pleasure in watching Jess eat. He remembered thinking earlier that there was something sexy about a woman with a healthy appetite. It suggested an appetite for other things as well, such as . . .

But once again, he wasn't about to go there. Despite last night's gasket-blowing kiss, he and Jess were a long way from becoming lovers.

Weren't they?

He remembered the moment before he'd kissed her, remembered what she'd said.

You don't know me. You don't know anything about me.

It was true. Jess had volunteered little about her recent past except that she'd come from Kansas City and that she'd been married before. Before he let things go any further, he'd be a fool not to learn as much as he could about her.

When he'd pulled up behind her broken-down car, he'd run a scan on her plates. Nothing had come up—no outstanding warrants, no indication that the car wasn't hers or that she wasn't who she claimed to be. But the fact that she had access to money and that she seemed to be hiding something were red flags.

Tomorrow he was due back at work. It would only take him a few minutes to run her name and the information on her driver's license through the FBI's National Instant Criminal Background Check System. If any kind of record came up, at least he would know about it and could decide what to do.

Across the table, Jess was laughing at something Ethan had said. Her eyes were sparkling, and she had a tiny dab of mustard on her upper lip. Ben ached to get her alone and kiss her till she went molten in his arms. But he couldn't be swayed by emotion or desire. Not until he'd found out what he needed to know.

He was a lawman. Suspicion came with the job. He was also a man with a man's heart. He didn't like himself for what he was about to do, but he couldn't rest easy until it was done.

*   *   *

Jess had taken some photos of the house with her phone. Now she held them up to the bars of the cell to show her mother. "This is the bathroom. Everything works, it just needs some paint and a few touches to make it look nice. And here's the kitchen."

Francine responded with smiles and nods. Was she truly interested or just being polite? Jess wondered. In a few more days her mother would be free. Would she settle in and help, or would she get the full treatment at the beauty shop and go back to her old ways without a backward glance?

"Here's your room." Jess showed her another photo. "At least it'll be yours till we move upstairs. It doesn't look like much yet, but I plan to paint it and have it ready with a bed for you."

Francine frowned and nodded. "The bed in my trailer's built in. But if you can get a frame, the mattress and bedding should be okay to use."

"Great." Jess wasn't sure she wanted bedding that had been in that trailer, but at least the sheets and blankets could be laundered. "Here are some paint chips I got at the hardware store," she said. "What color would you like for your room?"

Francine accepted the paint chips through the bars and fanned them like a hand of playing cards. For a long moment she studied them, as if overwhelmed by being given a choice. "They all look pretty, honey," she said at last, thrusting them back at Jess. "You decide."

"How about this one?" Jess held up a soft shade that blended feminine tones of pink and peach. In fact, that's what it was called—Peachy Pink.

"That's lovely, dear. Kind of like the sky in the morning, just before the sun comes up. It'll be fine."

"Great. I'll get to work." Jess wanted to have a nice room waiting for her mother, even if it took time and money from more urgent needs. It was important that Francine feel welcomed and cared-for.

After leaving the jail, she drove home with the electric Weedwacker she'd bought at Hank's Hardware. Since Hank, an affable, middle-aged man who walked with a limp, didn't rent tools, she'd been left with no choice except to buy it, along with a pair of safety glasses and the heavy-duty extension cord needed to reach the tool from the nearest outlet in the house. The items had cost more than she'd expected. But at least she'd have them when she needed to clear the yard again next spring.

Next spring . . .

Would she still be here by then, with a thriving business, a recovering mother, and an amazing man dropping by? Or was the whole rosy picture destined to shatter and blow away on the winter wind, like so many other things in her life?

At the house, she strung the extension cord to an outlet inside the front door and connected the machine. For a moment, she stood looking at the house, realizing that cutting back the weeds wouldn't be enough. The place looked so drab and run-down. There had to be something she could do to make it more inviting.

Not much could be done about the siding till spring, at least. But if she got right to it, she should be able to paint the front window shutters and the door. A few touches of bright, cheerful color would do wonders for the place. But what color? Green? Blue? Even orange?

She'd need to do it while the good weather held, which meant that, as soon as she got the weeds cut down, she'd have to run back to Hank's for paint supplies. She was going to be the man's best customer.

Pressing the trigger on the Weedwacker, she waded into the rank, dry growth that had taken over the gravel driveway. It took a few minutes to work out the technique of sweeping the machine ahead of her, back and forth in wide arcs. Once she'd mastered it, the knee-high weeds went down fast. But her hair and clothes were covered with flying weed fragments. Sneezing, she paused the machine long enough to wipe her face. She was going to need a shower and a change of clothes when she finished.

She'd just started again when she felt a touch on her shoulder. Startled, she gasped and swung around. Ben was standing behind her, an amused expression on his face.

"Whoa, there." He grinned down at her as she released the trigger and raised her safety glasses. "That machine's for cutting weeds, not fighting off visitors. You could've mowed me down like a bramble."

Jess recovered with a little laugh. "After lunch, I figured you were done with me for the day. Where's Ethan?"

"He's home watching TV, pretty tuckered out after the long trip yesterday. My excuse for showing up now is that my mother tried to call you. When you didn't answer your cell, she got worried and sent me to check on you."

She willed her pulse to stop its crazy fluttering, not that it helped. "My phone's in my purse, in the house. And even if I'd had it with me I wouldn't have heard it. Did your mother say what she wanted?"

"She just wanted to remind you that the Christmas Ball committee is meeting at her house tomorrow at three."

"Oh, dear." Had Clara told her about the meeting? Jess couldn't remember, but how could she go with so much to do on the house, especially since she'd have to drop everything and get cleaned up.

"I know you're busy here. Should I tell her you can't make it?" Ben asked.

Jess thought fast. She was tempted to make her excuses and skip the meeting. But in including her, these ladies had offered a hand of friendship. If she let them down, she might not be given another chance. Busy or not, she'd be wise to show up and contribute.

"No need. Please thank your mother for the reminder and tell them I'll be there—even if I'm up to my ears in paint."

"Will do. Is there anything I can get you? Any help you need?"

Jess knew better than to take him up on his polite offer. Under different conditions, she would have welcomed his help; but Ben had better things to do—and she had her pride. "Thanks, but I'll be fine," she said. "After I finish these weeds, I'll be going for paint. Hank's going to get a lot of business from me."

"Hank's a good man. If you asked him to spread the word about your bed-and-breakfast, he'd probably be glad to. He might even let you put up a poster in his window."

"Good idea. I'll remember to ask him when I'm closer to opening." Turning away, she lowered her safety glasses and pressed the trigger on the Weedwacker. The electric motor whirred, then abruptly stopped.

"Blast!" She checked the connection and pulled the trigger again. Nothing.

"What's the trouble?" Ben was headed for his truck. He turned around.

"I don't know. It just stopped, and it won't start."

"Maybe the plug's loose. Let's take a look in the house." He strode ahead of her, up the porch steps and through the door. "The cord's still plugged in," he said. "Let's try something." He flipped the light switch next to the door. The lights didn't come on.

"You've probably thrown a breaker switch," he said. "Come on downstairs with me. I want to show you how to check it. Got a flashlight? If the basement lights are out, we'll need it."

"I do." Jess had bought a small flashlight at the hardware store. She picked it up as they walked through the kitchen to the basement door. "Watch out for Sergeant Pepper. We don't want to let him out while the door's open," she said.

A long string hung from a bulb above the stairs. The dim light had been left on for the cat. There was no sign of the Sergeant, but his food dish, at the bottom of the stairs, was partly empty, so Jess figured he must be all right.

Ben led the way to a metal box mounted on a wall with an electrical conduit leading out of the top. "Move in close and shine the light up here," he said. Opening the hinged door on the front, he showed her the array of switches and pointed out the one that was out of line with the others. As he turned the switch off, then on again, Jess was achingly aware of his closeness. She battled the urge to stretch on tip-toe and tilt her face for a kiss—a kiss that would go on till she was hot and dizzy with yearning. Was Ben fighting the same urge? Was his pulse racing like hers?

Closing the cover of the breaker box, he shifted away from her. "Damn it, Jess," he muttered, "if I don't keep my hands off you, we'll both be in trouble! Now let's get back upstairs and see if we fixed the problem."

Turning away to hide her burning face, Jess led the way up the stairs. He followed her, checking for the cat as he closed the door.

"The living room light's on!" she exclaimed as they came out of the kitchen. "It must've worked."

"If the breaker switch was the problem, your Weedwacker should work too. Probably a good thing it happened. Now you know what to check for and what to do if it happens again."

Outside, Jess gave the machine's trigger an experimental squeeze and felt the motor whir to life. "Thanks, I'll be fine now," she said, slipping on her safety glasses. "Tell Ethan hi for me, and tell your mother I'll see her tomorrow."

"You're welcome to show up for supper," he said. "We eat around six."

"Thanks, but I've got a lot to do. I'll warm up the pizza."

Still smarting, she watched him walk out to the truck. At least she hadn't made a complete fool of herself. But she'd come close. Too close. If Ben wanted to cool things between them, she was a girl who could take a hint. From now on, the sexy sheriff was strictly off-limits.

Turning on the Weedwacker, she tore into the remaining weeds. When she looked up again, the black pickup was nowhere in sight.

Ben turned the corner with a long, slow exhalation. In the warm darkness of the basement, with Jess just inches away, it had been all he could do to keep from pulling her into his arms and kissing her till they were past the point of stopping. She'd wanted it as much as he had, he could tell.

But he'd known the woman only a few days, and he was already getting in too deep. If the attraction had just been hot chemistry, he could've handled it. The trouble was, he really cared for Jess. With her courage and spunk she was like a feisty, adorable little kitten. And her determination to help her mother showed a good and generous heart. The last thing he wanted was to create a situation that would only end up hurting her.

Should he follow his heart or slam the brakes on the relationship right now? How could he make that decision when he knew so little about her?

He'd planned on checking the NICS at work tomorrow. So why not do it now, while it was on his mind? He already had her driver's license information. It shouldn't take long to run a check of police and court records for her, and maybe for her ex-husband.

As long as he had the tools to run a background check on Jess, didn't it make sense to do so? Of course it did—but that didn't mean it was a nice thing to do, especially to someone who trusted him. She'd be furious if she knew. But he'd be a fool not to do it.

Feeling lower than a snake, Ben changed direction and headed for his office.

Chapter Ten

Jess finished cutting down the weeds, cleaned up and drove back to Hank's Hardware to buy paint. The store, which had been crowded earlier, was cleared of customers. She found Hank in the plumbing aisle, scanning the shelves with a clipboard in his hand.

"Back so soon, young lady?" He appeared to be in his early fifties with graying hair, a nice smile and a few extra pounds around the middle.

Jess returned the smile. "I'm afraid you're going to see a lot of me. This time it's paint. I've got a sample of the interior semi-gloss I want. Then I'll need some color suggestions for the shutters and front door—and of course I'll need the brushes and things for the job." She could imagine what all this would cost. Her poor Visa card would be taking some heavy hits by the time the house was ready to open. She could only hope she'd have enough money in her account to pay off all the charges.

He took the Peachy Pink paint chip Francine had chosen. "I can mix this for you while you look at exterior colors. For an average bedroom, one gallon will do a single coat. I'd recommend two."

"Fine. Two, then." Maybe she'd have enough left over to do the bathroom. The color would be nice in there too.

He carried two gallons of color base over to the paint mixer. "I hear tell you're Francine's daughter," he said.

"That's right." No use asking who'd told him. By now the news would be all over town. "Do you know her very well?"

"I've known Francine most of my life," he said. "She broke my heart when she ran off with that redheaded cowboy. From the looks of you, I reckon he was your dad." He pried open the first paint can and squirted jets of red and yellow into the pale base, then replaced the lid, attached the can to the mixer and turned it on. "At the time, I wanted to marry the girl—I was older than she was and ready to settle down. But she wanted bright lights and thrills. I guess that's what she got. I married another gal who left me a few years later, after I lost my leg in a farm machine. Took our boy with her." Hank added color to the second paint can while he waited for the first to finish mixing. "I'm sorry, girl. You came to buy paint. You didn't come to hear an old duffer tell you his sad story."

"No, this is something I need to hear," Jess said. "So you never got together with Francine."

"Nope. I was already married when she came back to Branding Iron. Then, by the time my wife left, Francine was hitting the bottle pretty hard. I figured that even if she wasn't, she wouldn't want to be stuck with a one-legged man. What woman would?"

Jess left the store twenty minutes later with the Pontiac's trunk full of paint, brushes, rollers, masking tape and plastic drop cloths for the floors. Hank had also given her a pile of the old newspapers he saved for projects like hers.

Hank struck her as a good man who'd gotten a raw deal in life, just like Francine. Both of them had suffered tragic losses. But he'd loved her once. Maybe it wasn't too late for them to find some happiness.

She'd have to get her mother off the bottle, of course. After hearing what Hank had said, Jess knew he wouldn't want to deal with a woman who drank. But miracles had been known to happen.

Maybe a miracle—a Christmas miracle—was what she needed.

Alone in his closed office, Ben stared at the computer screen. The young woman in the police mug shot looked dazed and scared in the harsh light, her hair slicked back, her eyes huge in her colorless face. Reluctant to believe what he was seeing, he studied the image and the name below it:

Jessica Jane Ramsey McConnell.

Denial was useless. The woman was Jess.

With a sinking heart, Ben forced himself to read on. Jess had been arrested in St. Louis five years ago and charged as an accessory to fraud. However, she hadn't gone to trial or served time. Instead she'd made a plea deal—immunity in exchange for testimony against her husband, Gilbert McConnell.

Was this the woman who'd shared his mother's roof? The woman he'd kissed and come close to falling in love with? Numb with shock, Ben read the online file again. It appeared she'd helped her husband commit fraud, then betrayed him to save herself. From what he knew of Jess, he would never have believed the sordid story. But the evidence was there on the computer, right in front of him.

Feeling like a man walking into a dark labyrinth, Ben brought up the file on Jess's ex-husband. Smiling, even in his mug shot, he looked like the blond, blue-eyed all-American boy next door. His wholesome, movie-star features were the sort that would inspire trust. But this man had defrauded dozens of people, most of them elderly, by selling life insurance policies and pocketing the money. He'd deserved his seven-year prison sentence, and worse.

Had Jess been taken in by this man's obvious charm, or had she been a willing partner all the way? At least she knew enough to testify against the bastard. Maybe a call to the prosecutor on the case would clarify the picture.

Ben found the number in the file and made the call, but he learned nothing. The prosecutor had passed away two years ago, and most of the other people involved in the case had moved on. There was no one available who could tell him about Jess's part in the crime and the trial that followed.

Which left Jess herself.

Ben switched off the computer and sank back into his chair. Was it fair to pass judgment on Jess before he'd heard her side of the story? He owed her that, at least. But she'd be furious if he told her how he'd learned about her past. Anything she told him would be tainted by defensive anger. Worse, if she was innocent, she would never forgive him. He would lose a woman he truly cared about.

His best chance of learning the truth would be to bide his time, win Jess's trust and hope that she'd volunteer her story. But he'd be gambling with his heart. If he lost—if she didn't tell him, or worse, if she lied—he'd feel duty bound to confront her, and they'd both end up wounded.

After leaving his office, he walked out to his truck, climbed inside and turned the key in the ignition. "Have a Holly Jolly Christmas," the Burl Ives version, came blasting out of the speakers. Ben turned the radio off. He didn't feel very jolly right now. In fact, right now, he didn't even feel like Christmas.

By the next afternoon, Jess had finished painting Francine's bedroom. It wasn't an expert job, but at least the room looked clean and bright—maybe a little too bright. The color had looked more subdued on the paint chip than it did on the walls. Perhaps when the time came to turn it into a guest room, she could paint one wall, and the ceiling a different color. For now, she could only hope Francine would like it.

She had yet to paint the bathroom. But she planned to do that after the Christmas Ball committee meeting at Clara's. The door and shutters would have to wait till tomorrow. On Hank's advice, she'd chosen forest green for the shutters and door frame and a deep shade of teal for the door. The combination had sounded strange at first, but when she'd held the chips side by side, she had to agree that the rich colors would give the house a welcoming look.

After washing the worst of the Peachy Pink paint spatters off her hands and face, she changed into clean jeans, a red sweater and her good shoes. She still had paint in her hair and on the backs of her hands, but if she wanted to get to the meeting by three o'clock, and avoid Maybelle's scathing comments, she didn't dare spend any more time on her appearance.

She arrived at three and pulled up behind Kylie Taggart's station wagon. Kylie, balancing a covered tray and her purse, was just stepping out onto the curb.

"Here, let me take that!" Jess rushed to grab the tray, which was about to tip. Kylie gave her a friendly grin. "Thanks. I almost spilled sugar cookies all over the road."

"Just don't spill yourself." Jess took the pregnant woman's

arm with her free hand as they mounted the curb and came up the sloping sidewalk.

"Ben and Ethan are out at the ranch, riding horses with my crew," Kylie said. "Ben tells me you're fixing up the old Winslow place on your own, and doing a great job. And Ethan talks like you hung the moon. I think he was impressed when you didn't freak out over the spider he caught."

Jess laughed. "Believe me, that took some self-control. The thing was a monster!"

"Well, whatever it took, you've made a conquest." Kylie rang the doorbell, then opened the door without waiting for an answer. "Here we are! I even remembered the refreshments!"

Maybelle looked up from her notes. "It's about time. I was getting ready to call the meeting to order without you."

"Oh, you're fine." Clara rose to greet them, taking the tray. "My, don't these cookies look delicious, Kylie. So Christmas-y. Have a chair, dear. Katy can pass them around while we visit a few minutes. Then we can start the meeting."

Maybelle frowned but didn't object. There was no question of who was really in charge here. With an eager smile, Katy took the tray, along with the napkins Clara had given her, and began serving the iced sugar cookies.

Connie looked Jess up and down. "My goodness, it looks like you've been painting up a storm," she said. "I hope you got as much on the walls as you've got on yourself."

"Almost." Jess laughed at the exaggeration. "My mother's coming home in a few days. I'm trying to have a comfortable room ready to welcome her."

"That sounds like the nicest thing anybody's done for Francine in years," Connie said. "Say, could you use a bed and a dresser? We've got an old set that's just taking up space in our backyard shed. I've been after Silas to haul it off to give us more room. You'd be welcome to it."

The offer was like an answered prayer. "That would be wonderful!" Jess said. "Can Silas bring the pieces by? I don't have any way to move them."

"Oh, don't bother Silas about it," Clara said. "Ben can haul them in his pickup. I'll ask him when he gets home. It'll be no trouble at all."

Ben again. *It's almost as if Clara is matchmaking,* Jess thought. Not that it would make any difference. The last time they'd been together, when Ben had shown her the breaker box in the basement, she'd sensed he was distancing himself from her. Sooner or later, he was bound to suspect she was hiding a secret past. He would run a background check on her and decide to back off—fast. Maybe it had already happened.

She should've been up-front and just told him. But Jess had a feeling that it was too late for that now.

"Excuse me, ladies, but it's past time to get started." Maybelle cleared her throat. "I call this meeting to order."

The committee got down to business, with every member reporting in. Jess was glad she could say that every person on the calling list had been contacted and reminded of the dish they'd promised to bring. Kylie was in charge of the decorations—an easy job, since the same decorations were used every year. Except for the Christmas tree, which Hank always donated, they were stored at the school, to be put up, and later taken down, by students who'd volunteered to help.

The Cowboy Christmas Ball was a big production. Security would be handled by the sheriff's department, which meant that Ben would likely be on duty. It would be his job to confiscate any alcohol and drugs and ensure that everyone had a wholesome, trouble-free experience.

The mayor's office had arranged for the Badger Hollow Boys, a well-known Nashville band, to entertain and play as people danced. Most of the proceeds from ticket sales would go to pay the musicians.

"I hope you're planning to go, Jess," Clara said. "It's great fun, and the whole town will be there."

At Clara's suggestion, something shrank inside Jess. She wanted to fit in, but she'd never had the self-confidence to walk into a party, mingle, and have genuine fun—especially this kind of party. "It sounds lovely," she said. "But I don't have a date or anything to wear. And I don't know any of the dances."

"You don't need a date," Connie said. "It's not that kind of party. You just show up and have a good time."

"My daughter Ellie's Christmas ball gown is packed away in my sewing room," Clara said. "She's about your size, and she'll probably never wear it again. You're more than welcome to borrow it. And the girls' gym teacher at the high school teaches a class before the ball. If you want to learn the dance steps, just come early. So no more excuses. Just say you'll be there."

Still, Jess hesitated, thinking how awkward she'd feel, walking into the ball alone.

"Maybe you could volunteer to help with something." Kylie came to her rescue. "That way, you'd have a reason to be there and something to do."

"I could use some help with tickets at the door." Maybelle surprised Jess by speaking up. "You'd have to get there early."

"That shouldn't be a problem," Jess said. "Thank you, I'd be happy to help."

As the meeting continued, Jess tried to pay attention. But doubts were already creeping into her mind. Why had she agreed to go to the ball and help? What would she do about Francine? What would she do about the bed-and-breakfast? And what about the people who didn't know her but who might already have judged her? What would she do if they made her feel unwelcome?

But she'd already agreed to show up and help out; it was vital that she keep her word. Whether she liked it or not, this reluctant Cinderella was going to the ball.

Ben secured the bed frame, mattress and dresser in the back of his truck and climbed into the driver's seat. "Thanks," he told Silas, who stood outside. "I know these things will be used and appreciated."

"No trouble at all," Silas said. "My wife's been after me to get rid of 'em. She'll be glad for the extra space. I'd be happy to come along and help unload 'em if you want."

"Thanks, but I can manage fine." With a friendly wave at Katy, who'd come out onto the porch, Ben put the truck in gear and backed out of the driveway. This would be the first time he'd been with Jess since doing the background check and learning about her past. How would he feel when he saw her? Could he act as if nothing had changed between them?

He drove slowly through the twilight, struggling to sort out his thoughts. Did he have any right to judge Jess, especially before hearing her side of the story? Everyone was entitled to a few mistakes, and she'd clearly paid for hers. She had no legal entanglements, no record of any trouble since her original arrest. Nothing she'd said or done would lead him to believe that she was anything but a good, moral person.

So why was he tormenting himself?

Now that he thought about it, it wasn't what Jess had done that troubled him. It was the fact that she'd kept it from him. How could he let himself fall in love with a woman who kept secrets—a woman he couldn't trust?

Was he falling in love with her?

Along Main Street, the Christmas lights had come on. Twinkling through the dusk, they cast dancing patterns of red, green, blue and yellow light along the sidewalks. In the years since coming home to Branding Iron, Ben had always looked forward to Christmas. But this year was charged with uncertainty. Between the custody issue with Ethan and his budding relationship with Jess, it could turn out to be the best Christmas—or one of the worst—of his life.

Near the end of Main Street he turned into the short, narrow one-way street where Jess lived. Her car was parked in the newly cleared driveway. A light glowed through the shuttered front window.

Ben mounted the porch and knocked on the front door. His mother would have told Jess that he'd be delivering the furniture, but she might not be expecting him until tomorrow.

No one answered, but the door was unlocked. He could hear Christmas music coming from somewhere inside the house. Following the sound, he entered, crossed the empty living room and found Jess in the open bathroom. She was standing on the toilet lid, brushing pink paint along the angle between the wall and ceiling. Her hair was tied up in a paint-spattered bandanna. She had paint on her clothes, on her hands and arms and on her face. She looked damned adorable.

"Hi," she said, glancing down at him where he stood in the doorway. "Don't come in here. There's wet paint all over."

"I can see that. It's all over *you*. I'll keep a safe distance, thanks."

"How's Ethan? Kylie told me you'd taken him horseback riding at their ranch."

"He had a great time, but he's tuckered out. I left him watching PBS Nature with his grandma. How's it going?"

"Take a look at that second bedroom. Francine helped me choose the color. I finished painting it this afternoon, with enough paint left over to do this bathroom."

Ben stepped back into the hall. Through the open doorway, the newly painted bedroom glowed with fresh color. It was a little bright for his taste. But who was he to judge?

"You've been one busy lady," he said. "Did you do all this by yourself?"

"Uh-huh. I'm hoping Francine can help me with the other rooms, but I want her room to be ready for her when she gets here."

Ben looked up at Jess, this small, paint-spattered angel of a woman who was knocking herself out to please the mother she barely knew—a mother who might not even deserve her kindness. Was this the same woman who'd helped her husband cheat people out of their savings, then turned on him to save herself from justice?

Something didn't make sense. And it wouldn't make sense until he knew the whole story.

"I've got your furniture outside in the truck," he said. "It's not heavy, but I'll need help balancing the bigger pieces. I hope you won't mind giving me a hand."

"No, not a bit. But I don't want to get paint on anything. Hang on." She lifted the hem of her baggy, paint-smeared sweatshirt, which he recognized as an old one of his, and worked it off over her head. The black tank top underneath revealed more of her sweet little figure than Ben had seen before, but he made an effort not to ogle her.

"I'll just wash my hands and get a jacket—" She sudsed her painted hands at the sink, then dashed into the other bedroom and emerged wearing the jean jacket she'd had on the first time he saw her. "Ready," she said. "And thanks, I know you've got better things to do than babysit me."

With Ben doing the heavy lifting and Jess balancing the load, they managed to get the bed frame, mattress and box spring inside the house and down the hall to the bedroom. The plain wooden frame had some scratches but it was solid quality, and the mattress, as well as the box spring, had been wrapped in plastic sheeting to keep it clean. "I'm sure Francine's slept on a lot worse," Ben said with a grunt as he heaved the heavy pieces into place.

"Like in the jail, you mean?"

He gave her a grin. "The jail, the trailer, and who knows where else. I just hope she appreciates what you're doing for her."

"I'm not asking for appreciation." Jess pushed a corner of the mattress to straighten it. "I just want her to know that someone cares enough to make things nice for her."

He straightened, meeting her eyes. "I just hope she doesn't end up hurting you, Jess."

"If she does, believe me, it won't be the first time. I'm a big girl. I can handle whatever comes."

"Can you?" The fierceness in her eyes and the tilt of her chin made Ben ache to seize her in his arms and kiss her. But the time wasn't right, and she still had a lot of paint on her hands and face. He didn't want any raised eyebrows from his mother when he came home.

"Have dinner with me, Jess," he said. "Tomorrow night. And I'm not talking Buckaroo's. There's a good steak house outside Cottonwood Springs, forty miles up the road. You've been wearing yourself out. You deserve a decent meal and a few hours to relax before you have to deal with your mother full-time."

She hesitated, and his heart sank. "What about Ethan?"

"He's friends with a boy down the block. They're having a sleepover at his house tomorrow night."

"Well . . ." She hesitated another beat. "Sure. Okay. That sounds great. But I should probably treat you and your mother. The two of you have both done so much for me."

"Nope, that's not the deal. Just you and me, and it's my treat."

"All right," she said. "What time?"

"Seven?"

She nodded. "Is it fancy? What should I plan to wear?"

"Whatever you want. I'll be in clean jeans and cowboy boots. Now let's bring that dresser inside so you can finish painting and get some rest."

They took the drawers out of the dresser and carried them inside. Then they carried the empty dresser, with its attached mirror, carefully up the walk and through the door. There was even a small dressing stool to go with it.

"Thanks again," Jess said as they surveyed the arrangement of the furniture. "I just need to get a few things tomorrow, and the room will be ready for my mother."

"I hope Francine appreciates how lucky she is to have you for a daughter."

"That remains to be seen, I guess." Jess stood beside him, their shoulders not quite touching. Ben fought the urge to lay a protective arm around her. She was so determined to be strong, but her vulnerability tugged at his heart.

"You'd better go," she said. "I need to finish painting the bathroom tonight."

"I'll be working tomorrow morning and spending the afternoon with Ethan," he said. "But I'll see you at seven."

"Seven it is." She walked him to the door and closed it behind him. Ben felt a strange lightness in his step as he walked to his truck. It had felt good to do something for

Jess. It felt even better to know that she'd agreed to go to dinner with him tomorrow.

But he'd asked her out for a reason, Ben reminded himself. He hoped to make her comfortable enough to talk about her past. If she volunteered the story of her arrest and the deal she'd made, it could open the way to understanding between them. But he'd need to be on guard. If Jess suspected he'd been checking on her, she would never trust him again.

Chapter Eleven

B y the next morning the paint in the bathroom was dry. Jess stripped away the masking tape, surveyed the results and congratulated herself on a job well—if not perfectly—done. All it needed was a shower curtain, a mat and some pretty washcloths and towels.

There were plenty of other things she needed as well. As she breakfasted on instant coffee and the last slice of leftover pizza, she began making a list. She hoped she'd be able to find most of the items at Shop Mart.

Besides the things for the bathroom, she wanted to get a pretty bedspread and matching drapes for Francine's room. Maybe a rug too, if she could find one that wasn't too expensive. She was going to need more food and kitchen items—eggs, bread, bacon, jam, and milk, as well as a toaster and a few treats. She would also need laundry supplies—after she made certain the washer and dryer were working. Maybe she should do that now. She needed to go downstairs anyway, to check on the cat.

The dim light above the stairs was on. Closing the basement door behind her, Jess made her way cautiously down the steps. There was another light fixture above the washer and dryer, but the bulb was burned out. She would need to buy lightbulbs—as well as kitty litter and a scoop, she reminded herself, as her nose caught the pungent odor of the litter box. At least the Sergeant was using it.

Sergeant Pepper came running to rub against her legs as she refilled his food bowl. She reached down and stroked his scruffy coat, feeling the rumble of a purr that passed through his tough, old body. He seemed to be settling in. Maybe when she got home from shopping she would open the basement door and let him come upstairs to explore.

While the Sergeant was eating, she checked the connections to the washer and dryer. Hoping for the best, she turned each one on, feeling a rush of relief as the machines responded. One less worry. Now she could wash her things and get the bedding from Francine's trailer and launder it.

Tomorrow, her mother would be getting out of jail and coming here to live. Jess wanted everything to be ready for her. But there was still so much to be done. She needed to shop. She needed to get things from Francine's trailer and arrange for a TV connection. She also needed to paint the front door and shutters while the unseasonably mild weather held.

And at seven o'clock she was going out to dinner with Ben.

The more she thought about tonight, the more aware she became of the alarm bells going off in her head. She should have been eager and excited about a real date with the sexy sheriff. But somehow the thought of a fine meal in cozy surroundings with the man who made her pulse race seemed almost too good to be true. Her instincts told her that Ben wanted something from her—something she might not be prepared to give.

When Shop Mart opened its doors at nine AM, Jess was waiting outside. List in hand, she grabbed a cart and started on the nonfood items in the housewares section of the big-box store—the towels, curtain and mat for the bathroom, then the bedspread and drapes for Francine's room. She found a pink and green floral on sale that would look pretty and might do fine after the house was fully converted for paying guests. Lightbulbs, a bag of cat litter with a scoop, two wastebaskets, a toaster, extra sheets and towels—she checked off each item as she found it. Her cart was getting full when something that wasn't on the list caught her eye.

On the clearance rack was a single cast iron cook set, boxed and complete with lids and basic utensils. It was on sale for less than half price.

Sooner or later, she was going to need something like this. Why not buy it now? The box was large and heavy, but she managed to heft it onto the top edge of her shopping cart. Keeping it balanced with one hand, she steered the cart toward the checkout line. She would load her car and make a second trip inside the store for the food items.

There were two women, both strangers, ahead of her. As Jess pushed her cart into line, the big box cut off her view of them—and their view of her. But their conversation came through loud and clear.

"I hear Francine's getting out of jail this week."

"And now her long-lost daughter's shown up. From what I hear, they'll be living together in that old Winslow place."

"Well, there goes the neighborhood." There was sharp-edged laughter. "Give 'em time. Maybe they'll both end up back in jail."

"That wouldn't surprise me one bit. You know what they say. The apple doesn't fall far from the tree."

"Have you seen the daughter? A little redheaded floozy. She dresses like she's been livin' on the street."

"Maybe she just got out of rehab."

"Well, wherever she's been, she hasn't wasted any time goin' after the sheriff. I've seen his truck in front of that old house at all hours. Whatever she's givin' him, it must be pretty darn good."

Still chatting, the women paid for their purchases and left the store. Thankfully, if the young man at the register had been paying attention and recognized Jess, he gave no sign of it. She ran her credit card, declined any offers of help, and wheeled the loaded cart out to the parking lot.

She made it all the way to her car before her eyes began to sting. Tears spilled over to trickle down her cheeks as she loaded the cookware box in the backseat and the other items in the trunk.

What she'd heard didn't matter, she tried to tell herself. Any newcomer in a small town would be a target for gossip. Neither of those mean-spirited women had ever met her, or knew anything about her, except that she was Francine's daughter. Still, the exchange had hurt her, especially the part about Ben, who was only being helpful. And she certainly hadn't "given" him what those women were implying!

She would have to warn him, of course. Ben's career depended on the people who voted him into office. The slightest breath of scandal could tip the balance against him in the next election—especially if it was intimated that he'd accepted "favors" from the daughter of a prisoner in his custody.

She could tell him tonight—or better yet, she could call him now and get it over with. Given the gossip, it might be best if they didn't see each other alone at all.

Without giving herself time to change her mind, she slipped into the driver's seat, closed the car door and found her phone. But the only number she had for him was his work listing. If she couldn't reach him there, she'd be out of luck.

After a couple of rings, a woman's voice answered, "Sheriff's office."

"Could I speak with the sheriff, please?" Jess asked.

"Sorry, he's out on a call. Can I help you?"

Jess thought fast. She didn't want to leave her name, and they wouldn't likely give her his personal number. Even if she had it, she wouldn't want to interrupt him if he was making an arrest or dealing with an accident. And if she tried to reach him this afternoon, he'd be off somewhere with Ethan.

She certainly didn't want to worry Clara with her personal concerns. She would just have to wait and talk with Ben tonight. Meanwhile, she had work to do.

After ending the call and dabbing her eyes dry with a tissue, she wheeled the empty cart back to the grocery area and began filling her list, which was far too short for her needs. Jess found herself reaching for pancake mix, syrup, salt and pepper, flour, baking soda, butter, vegetables, cereal, sugar, canned soup and tuna, fresh tomatoes, mayonnaise, paper towels and more. By the time she was ready to check out, her cart was overflowing. As the checker rang up the total, Jess cringed. But it couldn't be helped. These were all things she needed. If she didn't buy them now, she would have to buy them later.

The grocery bags filled the remaining space in her trunk. As Jess drove back to the house, the exchange between the two women played over and over in her mind like an irritating song. How many other people in the town felt the way those two did? Could she prove her worth and change their minds? Or was their judgment already set in concrete?

But why waste time wondering? She'd bought the house and made a commitment to stay. And she'd found a few good friends. In time, she'd find more. But part of her still wished she'd stepped around the cart and given those two gossiping women a piece of her mind.

It took her twenty minutes to unload the car and stow the perishables in the fridge. Leaving everything else inside the door, she headed back to Francine's trailer.

The run-down trailer park looked even more forlorn than Jess remembered, the little camp trailer dingy and cold. If Francine had tried to warm it with the heater, what were the odds she'd have set the place on fire or released deadly carbon monoxide into the small space?

Francine's beloved tabloid magazines were piled on every available surface. Jess weighed the idea of bringing them to the new place, then decided against it. If her mother wanted to keep them, she could get them later. She would strip the bed, get the clothes and shoes, and maybe a few toiletries from the tiny bathroom, and leave the rest.

The clothes, which smelled like a bar, would need airing. At least Francine didn't appear to smoke. That would've been a problem in the bed-and-breakfast, and the poor woman had enough issues as it was. The half-empty bottle of cheap Scotch Jess found in the closet and the fifth of vodka under the kitchen sink attested to that.

She bagged the bottles for consignment to the trash bin next to the trailer park gate. Getting her mother into decent housing would be the first of many hurdles, she reminded herself. Helping Francine recover was going to take patience, understanding and plenty of tough, tough love.

Back home, she unloaded the car again and laid Francine's clothes out in one of the upstairs rooms with a window open. Then she found the laundry detergent she'd bought, took the sheets and quilts downstairs and started the first batch of washing. Sergeant Pepper seemed eager to follow her back upstairs, but she would need to leave him in the basement a little longer while she painted the open front door—which would have to be done right away if the paint was to dry before nightfall.

Rushing back to her room, she changed into her painting clothes, gathered gloves, tape, brushes, newspapers, and the half-gallon can of dark teal enamel paint and headed for the front door.

Ben's half day of work included filling out forms, testifying in a juvenile drug case, and breaking up a fist fight between two young hotheads after a fender bender in front of the high school. He was looking forward to an afternoon with Ethan. They'd made plans for cheeseburgers and shakes at Buckaroo's, then plinking at tin cans with a lightweight .22 out on the sage flats. He'd have his cell phone in case of a true emergency. But his staff knew how much he valued time with his son. He could count on them to handle routine matters while he was out.

Before leaving, he decided to check on Francine. Her release was set for tomorrow. He wanted to make sure she understood what was expected of her. The woman had been in and out of the jail so many times that Ben suspected she viewed it as a refuge. But this time would be different. This time she had a daughter waiting—a daughter who'd laid everything on the line for her.

"Hi, sheriff." Francine glanced up from her lunch, a tuna sandwich with a carton of milk and a bag of chips. "Guess we'll be partin' company tomorrow, won't we."

"Guess we will," Ben said. "And this time I want to make sure you won't be back here."

"Hey." She gave him a grin. "I got my little girl back. We're gonna be a team, me and her."

"Can you really be part of a team, Francine? Can you pull your weight and hold up your end? Jess is knocking herself out to make things nice for you. But she can't do it all. You're not elderly, and you're healthy enough to work. You can't expect her to take care of you, physically or financially."

"Hell, sheriff, I'm not stupid. And I'm not lazy either. I can work if I got somethin' to work for."

"But can you behave yourself? Your probation requires you to show up at AA meetings every week. We've been through this drill before—you go for a while, then you start slacking off, and pretty soon you're right back to square one. If this was anything but a small town where people know you and cut you some slack, you'd be locked up for months at a stretch, not weeks."

Francine's girlish pout would've done justice to a three-year-old. "Now, sheriff, honey, we ladies got our weaknesses. My weaknesses just happen to be good, cheap whiskey and handsome men like you."

Ben had heard it all before, and not just from Francine. At least he knew this woman was only joking with him. "I'm leaving now," he said. "But I've got one thing to say to you. You have a loving daughter out there who believes in you, a daughter who's willing to do anything to help you change. Don't break her heart. If you do, you'll answer to me!"

Francine stared at him through the bars. Suddenly she burst into hearty laughter. "Glory be, sheriff, it's as plain as the nose on your face! You're in love with my little girl, aren't you?"

"I'll see you tomorrow, Francine."

Ben turned away to hide the rush of color to his face, but Francine's question stuck with him as he walked outside to his truck. True, he was right fond of Jess. Kissing her had felt like a sky full of fireworks on the Fourth of July. But was he really in love with her?

The answer to that question could well depend on what happened tonight.

Jess stood at the foot of the front sidewalk, studying the effect of the newly painted door and shutters on the drab old house. *Not bad*, she decided. The combination of dark green on the shutters and frame harmonized with the deep teal on the door, lending the entrance a fresh, inviting air. She could hardly wait to see how it looked in broad daylight with the masking tape stripped away, but that would have to wait until tomorrow, when the paint was dry.

Next spring, if she was still here and had the money, she would have the rest of the house painted—maybe a light storm gray to cover the dingy siding. For now these touches of color would have to do.

She'd finished the job just in time. The setting sun had left a chill in the wake of its meager warmth. Jess had left the radio on in the house to help her keep track of the time. The local station was broadcasting the six o'clock news. Ben would be picking her up for dinner in less than an hour.

She pounded the lids onto the paint cans and carried everything inside. Today she'd painted only the front and back of the door, leaving the edges for later, so she was able to close it without the paint sticking to the frame. With luck, she'd find time to paint the rest tomorrow, but with Francine moving in, anything could happen.

After turning on the porch light, she stripped down and

headed for the shower. She'd worn latex gloves and old clothes but still managed to be splotched with green and teal paint. She scrubbed off the colors as best she could and washed her hair.

She was hungry and should've been looking forward to dinner. But the thought of being stuck there, answering any question Ben chose to ask her, sent her stomach into flip-flops. Maybe she was nervous for nothing. Maybe all the man wanted was a tasty meal, some pleasant conversation, and a few good night kisses at the door. But knowing Ben, she'd wager against it. The sheriff, she sensed, was a man with an agenda.

Since she'd left Kansas City only with what she could load in her car, she'd had to abandon most of her clothes—not that they were worth missing. She'd kept just two dresses—a prim navy blue shirtdress that would do for a church meeting or job interview, and a simple black knit designer sheath she'd bought at a consignment shop and loved too much to leave behind. The draped bodice revealed a hint of cleavage without being immodest, the above-knee length showing just enough leg in the fishnet tights that had been a splurge back in Kansas City.

In her room, she held up the black dress, recalling how confident she'd always felt in it. If ever she'd needed confidence, it was tonight. Ben had mentioned he was going to wear jeans, but if she wore the dress with her low-heeled ankle boots and plain silver earrings, she shouldn't look too dressy.

As she pulled up her tights, she suddenly remembered the two gossiping women in the line at Shop Mart. She'd been so busy all afternoon that she'd almost forgotten them. But Ben needed to know about the rumors before they damaged his career. She dreaded the thought that he might have to stop seeing her, but at the very least they would need to be more careful. Of course, if this dinner was the kiss-off, that wouldn't be an issue.

By the time she'd blow-dried her hair and put on her clothes it was nearly seven o'clock. She'd just finished dabbing mascara on her eyelashes when the doorbell rang.

Mindful of the wet paint, she opened the door. Ben stood on the threshold dressed in jeans, boots, a plaid Western shirt and black leather jacket. His hair was still damp from showering, his jaw freshly shaved. He looked as delectable as a hot fudge sundae.

His warm, brown eyes took her in, from her hair to the toes of her boots. "Wow," he said. "Don't tell me you're the girl who just painted this door."

She looked down at the hand he extended. The tip of his index finger was green. Jess giggled. "You just had to touch it, didn't you?"

"You could've put up a sign."

"Would you have paid any attention to it?"

His laugh loosened the knot of nerves inside her. "Let's get your coat," he said. "I've spent all day imagining a couple of steak dinners with our names on them."

Jess's quilted coat hung on the wall rack next to the door. Ben held it for her, his knuckles brushing her shoulders as she slipped her arms into the sleeves. "Did I mention you look stunning?" he murmured next to her ear.

Like a light caress, his breath awakened a tingle that spread and deepened. "I hope I'm not overdressed," she said, recovering. "I could change."

"You're beautiful. Don't change a thing. Let's go."

She found the key in her purse and, avoiding the wet paint, locked the door. By now it was dusk. His arm guided her down the uneven sidewalk to his truck, where he opened her door and helped her climb into the passenger seat. He was doing his best to be gallant, but she sensed a thread of tension in his manner. Something was troubling him. Was it her?

As the truck pulled around the corner, onto Main Street with its bright strings of Christmas lights, Jess decided to address the painful issue and get it out of the way. "I overheard something today in Shop Mart," she began, and told him about the two women. "I almost wish I'd called them out and put them in their places. They were implying terrible things—things that could damage your reputation if they got around."

"And what about *your* reputation?"

"That too. But I'm not holding public office."

He exhaled slowly. "Jess, this is a small town. There'll always be people looking for something to gossip about. But we're both adults. We haven't done anything wrong, let alone anything illegal. If I want to spend time with an attractive lady, that's nobody's business but yours and mine. As for the way they talked about you . . ." He swung the truck onto the highway. "You're young, you're pretty and you're taking risks. Of course people are going to talk about you. Some of them will even be jealous. Give them time. After a while you'll be old news."

"I can hardly wait." Jess gazed out the window into the deepening twilight. At least Ben hadn't been concerned about the gossip. Maybe he was used to it. But what would he do if he knew the truth about her past?

"How's Ethan?" she asked, changing the subject. "Did he have a good time with you this afternoon?"

Ben was silent for a beat. "I hope so. He had a lot on his mind. His mother phoned him while I was at work this morning. She's definitely getting married again—maybe soon, or so Ethan tells me."

"Is that a good thing—or not?" Jess asked.

"That depends. Ethan doesn't care for the man. Frankly,

neither do I. Eastern type, old money. He wants to move Cheryl and Ethan back to Boston where he lives and send Ethan to boarding school—to make a man of the boy, he says."

Jess recalled what she'd heard about many boarding schools—the loneliness, the discipline, the abuse and bullying, more than enough to break a spirited little boy like Ethan. "But that's awful! What does Ethan's mother have to say about it?"

He shrugged. "I get the impression Cheryl is so smitten with the idea of becoming a Boston society wife that she's ready to do whatever it takes. That's why I'm planning to call her in the morning, try to talk her into letting Ethan live with me. If she digs in her heels, the next step will be getting a good lawyer to challenge the custody agreement. Whatever it costs me, I'm not letting them pack my son off to a place that's not much different from prison."

"Oh, Ben!" Jess laid a hand on his shoulder, feeling the tight knot of his muscles through his jacket. "I'm so sorry. I wish there was some way I could help."

"At least you're listening. I can't talk to my mother about this. The worry would make her sick."

At a loss for words, Jess kept her hand on his shoulder. Ben had just shared a crushing concern. He'd trusted her to listen and understand. It was almost as if he needed her.

That awareness touched Jess more deeply than she could have imagined. What she felt for this man was real and true. But was it enough?

The chemistry was there—the sweet, hot tingles that passed between them with every look, every touch. But chemistry was the easy part. A lasting relationship depended on complete trust and honesty. Unless she could offer him that, she'd be better off walking away now.

The truth was painful, but it had to be faced. If she

wanted a chance with Ben, she had to put her heart on the line. She had to tell him about her past—tonight.

She could speak up now and get it over with. But no, Jess reasoned, it would be better to wait. On the way home, after they'd enjoyed a relaxing dinner, she would tell him. By the time they reached her door, Ben would know the whole ugly, sordid story.

What happened after that would be up to him.

Chapter Twelve

Set back from the highway and sheltered by hundred-year-old cottonwoods, The Trail's End Steakhouse was, in Ben's opinion, the best restaurant in three counties. The rustic, ranch-style log structure was nothing fancy, but it was cozy inside with friendly servers and good food. Tonight Christmas lights framed the big stone fireplace and glowed softly from the open ceiling beams. Christmas songs played low in the background.

As he ushered Jess to a booth near the crackling fire and helped her with her coat, he sensed envious glances from the men in the room. *Eat your hearts out, boys,* he thought. *I'm with a queen tonight.*

Jess slid into her seat. She looked flat-out gorgeous in that simple black dress, which showed off her trim figure. And the fishnet stockings on those legs triggered thoughts that, if spoken out loud, would be liable to get his face slapped.

Cheryl had taught him how to order wine. Ben chose a vintage Merlot, which caused Jess to smile. "I thought they only drank beer in this state," she said as the server filled her glass.

"You'd be surprised."

"What's good here?" She studied the menu.

"Everything. But knowing you're hungry, I'd recommend the twelve-ounce prime rib or the New York strip."

"I'll go with prime rib, medium rare."

"Then I'll have the same." Ben gave their order to the server, then turned back toward her. He enjoyed simply looking at her, watching the firelight flicker across her elfin face as she sipped her wine. It was all too tempting to forget he'd asked her out for a serious reason.

"Are you ready for your mother to join you tomorrow?" he asked, making conversation.

"The house is ready. Whether *I'm* ready remains to be seen. If she wants to cooperate, we should be fine."

"And if she doesn't? Francine can be a handful."

"I'll cross that bridge if and when I come to it. Right now I'm trying to think positive thoughts."

"I gave her my prerelease lecture this morning—told her you were counting on her to behave and I didn't want to see you disappointed."

"What did she say to that?" Jess gazed at him over the rim of her wineglass, her stunning eyes holding glints of reflected flame.

She said I was in love with you.

Ben suppressed the true answer. "She told me that you and she would make a good team."

"I hope she's right. I understand that I may need to get tough with her."

"Yes, you probably will. Let me know if you need any help."

Their salads and bread had arrived. Jess dug into the fresh greens and hot, buttered sourdough with a gusto that would do credit to a starving urchin.

"I love watching you eat," Ben said. "You seem to enjoy it so much."

She gave him a grin. "I bet you say that to all the ladies you take out."

"Actually, no. What few there've been were all on diets. You must have a furnace inside you, burning up all that energy."

She laughed. "No, I'm just hungry."

"My mother says you're going to the Christmas Ball."

"That's right. I was more or less bullied into it. Maybelle said she needed help taking tickets, and your mother offered to lend me your sister's dress. How could I say no?"

"You'll look great in that dress. But Ellie's taller than you are. You'll need to shorten the skirt."

"No problem. I can sew up a hem." She broke off another piece of bread and slathered it with butter. "Will you be there?"

"I'll be working security. I usually volunteer for that job so my deputies can enjoy the party with their spouses. But I won't be busy all night, and neither will you. I hope you'll save me a dance."

"Dance?" She looked startled. "But I can't dance. I mean, I can go to a club and sort of move to the music, but I don't know any of those old-time Texas dances."

"They're not that hard. I could teach you the Texas two-step in no time at all."

"Even if I'm a lady with two left feet?"

"It's simple. I can show you when we get back to your house." Would she even be speaking to him by the time he got her home? If he confronted her about her arrest, and she found out he'd run the background check, she might not ever want to speak to him again. But one way or another, he needed to know the truth.

The server brought out slabs of juicy prime rib with loaded baked potatoes. They feasted, making small talk between bites and sharing a slice of apple pie for dessert. The evening, so far, had gone wonderfully. Ben found himself dreading the moment when he would have to ruin it by bringing up her past. He wouldn't do it in the restaurant. But maybe later, on the way home, or even when they arrived at her house, he would find the right moment.

Damn!

Toward the end of the meal, Ben sensed a change in Jess. She seemed to withdraw, her conversation becoming fragmented and strained. Reading people was part of his job, and he could tell something was troubling her. Had she guessed what might be coming?

He paid the check, helped her with her coat and escorted her out to the truck. By then she'd fallen silent. She gazed out the side window, into the darkness, as he pulled out of the parking lot and turned onto the main road.

"Are you all right, Jess?" he asked.

"Almost." She gave a nervous little laugh. "But there's something I've been meaning to tell you—something you need to know about me."

Ben felt a rush of relief, like the lifting of a heavy load. He'd waited, hoping against all odds that Jess would volunteer her story. Now it appeared he was going to hear it—and knowing Jess, he had to believe it would be the truth.

"I'm listening," he said.

"You're not going to like it."

He reached over and squeezed her hand. "Let me be the judge of that."

Jess's heart was pounding. It was as if she were spinning through time, her hold slipping as she groped for a solid place to begin. She'd done some hard things in her life, but baring her shameful past to this man, whose good opinion meant so much, was one of the hardest.

Closing her eyes for an instant, she took a deep breath.

"It was after my mother died. I'd managed to graduate from high school and enroll in some community college classes. I was living in Saint Louis, with roommates I barely knew, waitressing nights, when I met Gilbert—Gil, as he liked to be called."

Jess shook her head, remembering how young and naïve she'd been. "I don't know what he saw in me—probably that I looked like an easy mark. Whatever it was, his charm swept me off my feet. He was a few years older than I was, with nice clothes and an expensive car. And he had a way of saying exactly what I needed to hear, building me up and making me feel special. Later on I realized he could turn that charm on and off like a switch, to use whenever he needed it. But by then it was too late."

Jess fell silent, collecting her thoughts. Her gaze traced the rugged outline of Ben's profile in the darkness of the cab. His eyes were on the road, his expression unreadable.

"Gil was selling life insurance policies when I met him," she said. "He even showed me his Salesman of the Year award. But he told me he'd always wanted his own agency. After we were married—three months after we met—he leased an office and went into business for himself. I became his secretary—I had to drop out of school, but at least it was a step up from waitressing.

"The office was in a neighborhood with lots of older people. We rented a place nearby and even started going to church there, something I hadn't done in years. Gil was at his charming best. Pretty soon he was selling term life policies to the old people in the congregation and to their friends and neighbors. I took their payments and made out the receipts, but he always insisted on forwarding the checks to the company himself."

She took a ragged breath to settle her nerves. "I should've guessed by then that something was wrong. But I was in denial—about Gil and about the marriage. He doled out my household allowance in cash, and he told me how to dress, where to go, who to see. If I disobeyed him, I paid for it. He never hurt me physically, but there were other means of abuse, and he knew how to use them. Gil was a master manipulator."

Jess broke off, the memory a rising knot of anger in her throat. She would skip the part about his "working" late, the cloying scent of perfume that had lingered on his skin when he came home and fell into bed beside her.

"It's all right, Jess. Take your time." Ben's voice was gentle. But the brief look he gave her was narrow-eyed. Ben Marsden was a lawman. There was no way he wouldn't have run the background check on her, and maybe on Gil, Jess realized. Ben already knew *what* had happened. What he didn't know was *why*.

"You're probably wondering why I didn't leave," she said. "But when you're on the inside, it's all too easy to believe the problems are your own fault, and that if you try harder, things will change. I know better now, but I didn't then.

"The wake-up came one day when I was at work and Gil was out. An elderly woman from our church came storming into the office, terribly upset. She'd lost her husband two days earlier, and when she'd called the insurance company, using the phone number on her policy, they'd claimed they had no record of her payments. When the woman told her neighbors what had happened, they called the company and discovered the same thing. Those poor, old people! Gil had pocketed all their money! The woman was threatening to call the police if she didn't get her benefit right then."

"So what did you do?" Ben asked.

"I dialed nine-one-one and handed her the phone," Jess said. "I think you know what happened after that."

"Yes, I do know." His confession came in a taut, flat voice, as if he was braced to defend his action. But Jess continued as if he hadn't spoken.

"The police showed up, took me in, and charged me as an accomplice. By then Gil had gotten wind of the trouble, cashed out his secret bank account and was on the run with the money. They caught him with the cash two days later. Meanwhile, I'd turned over the agency's records to the police and promised my full cooperation in exchange for immunity. That same week, I filed for divorce."

The only sound in the cab was the steady thrum of the truck's engine. Jess had finished her story, but Ben seemed to be waiting for something more.

"How do *you* think I should've handled it?" she demanded after a moment's silence. "Short of not marrying the man in the first place, what could I have done differently? Or maybe you don't even believe me."

Ben tapped the brake as a deer flashed in front of the truck and bounded into the darkness. A dozen yards ahead, a rough farm road branched off the highway. Turning onto it, he pulled to one side and switched off the engine. Jess braced for the worst—a humiliating lecture and, most likely, a brusque good bye before he drove her home and dumped her at the curb like a bag of trash.

Eyes deep in shadow, Ben unbuckled his seat belt and turned toward her. "Come here, Jess," he said.

Heart thundering, she unhooked her belt and leaned near enough for him to draw her into his arms. Her eyes closed as he pulled her against his chest. Tears moistened her cheeks.

"I believe you, girl," he murmured against her hair. "Even after I found out about your arrest, I couldn't help feeling you'd done the best you could. I just needed to hear it in your own words."

"You could've asked me."

"I wanted it to be your idea."

Jess pressed her face against his jacket. At least he hadn't denied running the background check. For that, she had every right to be angry. But reliving her painful past had drained her of emotion. She had no anger left—only need.

She raised her head, her lips parting in an invitation no man could misread. Their kiss was long, deep and tender, filled with passion and promise. Still, the uncertainty was there, and the fear. Jess had been through too much heartbreak to take anything for granted. So, she sensed, had Ben. The happiness that was almost within reach could be gone tomorrow.

His arms tightened around her as the kiss ended. "We've got a long road ahead of us, Jess," he murmured. "Right now all we can do is see where it leads. But I can't help hoping you'll still be here at the end of it." His second kiss was brief but warm. "Now let's get us both home. We've got a busy day tomorrow."

Minutes later they pulled up to the curb in front of Jess's house. Jess yawned. "I hope you'll give me a rain check on the Texas two-step lesson," she said.

"Good idea. Get me alone in that house with you and you might have a hard time getting rid of me."

"Or you might have a hard time getting away." She gave him a smile. "What time can I pick up my mother in the morning?"

"There'll be some paperwork and an interview with her probation officer. If you come around ten, she should be ready to go."

"Wish me luck," she said.

"You're going to need it." He climbed out of the truck, came around to her door and helped her down. At her front door he swept her into his arms and gave her one last, lingering kiss. "Just in case those gossips have got your house staked out," he joked as he let her go. "Now they'll have something to talk about."

She stood in the open doorway, watching him drive away. The "walking on air" feeling lingered as she locked the front door and wandered into her bedroom. Were they falling in love? Surely it was too soon for that. But even after hearing the worst about her, Ben was still around. That had to be a good sign.

Jess slipped off the black dress and hung it in the closet. Life was full of cruel surprises and disappointments, she reminded herself. Given her usual luck, the magic might not last long. But while it did, she meant to savor every minute.

When Jess arrived at the jail, Francine was waiting on a bench opposite the check-in counter. Her black stretch pants and sequin-trimmed sweater looked out of place with her straight, mousy hair and makeup-free face. But Jess had honored her mother's request. Francine had an appointment to go straight from the jail to the beauty parlor.

"Hello, sweetie!" Francine stood, dropped her overstuffed purse on the bench, and held out her arms. "Come give your mama a hug!"

Jess obliged with the hug, though it felt a little strange. She had a lot to learn about this mother she barely knew.

"Ready to go?" Jess glanced around, hoping to see Ben. "If you're looking for that handsome honey of a sheriff, he got an emergency call and went chargin' out of here. But he asked me to tell you hi for him." Francine raised an eyebrow. "Is there somethin' goin' on here that I should know about?"

"It's too soon to tell," Jess said, dismissing the question. "Let's go. Your appointment's waiting."

"Thanks again. Can't wait to get out of this hole and have you see me lookin' decent." She grabbed her purse and followed Jess through the exit door, wobbling a little in her four-inch black stilettos, which she must've been wearing when she was arrested. "Somethin' I need to clear up now," she said. "I know I haven't earned the right to have you call me mother. It's fine if you just call me Francine."

"Thanks . . . Francine." That did ease things a little, Jess thought. "Now let's go get you prettied up."

Roxanne's Beauty Salon was located in the basement of one of the small, neat homes Jess had driven past. Jess had made the appointment with the owner, who knew Francine well. "I know just what she'll want," the woman had said. "You can plan on her being here about two hours. If you'll give me your number, I'll call you when she's ready to go."

Jess had paid in advance with her credit card. The price had been double what she'd planned on, but it would be worth the extra expense to make Francine happy and celebrate her homecoming. Meanwhile, she could use the time to get more work done. After dropping her mother off, she headed home.

Jess started her work by painting the edges of the door, leaving it partway open to dry. The living room would be next—a major project, to be done before tearing up the carpet and finishing the hardwood. Hank had already suggested she start with a coat of primer on the walls to cover the graffiti.

She was counting on Francine to help her with the color choice and the painting. While she waited, she could at least start masking around the windows and doors. First, however, she wanted a better look at the furniture in the backyard garage. If it wasn't usable, she would need to start shopping for bargains right away.

After checking the paint on the door, she went around the house to the back. A chilly wind had sprung up, blowing in a bank of clouds from the west. Was the first winter storm arriving at last? If so, maybe she should get the furniture into the house now and plan to work around it.

Clutching her jacket around her, she opened the garage. The furniture inside had been hastily piled any way the pieces would fit. The overstuffed sofa and armchairs were worn and likely mouse-infested. But the large dining room table would be perfect for the bed-and-breakfast. Jess counted at least six matching chairs, some of them missing rungs and braces but nothing that couldn't be fixed. The bed frame she'd seen earlier looked usable too, although she'd want to buy a new mattress for it. All in all, she felt encouraged by what she found.

Stepping outside again, she closed the door and studied the sky. This late in the year, storms could move in fast. If she wanted to get the furniture in the house, and didn't want to drag it through the snow, she would have to make some quick arrangements. Ben had offered earlier to recommend some husky boys she could hire. The sooner she got them here the better.

She didn't want to phone Ben's office, not even to leave a message. It wouldn't go over well with his staff if she kept calling him. But she knew he usually checked on his mother. Maybe she could leave a message with Clara. Back in the house, she made the call.

"Hello?" Clara's voice sounded strained. Jess was instantly concerned.

"Are you all right, Clara? Should I come over, or maybe call a doctor?"

"No, I'm fine, dear. I just had some upsetting news, that's all."

Jess's heart slammed. "Is Ethan all right? Is Ben—?" She couldn't finish the question.

"Oh, yes, they're fine. It wasn't that kind of call." Clara sighed. "So you won't wonder, the call was from Ellie. She found out her husband's been having an affair. She's just devastated."

"Oh no. I'm so sorry." Jess's sympathy was real. She knew how it felt to be betrayed by a man you loved and trusted.

"When I first met her husband, Brent, they'd just become engaged. Ellie was head over heels in love. But I didn't have a good feeling about him, and I made the mistake of telling her so. Things have been strained between us ever since. At least she called me. I should be grateful for that. But after all this time, I was hoping I was wrong."

"What's she going to do?" Jess asked.

"For now, she's decided to try to get through it. Brent insists the affair's over, and he's agreed to counseling. All I can do is hope for the best. I had a wonderful marriage for the years my husband was with us. It makes me sad that my children weren't as lucky. But that's enough about my troubles. What was it you were calling about, dear?"

Jess relayed her need for help moving the furniture. "Ben said he might know some boys I could hire."

"I'm sure he will," Clara said. "He works part-time most days when Ethan is here, so he should be home around lunchtime. I'll have him call you." She paused, as if weighing her words. "Ben seemed preoccupied when he left for work this morning. Did something go wrong last night?"

"No." Jess's heart dropped. Was Ben already having second thoughts? "We had a lovely evening. As far as I know, everything was fine."

"Well, maybe it was nothing," Clara said. "I'll mention to Ben that you need help."

"Thank you, Clara. And I'm so sorry about Ellie. I hope things work out for her. If you need to talk—"

"I'll be fine. Come by anytime, dear. You're always welcome."

"Thank you." Jess ended the call, battling a vague sense of foreboding. Things had seemed so good with Ben last night. But she'd told him some ugly things about her past. Maybe she'd revealed too much.

If their relationship couldn't stand up to the truth, maybe that was just as well, she told herself. For now, she had work to do.

Grabbing a roll of masking tape and a chair, she began prepping the living room for its new coat of paint.

Domestic calls were Ben's least favorite thing to deal with. This one had been bad—a man who'd broken his wife's cheekbone because she burned his breakfast. Now the man was in jail, his wife was at the clinic, and their two young children, who'd witnessed it all, were with the woman's sister.

As he drove back to his office, the happy sound of Christmas music drifted from the SUV's radio. Ben switched it off. He wasn't in a Christmas mood today.

This morning he'd phoned Cheryl about his keeping Ethan for the school year. Reasoning with her had been like talking to a brick wall. A vacancy had come up at the prestigious boarding school Nigel had attended. Weighted by Nigel's influence, the last-minute application for Ethan had been accepted. He'd be starting school right after Christmas vacation.

"Think about the advantages he'll have," Cheryl had argued. "Ethan is a bright boy. Graduating from a prestigious boarding school will open the door to any Ivy League college he wants to attend. What you're asking is to raise him in Podunk, Texas, where he'll grow up chewing tobacco and using bad grammar. That's just plain selfish, Ben!"

At least he wouldn't grow up to be a self-important prig like Nigel. Ben had known better than to voice that thought.

"Don't do this to him, Cheryl," he'd pleaded. "I want Ethan to grow up happy, with people who love him. When the time comes, he can go to college anywhere he wants. For Pete's sake, he's only eight years old!"

"Forget it, Ben, it's a done deal. He'll be starting school the first Monday in January."

"Aren't you rushing things? You're not even married to the guy yet."

"I will be . . . and very soon." She'd let the implication hang till it sank in.

"Oh, hell," Ben had groaned. "Don't tell me you're pregnant!"

The connection had gone dead. She hadn't even said good bye.

Now, as Ben pulled into his parking space at the jail, his thoughts were far from his work. It was time he gave serious thought to finding a good lawyer. Fighting for his rights as a father wouldn't be cheap, but he'd go bankrupt before he'd let Cheryl take their son across the country and send him to boarding school.

The worst of it was, what was he supposed to tell Ethan? Could he wait till after Christmas to break the bad news, or would Cheryl do that for him?

He would do everything in his power to give Ethan a happy Christmas, Ben resolved. But meanwhile, he would explore every possible means of keeping the boy here in Branding Iron. The game of life was unfair at best, and this time Cheryl was holding the high cards. But his son's happiness was at stake. As long as there was a chance, he couldn't give up.

Chapter Thirteen

J ess had just finished masking the door frame when the phone rang. The caller was Roxanne from the beauty shop. Francine was ready and waiting to be picked up.

Driving across town, Jess felt a vague unease. She'd dealt with her mother in a controlled situation, but from here on out, it would just be her and Francine. She'd been warned again and again that her mother could be hard to handle. But she'd made a commitment. It was too late to walk away.

Be prepared for anything, Jess told herself as she pulled up to the curb and climbed out of the car. *Take this one step at a time.*

It was good advice. But the thought fled her mind when she saw the woman who'd just stepped out of the beauty salon. Jess's eyes took in the fluffy platinum curls, ruby lips, creamy skin and long false eyelashes. It was as if the winner of a Dolly Parton look-alike contest were walking toward her.

"Well, honey, what do you think of your old lady now?" Francine strutted down the sidewalk in her black stilettos. The hand she held out for Jess's admiration sported inch-long fake nails, painted flame red and decorated with bits of sparkle.

Those nails were going to be a problem.

"You like?" She made a teetering pirouette in front of Jess.

"Wow! You could walk onstage at the Grand Ole Opry!" It was the most sincere compliment Jess could come up with. Francine was an attractive woman. In an overblown way, she looked spectacular. But for a daughter who needed help refurbishing a run-down house, her new look was disastrous.

"Where to now, sweetie?" Francine traipsed around to the passenger side of the car and climbed in.

Jess slipped back behind the steering wheel. "Are you hungry? I thought we could celebrate your release at Buckaroo's."

"Well, it isn't Vegas, but at least it's food. I'm so hungry I could eat a whole barbecued steer!"

"After that we'll be dropping by the hardware to pick up some paint for the living room. I've got paint samples in my purse. You can help me choose the color while we're waiting for our meals."

Did Francine's interest sharpen when Jess mentioned the hardware store? Jess couldn't be sure. But maybe it was, at least, a move in the right direction.

They pulled into the parking lot at Buckaroo's and went inside. The regulars, including Smitty behind the counter, greeted Francine with a round of grins and howdys. Evidently, the way she looked was old news to them.

They took a booth and studied the menu. Jess was about to ask her mother what she wanted when a voice startled her.

"How would you pretty ladies like some company?"

Ben stood outside the booth with Ethan at his side. Francine gave them a welcoming grin. "Sure thing. Good food always tastes better with a couple of handsome men to share it."

"How about pepperoni pizza all around? And a big pitcher of root beer? My treat." Without waiting for a reply, Ben gave the order to the waitress.

"Sounds good to me, sheriff." Francine gave him a playful wink as they sat down—Ben next to Francine, Ethan next to Jess.

"Thank you, Ben, that's awfully nice of you," Jess murmured. After Clara's mention that Ben was preoccupied, she'd worried that he'd gotten cold feet about their relationship. That could still be true. With Francine and Ethan here, there was no way to tell how he was really feeling toward her.

"What are you two gents up to?" Francine asked.

"We were going to a movie," Ethan said. "But I've already seen the one that's playing, so we're just hanging out. Somebody needs to build a megaplex here. I bet a lot of people would go."

"Sounds like a good idea to me," Ben said, then turned to Francine and drew a folded paper out of his jacket. "I didn't get a chance to give you this before you left. It's the schedule for your AA meetings. Post it somewhere to remind yourself. I'm sure Jess will help too. Maybe she'll even go with you." He gave Jess a meaningful glance.

"Why don't you give me that?" Jess said. "I'll see that it gets put up in the right place." She took the paper and slipped it into her purse. "Did your mother tell you I called?"

"She did," Ben said. "I recruited a neighbor boy to come later today and move the furniture—I'll come with him to lend a hand. He says he can come back later, when you're ready, to drag the carpet out and haul it off."

"Thanks for finding him," Jess said. "But if there's only

one boy, I can help him balance things. You've got better ways to spend your time than hauling my furniture."

"Dad said I could help too." Ethan piped up. "I can carry some of the chairs and easy stuff."

The boy looked so eager that Jess was sorry she'd spoken so hastily. "That would be great, Ethan," she said. "And you can catch any spiders we find."

They finished their meal, spent a few minutes looking at paint chips, and set a time for Ben and the neighbor boy to help haul furniture before going their separate ways.

Back in the car, Francine couldn't stop talking about Ben. "I can tell he really likes you," she gushed. "A man doesn't bring his kid around to see a woman unless he's got plans for her. You should latch onto him while you can, honey. That handsome sheriff is the best catch in town! If I was a few years younger, I'd go after him myself!"

Jess shook her head. "I don't think Ben plans to get caught anytime soon. He's got too much on his plate for that."

"Maybe, but I know a lot about men, and that one's got a spark in his eye. Want to bet he'll propose by the end of the year? Come on—a trip to Vegas if I'm right."

"And what if you're wrong?"

"Name it, girl. It's yours."

Jess chuckled. "Sorry. I'm not a betting woman."

"Suit yourself. But I know what I see."

They pulled up to the hardware store and went inside. Hank was up front when they walked in. His face lit in a smile when he saw Francine.

"Hi, Hank." Her greeting to him was subdued, almost ladylike.

"Hello, ladies," he said. "How's the house coming along?"

"I haven't seen it yet," Francine said. "But I'm excited

about it. With my girl here to give me a new start, I just might make it this time—AA meetings and all."

Jess listened in surprise. She was accustomed to having Francine make a joke of everything. To hear her express what sounded like hope and gratitude was oddly touching. Maybe coming to Branding Iron and buying the house would turn out to be worth it after all.

They'd agreed on a warm, creamy beige color for the living and dining areas. Jess picked out more supplies while Francine chatted with Hank. They left with three gallons of paint, a gallon of primer, fresh brushes, rollers and drop cloths, and more newspapers. Jess had resigned herself to painting the whole large room. With those long, expensive fake nails, there was no way Francine could do the job. She couldn't even wear gloves.

"I know I can't paint or scrub with these beauties," Francine said when Jess broached the subject. "But I can still help. I can do laundry. And I'm a pretty good hand in the kitchen. I'll pull my weight. You'll see."

"I hope so," Jess said. "I'm going to need you. I can't do this job alone."

"You won't have to, dear," Francine said.

A few minutes later they arrived home. Grabbing what she could carry of the paint supplies, Jess ushered her mother inside. She'd left the basement door open so Sergeant Pepper could come upstairs. The scruffy ginger cat came running to meet Francine, purring and rubbing against her legs.

"Well, how about that!" Francine reached down and scratched his head with her long fingernails. "This place feels like home already. Where do I bunk?"

When Jess opened the door to her newly decorated bedroom, Francine gasped. "Oh! You did all this for me? I haven't had a room this nice since I was a girl! C'mere, honey, let me give you a hug!"

When her mother squeezed her tight, Jess felt the wet-
ness of tears on one rouged cheek. There would no doubt
be some bumps in the road ahead, but so far she had no
regrets.

After seeing the rest of the house, Francine declared that
she was tired and needed to lie down. She kicked off her
stilettos and stretched out on her bed, with the Sergeant
curled next to her. Jess closed the door so she wouldn't be
disturbed, then changed back into her paint clothes,
hauled the rest of the supplies out of her car and went to
work.

It felt good to roll the primer over the ugly spray-painted
graffiti on the walls. The room looked better already. She
could hardly wait to see it all painted, with the filthy carpet
gone, the hardwood floor polished, and the furniture in
place. She would throw out the old overstuffed pieces in
the garage and splurge on a new sofa and armchairs for
guests. Some colorful curtains and framed prints for the
walls would complete the homey look.

But it was already December and she was weeks away, if
not longer, from having the house ready for paying guests.
Time was running out, and so was her money. True, she'd
likely get the line of credit from the bank. But using that
fund would only put her in debt. Somehow she had to get
this place to make a profit.

She'd finished with the primer and was about to start on
the ceiling when the front door opened and Ben walked in,
followed by Ethan and a teenage boy who looked like a
natural for the local football team.

"Wow, it looks better already," Ben said. "If you're ready
for a break, we'll need you to come outside and show us
what to haul in."

Jess put a finger to her lips and pointed toward the
closed bedroom door. "Francine's resting," she said softly.

Ben didn't speak again, but the look on his face said enough. Clearly he thought she was letting Francine take advantage of her. Well, right now that couldn't be helped. Jess pulled on her old jacket and followed her helpers outside.

The dining room table came inside first. Jess was delighted to discover extra leaves to make it even larger. Ethan helped carry in the leaves and the chairs, which they piled in the middle of the living room. The chest of drawers, bed frame and spring went into Jess's room, the mattress being too far gone to use. There were boxes filled with mismatched dishes and cutlery. Jess had them carried into the kitchen for sorting—something Francine should be able to do. Aside from some boxed books and odds-and-ends of shelving, most of what remained was junk. She could have it hauled away later.

The job had taken about half an hour. She took the boy's phone number and gave him the $10 bill in her purse, which seemed to please him. She might have paid Ethan as well, but Ben caught her eye and gave a subtle shake of his head. "I want Ethan to experience the satisfaction of helping people," he said quietly.

After the three had left, Jess checked on Francine and found her fast asleep. She couldn't have rested well on that jail bunk, she told herself. The poor woman was probably exhausted.

Closing the door again, Jess covered the piled furniture with the drop cloth, mounted the roller on the long pole she'd bought, covered her hair with a bandanna and began rolling paint on the ceiling. It was hard work, and messy, but she loved seeing how every stroke of fresh paint brightened the dingy surface.

She'd been painting for an hour and was about half done

with the ceiling when Ben and Ethan walked in again, wearing grubby old clothes. Ethan was grinning. Ben was carrying a pan of something that smelled like fresh cinnamon rolls, covered with a towel.

"We thought you could use some help," Ben said. "And my mother sent these. Nice color on you, by the way, especially on your nose."

Jess's knees went wobbly with gratitude. "You can put those yummy rolls in the kitchen," she said. "And thank you. I would have been painting all night."

Ben took charge at once. "I'll take over the ceiling for now," he said. "Jess, the walls might be easier for you. Ethan, you can take a brush and go around the bottom. Paint those baseboards and a few inches above them. If you get paint on the carpet, that's fine. Okay?"

"Okay!" Ethan took the brush and the partly filled paint can and went to work. Ben took the long-poled roller Jess had been using and began painting the ceiling in long strokes. His added height and strength made the work go twice as fast as it had for her.

Jess dipped a fresh roller in the spare pan and started covering up the primed walls, which by now had dried. Until she'd bought the house, she'd never painted anything. She hadn't expected to enjoy it so much. It was like having a magic wand that made everything look bright and new. But it was hard work. After an hour, with two walls left to do, she was starting to flag.

That was when Francine woke up and came tottering out of her room. When she saw the paint crew, her face broke into a grin. "Hey!" she exclaimed. "Why didn't somebody tell me there was a party goin' on? We need music!"

She hurried back into her room. A moment later the country version of "Rockin' Around the Christmas Tree" blasted through the house, loud but energizing.

"Now, that's more like it!" Francine disappeared into the kitchen. A few minutes later she came out with the pan of cinnamon rolls, a stack of paper cups and a carton of milk. "Break time!" she called. "C'mon, all you painters!"

They sat on the rolled-up rug from the bedroom and feasted on warm, sweet rolls, washed down with ice-cold milk. Sergeant Pepper showed up to meow for attention and leave painted paw prints across the carpet, which made Ethan giggle.

The break was a short one, but it recharged them all. While Francine cleaned up the food, Jess, Ben and Ethan, moving to the music, finished painting the room. By the time they'd bagged the newspapers and set the brushes and rollers to soak, it was well after dark.

"It's past Ethan's bedtime," Ben said. "We need to be going."

Jess gave him the empty roll pan to take home. "Please thank your mother," she said, meeting his warm, sarsaparilla eyes. "And thanks to you both. You saved my life tonight."

"Our pleasure," Ben said. "Call you later. Come on, Ethan."

As they were going out the door, Ethan gave Francine a wave. "Thanks for making it fun," he said.

"Anytime, sweetie." Francine watched the door close, making sure the cat was in. "What a little gentleman! He's going to be a heartbreaker when he grows up, just like his daddy!" She turned to Jess, frowning slightly. "You look like you just fell off the back of a wagon, girl. Run along to bed and get some sleep. I'll be staying up awhile to sort out my room, but don't worry. I'll turn the music way down so it won't bother you."

With a muttered "thanks," Jess stumbled off to shower and get ready for bed. She was still sleeping on Ben's camp cot with the air mattress, but tonight she was so tired she could've slept on a bed of rocks. She'd had a long day. There was still so much to do, and she'd already learned she couldn't count on her mother for much. But at least Ben had shown up to help, and he'd said he would call her. Dared she hope that he meant it? Or was he just getting ready to cut her loose?

She had yet to meet a man who didn't end up hurting her. And Ben was almost too good to be true. Would he turn out to be the one who didn't let her down? Or was she just making one more trek along that winding road to heartache?

Only time would answer that question.

"I'm proud of you," Ben told his son as they drove home. "You did a great job tonight."

"Thanks. It was fun for a while. But I got pretty tired." Ethan yawned. "Jess is nice. Maybe you ought to marry her."

Startled, Ben stomped the clutch to keep from killing the engine. "What put that idea into your head?"

"Well, if Mom can get married again, so can you. And I like Jess a lot better than I like Nigel."

"That's not saying much. Anyway, what if Jess doesn't want to get married? She just bought a house and moved into it with her mother. Does that sound like a woman who wants to get married?"

"It sounds like you've thought about it—maybe a lot."

"No, it doesn't. I'm just talking."

"Okay." Ethan yawned again and lapsed into silence. When Ben glanced over at him a minute later, he saw that Ethan had fallen asleep.

Looking at the boy, Ben ached with love and dread. That afternoon he'd phoned a lawyer friend to ask about his chances in court. The news hadn't been good. "Unless you can prove Cheryl's an unfit mother—which, I gather, she isn't—you'd just be wasting time and money," his friend had told him. "If she won't agree to a change for the boy's sake, I'm afraid you're out of luck."

Heartsick, he imagined his son in Boston, with a cold, authoritarian stepfather and a mother busy with her social life and a new baby. He imagined Ethan in boarding school, lonely, regimented, possibly bullied or even abused. He couldn't let that happen. But how could he convince Cheryl to change her mind?

Ben hadn't prayed or gone to church in years. Maybe that had been a mistake, because what he needed now was a damned miracle.

How was he going to tell Ethan? He hated to spoil his son's Christmas. But the boy would need time to prepare. Time might even give Ethan a chance to talk his mother into leaving him here. If there was any chance at all. . . .

He swung the truck into the driveway, climbed out and walked around to the passenger side. Ethan was still asleep, his head drooping to one side like a tired puppy's. Ben unfastened the seat belt, eased his son into his arms and carried him into the house. He would wait a day or two longer, let the boy relax and enjoy the holiday before breaking the news, he resolved. In the meantime, he would hope for that miracle.

Right now, hope was all he had.

Jess woke to the wafting aromas of fresh coffee and frying bacon. She blinked, sat up and took a deep breath. Was she dreaming?

Raising her arms and arching her back, she stretched. Her muscles ached from last night's painting marathon. If the pain was real, that mouth-watering smell could be real too. Standing, she opened the bedroom door and padded into the kitchen.

Wrapped in an old chenille bathrobe, her face bare of makeup, Francine stood at the stove. She'd unpacked the cast iron cookware set and was using one of the skillets to fry a half-dozen strips of thick-sliced bacon. Fresh coffee dripped into the glass carafe on the coffeemaker.

"Hi, honey," she said, giving Jess a grin. "Have a chair. I was about to scramble you some eggs."

Still groggy, Jess stared around the kitchen. "Chair?"

"In the other room! Your place is all set! Go on, girl!"

Jess wandered into the living room and stopped short. The table had been uncovered and wiped clean, the chairs set up around it. Two places were set at one end—mismatched plates, cups and cutlery, freshly washed, with folded paper towels for napkins. A carton of milk, a jar of raspberry jam and a cube of butter sat on the table. Jess had just taken a seat when Francine waltzed in with the coffee and a plate of buttered toast.

"The rest is coming right up. This morning I wanted to treat my girl to a good, old-fashioned breakfast!"

Jess had never been a big breakfast eater, but Francine had gone to a lot of effort, and everything did smell wonderful. She poured a cup of coffee, added milk and spread jam on a slice of the warm toast. She was beginning to feel hungry.

Minutes later, Francine came out of the kitchen again. This time she balanced a plate piled high with golden scrambled eggs and strips of bacon. Taking the empty chair, she pushed the plate toward Jess. "Eat up, honey. We've got a long day ahead of us."

Jess took two strips of bacon and a few modest scoops of scrambled eggs. The eggs were light and tender, almost airy. She tried a forkful. At the first taste, they almost melted on her tongue. The bacon was perfectly cooked—

crisp but not overdone. She took a second bite, then a third.

"My heavens, Francine, this food is wonderful!" she muttered between bites. "Where did you learn to cook?"

Francine smiled. "Oh, here and there. I'm not much on lunches and dinners, but I do love to cook breakfast. I wasn't sure I'd remember how. It's been way too long since I had anybody to cook for. But it all came back once I got in that kitchen. Wait till you taste my flapjacks, and my hash browns."

Jess was heaping more eggs on her plate when the idea struck her like a thunderbolt. She stared at her mother. "Francine, I've been worried about getting this bed-and-breakfast up and making money. What if we started with just breakfast? The bed part could come later, when we're ready."

"Hmmm." Francine looked thoughtful. "I don't know if—"

"Think about it," Jess said. "The only place in town to sit down and eat is Buckaroo's. And they don't open till lunchtime. I'll bet a lot of people would enjoy a good breakfast and a cup of coffee to start the day. Just breakfast—we could close at ten or eleven and not be competing with Buckaroo's at all. You could cook. I could serve, help clean up, and handle the management. What do you think?"

Francine was silent for a moment; then she brightened. "You know, it just might work! I can see it now—" Her hands framed an imaginary sign. "Branding Iron Breakfast! We could add the bed part later."

"That's perfect!" Jess said. "So, are you in?"

"All the way!" Francine reached over and clasped her hand. "Now eat your breakfast before it gets cold."

*   *   *

While Francine cleaned up after breakfast, Jess sat down with a notebook and made a list of things that needed to be done before they could open for business. They'd need to finish the living and dining rooms and buy more furniture. The big table would do for those who wanted to eat family style and visit. But she'd also need a couple of small tables, with chairs. They were going to need a business license, as well as TV and Internet service. A wall-mounted TV would be nice for people who liked to watch the morning news.

For now they could make do with the dishes they had—the mismatched plates and cups would add a homey touch. But sooner or later they'd need to upgrade. And they'd need something on the tables—maybe a spill-proof cloth with colorful placemats. And she'd need a couple of high chairs and booster seats for the little ones. The list was getting longer and longer.

"What about advertising?" Francine asked. "If you'll get me some supplies, I can make posters. I'll bet Hank would let us put one up in his store."

"I could talk to the woman who owns Merle's Craft and Yarn," Jess said. "Since it's right around the corner on Main Street, that would be the perfect place to advertise. I could offer to pay her, or maybe advertise her shop here."

"We'll need menus with prices," Francine said.

"I could buy a printer and do them on my laptop." Jess was beginning to feel overwhelmed.

"How about if, for now, we just get a chalkboard and write our menu on it," Francine suggested. "That should work fine, and we can change it anytime we need to."

"Perfect." Jess added a chalkboard to the list. And she'd

need a way to run credit cards. At least she knew how from her waitressing days.

The idea had seemed so simple at first. But nothing was simple these days. Never mind, they had the basics. Now it was time to get going on the rest.

Chapter Fourteen

Ben was almost always on call for emergencies. But at least Sunday, a regular day off, gave him a rare chance to sleep late. This morning he was taking full advantage, drifting in and out of slumber, remembering how Jess had felt in his arms and plotting to get her back. Three days had passed since he'd helped her with the painting. Maybe today he'd have time to drop by the house and see how the project was coming along. They'd played phone tag a couple of times but hadn't managed to connect. He'd been busy, and he knew that she'd been busy too.

He'd just rolled over for a few more winks when he felt a light touch on his shoulder.

"Wake up, Dad." Ethan's voice quivered with distress. Ben opened his eyes and sat up. His son's eyes were red and swollen from crying.

"What is it?" Ben reached out and pulled him close. From the kitchen downstairs, he could hear the muted rattle of pans and dishes and smell the faint aroma of bacon, a sign that his mother, at least, was all right.

Ethan quivered in his arms. "Mom called me this morning," he blurted between sobs. "She and Nigel got married yesterday. She says I have to come to Boston after Christmas. They already signed me up for boarding school. Dad, I don't want to go! I want to stay with you!"

He flung his arms around Ben's neck and held on with all his strength. Ben's heart broke for his child. He'd meant to tell Ethan when the time was right, but Cheryl, in her brusque, no-nonsense way, had beaten him to it. "Did you tell her you want to stay here?"

He nodded. "I begged her. But she said they'd already paid the money. She said I'd thank them for it later on because it would give me advantages." His wiry little body quivered. "I don't even know what that word means."

Ben held his son tight, silently cursing Cheryl for her unfeeling decision, and himself for his inability to change things. Where was that miracle when he needed it?

"Can you talk to her?" Ethan asked. "Maybe Mom will listen to you."

"I already tried. She wouldn't budge. I even talked to a lawyer, but he didn't give me any hope. Unless your mother changes her mind, there's nothing we can do. I'm sorry, son. I hadn't told you yet because I didn't want to spoil our Christmas."

Ethan unwound his arms from Ben's neck and drew back. His nose made a snuffling sound as he sucked back his tears. "It's okay, Dad," he said. "We can have a good Christmas anyway. Maybe Mom will change her mind."

Ben had never been more proud of his son. But Cheryl had a mile-wide stubborn streak. Once she made up her mind about something, an army of Supreme Court justices would be hard put to change her thinking.

Breaking the mood, he rumpled Ethan's cowlicked hair. "Hey, didn't you promise your grandma you'd go to church with her this morning?" he asked. "You'd better wash up and get ready."

"You could come too," Ethan said.

Ben had stopped going to church in college and had

never taken up the habit again. Since moving back in with his mother, his contribution to the Sabbath had been preparing an easy Sunday dinner for her. "If I walked into church, people would think I was there to arrest somebody, and they'd all be nervous," he said. "That's my excuse and I'm sticking with it. We can do something fun this afternoon."

"Like what? We can't go sledding, because there isn't any snow."

"That's true." Ben thought fast. "But I'll bet you've never tied fishing flies. Your grandpa taught me how years ago, and I've still got his old kit, feathers and all. It isn't easy to do a good job, but if you can make a few flies, we'll use them to catch fish next summer."

With so many changes in the wind, would they still have next summer together? Ben willed the question away. All he could do was hope.

"I'd like that," Ethan said.

"Great. I'll find the kit and set it up."

Ethan started for the door, then turned back. "I've seen my grandpa's picture, the one next to Grandma's bed. What was he like when he was alive?"

"He was gentle and brave and funny—the best father ever. You and he would have been great pals."

He was the kind of father I want to be—except that he was gone when I needed him. And if you have to go away, I'll be gone when you need me too.

The thought raised a lump in Ben's throat. He suppressed the rush of emotion. "Now run along and get ready to go with your grandma," he said.

As Ethan scampered down the hall, Ben thought about going back to sleep. But he was wide awake now and, after his son's news, aching with the need to hear a certain sweet, sexy voice.

He found his cell on the nightstand and punched in Jess's number.

"Hi." She sounded warm and sleepy. Ben felt the tension in his body begin to ease.

"Did I wake you?"

"No. I've turned up the heat, and I'm waiting for the place to get warm. Are you at work?"

"I'm in bed. How's it going with the house? Do you need any help today?" Jess had called him yesterday, bubbling over with her plan for a breakfast café.

"Thanks for the offer, but the muscle work is pretty much done. It's the details that are giving me fits now—the final decorating, the paperwork, the supplies, the promotion . . ." She gave a wry chuckle. "We plan to open this coming Saturday, with free coffee for bait. I hope this works, Ben. I don't know what I'll do if it doesn't."

"A breakfast place is a great idea. You should do fine." He wished he could give her an ironclad promise. Damn it, he'd give her the moon and stars if he could. After the bad breaks she'd had, Jess deserved some happiness.

"How's Francine doing?" he asked.

"All right, I think. She's not much for cleaning or painting or hauling. But she seems excited about the business. And wait till you taste her flapjacks and scrambled eggs!"

"Changing the subject," he said, "could you use a break tonight? Maybe take a drive somewhere, get something light? With all this craziness Cheryl is causing, I need some time alone with you, just to talk if nothing else, and maybe take up where we left off the other night."

There was silence on the other end of the call. Ben's heart dropped. Had he assumed too much?

After a moment's hesitation, she spoke. "That would be wonderful. I mean it. But we'll have to take a rain check. Tonight is Francine's first AA meeting in the basement of the church. I need to drive her there and make sure she stays."

Ben sighed. "Yes, you'd be wise to do that. You're learning fast. But will you promise me some time for another night—soon?"

"I promise. If you don't call me, I'll call you."

"I'm holding you to that," he said, wishing he could hold her in a more intimate way. "I need you, lady."

He heard the subtle intake of her breath. "I need you too," she said.

Ending the call, Ben lay back and allowed himself a moment of sprawling contentment. At least something in his life was going well. Jess Ramsey made him feel as giddy as a teenager with a crush on the girl next door. Dared he hope that this beginning would lead to something good? Or was he headed down the familiar road to disappointment?

The voice of hard experience cautioned him to be wary. Ben tossed the warning aside like a piece of junk mail. For however long it lasted, he was enjoying the ride—and so far it felt damned good.

Jess had spent most of Sunday afternoon making posters to advertise her new business. Since she couldn't afford a commercial printer, she was making do with colored poster board, markers, glue and pictures cut from Francine's old magazines.

Hank had agreed to their putting up a poster in his store. So had the elderly woman who owned Merle's Craft and Yarn, in return for Jess's advertising her shop in the restaurant. Silas at the garage and Roxanne at the beauty parlor had accepted the same arrangement. Clara had donated a discarded bulletin board from her days at the library. It would go on one wall to serve as a community center for ads, public notices and messages.

Francine had helped with the posters early on, finding pictures and adding details in her surprisingly elegant hand. But after a couple of hours she'd tired of it and gone into her room to lie down. Left to finish alone, Jess lost track of time until she realized it was getting dark outside. She glanced at the clock. It was almost seven, time to get ready for Francine's seven-thirty AA meeting.

Leaving the poster supplies on the table, she stood, stretched the kinks out of her back and hurried down the hall to the closed door of her mother's room.

When a light rap got no response, Jess opened the door and stepped inside. Francine lay sprawled on her bed, fast asleep.

Leaning over her, Jess gave her shoulder a gentle shake. "Wake up, Francine," she said. "We need to leave in a few minutes."

"Huh?" Francine's false eyelashes fluttered as her eyes opened. "Leave for where?"

"Your AA meeting. You've known about it all week. We've got twenty minutes to get there."

"Lemme sleep." Closing her eyes again, she rolled toward the wall.

Jess shook her more firmly. "Come on," she said. "You have to go. It's one of the terms of your probation."

Francine rolled onto her back again and opened her eyes. "Listen, honey, I don't need that crap anymore. I've been cold sober for a month, ever since your boyfriend threw me in jail. Let's just say I went to the meeting, and we'll both be happy."

It was definitely tough-love time. Jess folded her arms. "Do you want to end up back in jail?" she demanded. "You're coming with me now, or I'm phoning your probation officer first thing tomorrow."

Francine didn't even twitch. "You wouldn't do that to

your mother, honey. I know you better than that. Besides, you'll need me in that kitchen when we open."

"Don't bet on that. If you aren't around, I can always hire somebody else—even if they can't cook like you do. Come on, we're wasting time."

Francine's lower lip thrust outward in a childish pout. "If you're so all-fired determined, why don't you just go to that meeting yourself? Tell them I'm sick."

"No you don't!" Jess could feel the frustration boiling inside her. "You owe me this, Francine! I've found you, taken you in, given you a home and a job! The least you can do is behave yourself!"

"I owe *you?*" Francine sat up. "Listen, girl, when I got pregnant with you, I could've had an abortion and been done with it. Instead I chose to have you and give you up so my little girl could have two parents and a good life."

"*A good life?*" Jess's seething temper boiled over. "Lord, is that what you think I've had?"

The whole story came spilling out of her—the absent father; the depressed mother; the motel rooms; the dreary, grinding jobs; the miserable marriage. "I might've been better off if you'd kept me!" She hurled the bitter words at her mother. "And you might have been better off too! Now you know!"

Francine didn't reply. Her face, through too-heavy makeup, looked drawn and weary, as if she'd just aged ten years. Jess had never planned to tell her mother the truth. Even now, she was sorry for the pain she'd caused. But the story was out, and it was too late to take it back.

For the space of a long breath, Francine sat in rigid silence. Then her shoulders sagged. She raked a hand through her Dolly Parton curls. "All right, you win," she muttered. "I'll go to the meeting with you. Just give me a minute to check on the Sergeant. I want to make sure he's got food."

She stood, picked up the fleece jacket she'd tossed over the dresser bench and slid her arms into the sleeves. "Go on and finish getting ready. I'll only be a minute," she said, heading through the kitchen toward the basement stairs.

Jess ducked into the bathroom for a few minutes. When she came out, Sergeant Pepper was in the hall. Rubbing against her leg, he gave a rusty *mrowr*, his usual signal that he was hungry.

"What are you doing here, boy?" she asked. "You're supposed to be getting food downstairs."

As she spoke, realization slammed her.

"Francine!" She raced back through the kitchen and down the basement stairs, but there was no sign of her mother. Only the unlocked back door told Jess which way she'd gone out.

"Francine, come back!" Calling, she rushed out into the yard. But Francine, who would know every shortcut and back alleyway in town, had already disappeared.

Ben was tucking his son into bed after a Sunday afternoon of tying flies, watching videos and feasting on popcorn and root beer floats. "So, did you have a good day?" he asked.

"You bet." Ethan's eyelids were already drooping.

"How was church with Grandma? Did you learn anything?"

"Uh-huh. The preacher said that if you want something, and it's something good, you should pray about it. I'm going to pray that Mom will change her mind and let me stay with you."

Good luck with that. Ben was moved by his son's childlike faith, but knowing Cheryl, Ben knew even God would have a hard time persuading her.

"Do you think that might help, Dad?"

"Couldn't hurt. We need all the help we can get." Ben

leaned over and skimmed a kiss on the boy's forehead. "Go to sleep, now. We'll talk more tomorrow, when we go to buy your new cowboy boots for the Christmas Ball."

Ethan closed his eyes and snuggled deeper under the covers. For a moment, Ben stood gazing down at him, thinking how fast his son was growing up, and how many precious changes he would miss when they were half a continent apart. How could this be happening? Where was that miracle he needed?

He had left the room and reached the top of the stairs when his cell phone rang. The caller was Jess.

Even before she spoke, some sixth sense warned him of trouble.

"What is it?" he asked.

She drew in a ragged breath. "It's my mother. We had an argument, and she left. I've been driving around for the past hour looking for her. But I don't know the town that well. I can't find her anywhere." Her voice wavered. Ben imagined her fighting tears. "I . . . need your help."

"Where are you?" He was already reaching for the keys in his pocket.

"I'm back at the house. I thought she might've come home. But she's not here."

"I'm on my way." After a quick word to his mother, he sprinted out the door to his truck. Minutes later he was turning onto Jess's street. He couldn't say he was surprised. It would be just like Francine to run off at the first sign of discord and take refuge in a bottle of booze. But he felt for Jess, who was trying so hard to help her.

She was waiting for him on the porch. As he pulled the truck up to the curb, she ran down the sidewalk, opened the door and clambered in beside him. In a few breathless sentences, she told him what had happened.

"Did you happen to notice whether Francine took her purse?" he asked, pulling away from the curb.

"I was in the bathroom when she left. Afterward, I didn't think to look. Why?"

"If she's got money and wants a drink, she'll head for Rowdy's Roost, a dive on the edge of town. That was where she got arrested last time. We could check there."

"Let's go. I already checked the AA meeting. She wasn't there—not that I expected her to be." Jess raked her hair back from her face. "I should never have told her the truth about my adoption. If anything's happened to her, I'll never forgive myself!"

"Don't beat yourself up, Jess, it's not your fault." He swung the truck onto a back street, leading to the far side of town. "Francine's been an alcoholic more than half her life. Sooner or later, some crisis was bound to come along and knock her off the wagon. All you can do is get past it and move on."

A cold wind battered the outside of the pickup. Jess stared through the side window at the whipping trees. "Francine wasn't dressed for this weather. What if she falls or gets stranded somewhere? What if we can't find her?"

"We'll find her, Jess." He reached over the console and squeezed her small, cold hand. "We won't stop looking until we do."

Rowdy's Roost, a place Ben knew all too well, sat just outside the city limits, next to a rusty railroad line that no train had used in twenty years. It was three-quarters of a mile from the center of town, a long walk on a cold night. But even in high heels, a determined Francine could get there. She'd done it plenty of times before.

Low-slung, with clapboard siding and a metal roof, Rowdy's was busy tonight. The weedy gravel strip for parking was crowded with pickups, SUVs and a couple of motorcycles. Even if she didn't have money, Francine could've come here in the hope of bumming a few drinks. Ben could only hope he didn't have to drag her out of the place, with Jess waiting in the pickup.

He parked a few yards away from the other vehicles. "Stay here and lock the doors," he told Jess. "I won't be gone long."

Huddled in the front seat, Jess watched Ben stride across the parking lot and into the ramshackle bar. The place looked like something out of a bad biker movie, she thought. Ben was man enough to handle anything, but tonight he wasn't in uniform. He didn't even have his gun. What if he ran into trouble? What if he found Francine and she wouldn't come with him?

Seconds crawled past, stretching into minutes before she saw Ben trotting back across the parking lot—alone. "She wasn't in there," he said, climbing back into the truck. "Nobody's seen her tonight."

Jess's relief surged, only to be swept away by worry. At least her mother wasn't drinking in the bar. But where was she? What if she'd set out for the bar, taken a fall, and was lying somewhere along the road, injured and freezing? Or worse, what if she'd been picked up by some predator who would do her unspeakable harm?

Ben seemed to read her thoughts. "We'll take it slow on the way back," he said, switching the headlights to high beam. "Watch your side of the road. I'll watch mine. If we don't find her in the next half hour, I'll put out an alert."

The road was narrow, with no more than occasional traffic. The SUV moved at a crawl as they scanned both sides of the road. But they found nothing, not so much as a track in the half-frozen earth.

By the time they got back to town, the wind had risen to a howl. "Does my mother have any friends who'd take her in?" Jess asked.

Ben pondered the question. "Not that I know of. She's

pretty much a loner. But there's one place we haven't looked—her trailer. She liked to stash a few bottles there."

"I know. I threw away two or three when I cleared the place out. If she's there, she won't find anything to drink."

Ben shook his head. "I can tell you've got a lot to learn about that lady. She's got a rare talent for hiding things."

Minutes later they swung into the trailer park. Francine's tiny trailer was dark—as it would be, Jess reminded herself. She'd disconnected the power after moving her mother to the house. "We'll need a flashlight," she said as they pulled up a short distance away.

"Got one." Ben switched on the flashlight and stepped to the ground. "You might want to wait in the truck."

With a shake of her head, Jess followed him. Wind lashed her hair, biting cold through her denim jacket. A dark apprehension gripped her as they neared the trailer. Why had Ben suggested she stay in the truck? Did he know something she didn't? Could Francine have turned prostitute to support her drinking?

But never mind, she told herself. If it was so, not knowing wouldn't change the truth.

The door was unlocked. Ben gave it a gentle rap. "Francine?"

There was no answer. With Jess pressing behind him, he shone the light into the trailer.

Francine was alone, slumped in the old overstuffed chair. Her eyes were closed. Her mouth hung open in a rumbling snore. An empty gin bottle lay beside her on the rug.

"Thank heaven," Jess breathed.

"Come on." Ben stepped inside. "We've got to get her into the truck."

The trailer was frigid inside. With Ben shaking her shoulders and Jess rubbing her ice-cold hands, they managed to rouse Francine enough to get her on her pump-clad feet. Supporting her on either side, they walked her out to the truck and piled her onto the backseat of the club cab. By the time they'd tucked in her feet and closed the door, she'd collapsed on her side and gone back to sleep.

"Has she violated her probation?" Jess asked as they drove back toward the house.

"She's skated the edge. But at least she didn't go back to the bar. There are two more AA meetings scheduled later this week, Tuesday and Thursday. If she goes to those and stays out of trouble, I'll give her a pass this time. I know you don't want her back in jail."

"Thanks." Jess settled into the seat with a long sigh of relief. "Can you help me get her into the house?"

"Sure. Let me know if she gives you any trouble tonight."

"We'll be fine. This is just a bump in the road."

"I hope you're right." He reached across the console, probably meaning to squeeze her arm, but he was watching the road and instead his hand came to rest on her knee. The hand lingered, its warm weight sending a ripple of awareness through her body. Her gaze traced the clean, strong line of his profile as he drove. What would she have done without him tonight?

At the house, they woke Francine. She wobbled on unsteady legs and would have fallen if Ben hadn't caught her. Supporting her, they got her into the house and into her bedroom. Jess managed to turn down the bed before her mother collapsed on the sheet.

"Thanks," she said, giving Ben a tired smile. "You can go. I'll take it from here."

When Ben had left the room, Jess pulled off Francine's shoes and her fleece jacket. With effort, she tugged off her mother's black stretch pants and, with her blouse still in place, covered her with the quilt. Slipping out of the closet, Sergeant Pepper leaped onto the bed and curled at her side, a warm, purring bundle of comfort.

"Good boy. You take care of her." Jess scratched the

cat's scruffy head. Then, turning off the light, she left the door ajar and walked back to the living room.

She hadn't expected Ben to wait, but he was there, standing by the table, studying the posters. He glanced up as she came into the room. "How's she doing?" he asked.

"She's fast asleep. I hope she'll be sorry in the morning. Don't worry, I know what to expect. I'll have plenty of coffee for her." She crossed the room to stand facing him. "Thank you for your help. I couldn't have managed without you tonight."

"Thank you for calling me. I told you it wouldn't be easy."

"I know. But I still want to be here for her."

His hand moved to cup her cheek, tilting her face toward him. "You're amazing," he murmured.

His kiss started out as a tender nibble, his mouth tasting hers, his tongue just skimming her lower lip. Jess moaned as the contact deepened. She pressed upward, feeling the heat that burned through their clothes, flowing between their bodies, molding them together. Her pulse surged, pouring desire through her veins. Heaven help her, she wanted him, in all the ways a woman could want a man.

It wasn't going to happen—not tonight at least. But when they broke apart they were both breathing hard.

Stepping back, he gave her a lopsided grin. "To be continued," he said.

"If we can ever find the time."

"We'll *make* the time." With a quick peck on her lips, he was gone.

From the porch, Jess watched the red taillights of the pickup vanish around the corner. Things were good between her and Ben—so good it scared her. With so many complications in their lives, how could something *not* go wrong?

She'd been there before. Her father had left her, Gil had

turned out rotten, and there'd been other letdowns over the years, leaving her wounded and cynical. Now it was Ben's turn. He was everything she'd ever wanted in a man—but why should this time turn out to be any different?

From the speakers on Main Street, the sound of Christmas music drifted to her ears. A small, decorated tree glowed through the window of the run-down house next door. Christmas was a time of love and warmth and family. But for Jess, it had come to be a time for others to celebrate. For her, it was just another day. Time had taught her to lower her expectations—no hope, no hurt.

Ben's truck was gone, and the wind was cold. Struggling to deny the need in her heart, Jess walked back inside and closed the door.

Chapter Fifteen

The next morning, when her mother woke up, Jess was waiting to bring her coffee. Francine looked like a smeared portrait of her usual self, her lipstick smudged, her red-rimmed eyes sunk into dark pools of mascara.

"Hell, girl, why d'you even bother with me?" Sitting up, she sipped the strong, black brew. "After what I done to you, givin' you up to such a god-awful rough life . . ."

"Playing on my sympathy won't work, Francine." Jess found her mother's robe and draped it around her shoulders. "It was freezing last night. You could've died of hypothermia if we hadn't found you in that trailer. And you're on probation, for heaven's sake! You're lucky Ben didn't take you straight back to jail!"

"Uh-oh!" Francine looked startled. "Am I in trouble with the law?"

"You could be. But Ben said he'd give you a pass if you stayed sober and went to your AA meetings. The next one's on Tuesday, that's tomorrow night."

Francine muttered what sounded like a curse.

"Don't give me that." Jess was doing her best to show tough love. "Branding Iron Breakfast is set to open this weekend. That can't happen if the cook is drunk or in jail.

So get up and put yourself together. We need to take the posters around and get them up today. The first place we'll be going is the hardware store."

At the mention of the hardware store, Francine brightened a little, as Jess had hoped she would. Grumbling about her aching head, she shuffled into the bathroom. Moments later Jess heard the shower running. While her mother got ready to go, Jess made some toast, then spent some time with her laptop. On Saturday, they'd gotten Wi-Fi in the house. Jess was already using it to track her bank balance and check out supplies for the restaurant. The customers would appreciate having it too.

After an hour Francine appeared, made up, coiffed, and wearing a fresh outfit. Only her eyes betrayed the kind of night she'd had as she downed another cup of coffee, then helped Jess gather up the posters and load them in the car.

At the hardware store, she insisted on getting out and taking the poster inside. Hank took it from her.

"Branding Iron Breakfast. That's a dandy name," he said.

"We'll add the bed part when the place is ready for overnighters." Despite her hangover, Francine managed a sparkling smile. "Have you got a place to put our poster?"

"I'll stick it right in the corner of the front window where everybody will see it," Hank said.

"This gets you a free breakfast if you'll stop by," Francine said. Jess flashed her a surprised glance. Where had that come from? But never mind, Hank had been good to them. He deserved a treat.

"Do you like that man as much as I think you do?" Jess asked her mother as they drove away.

"Back in the day, I almost married him," Francine said. "But then your father came along, and that was that. Hank found somebody else, and we never got together again. Now we're just friends."

"Are you sorry you didn't marry him?" Jess asked.

"In a way, maybe. Hank would've given me a decent life and probably a pack of youngsters. But then I wouldn't have had you, would I? Honey, you're worth everything I went through."

Jess blinked away a tear, remembering the story Clara had told her. "Promise me you'll go to your AA meeting tomorrow night," she said.

"I'll go, honey. But only if you go with me."

By the time Tuesday night came, Francine was already dragging her heels. "Oh, sweetie, I don't need that soap opera stuff," she argued. "I'm not like those other folks. I can quit anytime I put my mind to it."

"Would you rather go back to jail?" Jess shook her car keys under her mother's nose. "Get your coat. We're going if I have to hog-tie you and throw you in the trunk!"

Muttering all the way, Francine allowed herself to be herded into Jess's car.

For a town as small as Branding Iron, the AA meeting in the basement of the church was surprisingly well attended. Jess counted sixteen chairs set up in a circle, with a few more seats in a short row behind. Most of the people there—twice as many men as women—recognized Francine. They greeted her and invited her to sit.

Unsure whether she was even allowed to be there, Jess took a seat in the back row. She'd never attended an AA meeting, but she'd seen enough on TV to know what to expect.

The leader, a man in his thirties, greeted the group. Then, one by one, each person rose and introduced themselves in the customary way. Francine was last to stand. When her turn came, she rose shakily, as if dreading the moment. "I'm Francine," she said. "And I'm . . . an alcoholic."

"Hi, Francine," the group echoed as she sank back to her chair.

The leader rose. "Francine, somebody has offered to be your new sponsor. He said he'd be here tonight, but I don't see . . ."

His words trailed off as a door opened at the back of the room. Jess checked the urge to turn around and look at the new arrival. But she didn't need eyes to recognize the heavy, uneven tread of footsteps or the familiar male voice that spoke from just behind her.

"Sorry to be late, folks. I'm Hank. And I'm an alcoholic."

Hank walked Jess and Francine to their car in the church parking lot. The AA meeting had gone well. Hank's support was already making a difference for Francine. He would be coming by the house to pick her up for the Thursday meeting.

"Almost like a date!" Francine primped and giggled as Jess pulled out of the parking space.

"Did you know Hank had a drinking problem?" Jess asked.

"I never thought much about it," Francine mused. "But it makes sense that a man who lost both his leg and his wife would turn to drink. He hasn't come all the time, which is why I've never run into him here. But he told me the meetings have helped keep him sober for the past five years."

"If he can do it, so can you."

"Don't lecture me, girl. I've heard it all." Francine grinned. "You know, I wouldn't be surprised if that hot sheriff of yours had a hand in this. How else would Hank have known I'd be there?"

"Don't look at me." Jess dismissed the question with a shrug, but she couldn't help thinking her mother was right.

It would be like Ben to pull a few strings and get Hank to the meeting as Francine's sponsor.

"Speaking of the sheriff—" Francine gave her a playful nudge as Jess turned onto their street. "What's his big, black pickup doing parked in front of our house?"

The truck was indeed Ben's. Wondering if something was wrong, Jess pulled into the driveway and jumped out of the car. Light filtered through the closed shutters on the front window.

"What do you think's goin' on?" Francine caught up with her at the foot of the steps.

"I don't know. Stay here till I check it out."

Maybe there'd been a break-in and a neighbor had called the sheriff. Jess braced herself for bad news as she tested the door, found it unlocked and eased it open.

"Surprise! Merry Christmas!" Ethan came bounding out of the hallway with Ben stepping into sight behind him. For an instant, Jess didn't realize what the fuss was about. Then she saw it—the Christmas tree, ablaze with lights, standing in front of the living room window.

"Oh, my stars!" Francine clapped her hands like a delighted little girl. "Will you look at that? It's gorgeous! And that pine aroma! The whole room smells like Christmas!"

Jess stared at the tree. It wasn't much over five feet tall. But its shape, down to the smallest branch, was perfect. Ben, she knew, wouldn't have settled for anything less. The tree was set on a sturdy crate covered with a white sheet that wrapped like snow around the trunk and the stand. The lights and ornaments looked old and well used. But that only added to the tree's beauty.

"This was Ethan's idea," Ben said. "We've always had our tree ready by the time he showed up for Christmas. This year he wanted to decorate a tree himself. So, since we already had one at our house . . ."

His words trailed off as his eyes met Jess's—the contact

so warm that she could feel the heat between them. Was this love or just sizzling physical chemistry? Whatever it was, the intensity was enough to send tingles all the way to her toes.

Dropping her gaze, she found her voice. "Thank you both. I didn't realize how much we needed a tree in here until you gave us one. I'd be happy to pay you for it."

Ben gave her a shake of his head. "No way! Consider it a housewarming gift. Every home needs a little Christmas!"

"Then let's have more! We need music!" Francine dashed into the bedroom. A moment later, the rollicking strains of "Here Comes Santa Claus," the old Gene Autry version, boomed through the house.

Dancing to the beat, Francine reappeared from the hall. "Now, we gotta have treats! Hot cocoa with marshmallows coming up!"

Jess hurried into the kitchen to lend a hand. Francine, while filling the kettle, gave her a wink. "See, I told you our sheriff had stars in his eyes. If you let that man get away, you're crazy, girl. God doesn't make 'em any better than Ben Marsden."

In the time it took to heat the water, gather the cups and mix the ingredients, the cocoa was ready. Jess carried the steaming cups to the dining room table on a tray, and they all sat down to enjoy. Sergeant Pepper padded his way under the table to rub against their legs.

"How did you two get in here?" Jess asked Ethan. "I know I locked the doors."

The boy exchanged a mischievous look with his father. "It's a secret," he said. "I promised not to say."

"We sort of broke in," Ben said, leaving the answer at that.

"We found the decorations in a box at the back of our closet," Ethan added. "Dad says he remembers them from when he was a little boy."

"Then they must be very precious," Jess said. "I'll make sure you get them back after the holidays."

When they finished their cocoa, Ethan got up to help Francine take the cups to the kitchen, leaving Jess alone with Ben for a moment.

"You're family's done so much for me," she said. "I can't thank you enough."

"You already have." Ben's eyes held hers again, but gently this time. "Tonight was for Ethan. He needed an adventure. The boy's been down ever since he learned his mother has married again and he's headed for boarding school."

"Oh, Ben!" Jess shook her head, feeling his pain. "If there's anything I can do—"

"All you can do is what Ethan has been doing—pray."

Ethan and Francine came out of the kitchen, putting an end to the conversation. "If you want to make a night of it, we can make popcorn, bring the TV in here and put in a video," Francine offered. "I've got *It's a Wonderful Life* packed away somewhere. It shouldn't take me long to find it."

"It's way past Ethan's bedtime," Ben said. "I need to get him home. But it does sound like fun. Maybe another night."

By the time they'd said their good nights, it was after ten. Francine had stayed up to watch TV in her room, but after a busy day and an emotional night, Jess was exhausted. She got ready for bed, then lay on the camp cot staring up into the darkness, too wired to fall asleep.

The bed frame from the garage stood propped against one wall. Maybe tomorrow she'd go online, order a mattress set from some big chain store and have it delivered. A decent bed might help her get the rest she needed.

But it wasn't the bed that was keeping her awake tonight. It was her worries, tumbling over and over like water in an old-fashioned millrace. Ethan, the business, her mother's recovery, and her relationship with Ben—so many dreams that could come true or turn into nightmares.

Like the little Christmas tree, tonight had glowed with promise. But the past had taught her that promises could be illusions and that one bit of bad luck could send her hopes toppling into ruin.

Right now, however, she needed to stop worrying and get some rest. Closing her eyes, she fixed her thoughts on the memory of Ben's face and the way he'd looked at her tonight—the hunger in his eyes, the unspoken tenderness . . .

At last she drifted into slumber.

Hours later, the jangle of her cell phone jarred her out of a deep sleep. Heart slamming, she sat up. The room was pitch-black, the house quiet except for the insistent ringing. What was it? Could Francine have stolen out in the night? Could something have happened to her?

The phone shrilled again. Jess's fumbling fingers found it on the nightstand and pressed the answer button. "Hullo?" she muttered.

"Hi, baby. It's me."

The unctuous voice was the very last one Jess had expected—or wanted—to hear. A sick dread welled in her throat. She forced herself to speak.

"Gil? Where are you?"

"I'm out, that's where. Early release for good behavior. And the number one thing on my list has been tracking down my wife." He chuckled. "Sounds like I've found her. Are you alone, or have you found a new bed partner to replace me?"

"That's none of your business," Jess snapped. "And I'm not your wife. The divorce was final years ago."

His cold laugh held no humor. Jess could only imagine what five years in prison would do to a man, and how much he would hate the woman whose testimony had helped put him there. But she mustn't let him scare her. She mustn't let him see her as a victim.

"How did you find me?" She struggled to keep her voice from shaking.

"I've got friends. They've kept track of you for me. No way you could run far enough or fast enough to get lost."

"What is it you want, Gil? If it's money, forget it."

"I know you aren't rich, baby. And I know I won't be gettin' any of what I really want—not from you, at least. I just called to let you know I was free and still thinking about you."

His words made her skin crawl. She wanted to fling the phone against the wall and smash it to pieces. But no, Jess reminded herself, the more she could learn from her ex, the less likely she was to be caught off guard.

"So, do you have plans? What are you going to do?" She willed herself to stay calm.

"Don't rightly know yet. Guess I could always go back to selling insurance." He laughed at his own bitter joke. "For now I'm just checking in with old friends to say hello. Maybe I'll drop by and pay you a visit one of these days."

Dread ran an icy finger down Jess's back. She'd changed her phone number early on, but he'd had no trouble finding the new one. Did he know where she lived as well, or was he waiting for her to give him a clue?

"Don't bother to come by," she said. "I wish you well, but I don't have anything to say to you."

His laugh was razor-edged. "Well, maybe I have a few things to say to you. And maybe you need to hear them. See you around, baby."

He ended the call. Jess was left sitting up in bed, her body quivering as she clutched the phone. Until now, she'd put

Gil behind her, like a bad dream. She hadn't given much thought to his getting out of prison, or what he might do to her given the chance. But she had to think about it now.

It didn't make sense that he would harm her physically. Gil was a white-collar criminal. He was mean, but he wasn't stupid. An assault charge would land him right back in prison. As for murder . . . Jess choked back a wave of nausea. If he was crazy enough to have her killed, or do it himself, he would be the number one suspect. He had to know he'd never get away with it.

In any case, Jess reminded herself, he'd be on parole. If he got caught leaving Missouri, he could be locked up again. Surely he wouldn't take that risk.

Gil was playing a mind game, she surmised—not unlike the control games he'd played when they were married. He wanted to reach out and make her uncomfortable, to unsettle her, even to terrorize her.

Should she tell Ben?

Not yet, she decided. Between his job and his son, Ben had enough worries. Besides, as sheriff, what could he do? Gil had paid his debt to society. Unless he began stalking her or threatening her, the man wasn't doing anything illegal.

She wouldn't tell Francine either. Her mother was liable to fly into a protective panic and go running to Ben with the story. For now, Jess decided, silence was the best option. Gil would do his best to push her buttons. No doubt he would call her again, maybe even show up if he knew where she lived. But he could rattle her only if she let him. And that wasn't going to happen.

She was no longer the submissive little wife he'd browbeaten and bullied for years. She could stand up for herself—and she would.

* * *

The following Saturday morning, at 7:30 AM, Branding Iron Breakfast opened its doors for business. The tables were set. The tree was glowing. Christmas music drifted from Francine's boom box. A bayberry candle scented the room. The first batch of coffee was brewed, the bacon fried and warming in the oven, the eggs ready for whisking, the pancake batter mixed, and the bread ready for popping into the toaster.

But now it was nearly eight. Where were the customers?

Jess and Francine stood at the newly installed storm door, their breaths clouding the frigid glass. The morning was overcast. An icy wind whistled through the bare trees. It wasn't the best of days, but the empty chairs and tables could hardly be blamed on the weather.

Jess tried to ignore her gnawing worry. "I thought for sure the free coffee would bring people in," she said. "Maybe we should've paid for an ad on the radio."

Francine sighed. "Maybe we shouldn't have opened so early. It's Saturday, you know. Some folks like to sleep late."

"You're probably right. For now, all we can do is wait and hope." Jess was nursing a headache. She'd been too nervous about the opening to sleep last night. To make matters worse, Gil had called her again at two AM, just to pull her strings. Refusing to play his game, she'd hung up on him and turned off her phone; but the call had left her with a knot in her stomach. If her ex-husband could find a way to ruin her life, he'd do it in a New York minute, laughing all the way.

Why did this have to happen now, right when she had so much to lose?

"Look!" Francine nudged her, snapping her attention back to the present. Three figures, bundled against the cold, were coming up the walk. Only when they got to the door and began to peel off their wraps did Jess recognize Connie, Silas and Katie.

While Francine dashed back to the kitchen, Jess welcomed them in. "My goodness!" Connie unwound her scarf and hung it on the coat rack. "Are we the first ones here? I thought the place would be packed by now."

"It's early yet." Jess's words came out breathless. "Have a seat. The menu's on the chalkboard. Do you want to sit at the big table or one of the small ones?"

"The big one," Connie said. "Maybe we'll get some nice company."

Jess took their coats, then darted into the kitchen for fresh coffee and toast. She came out again just as Ben, Clara and Ethan walked in the door. As Ben took his mother's coat and helped her to a chair at the big table, he caught Jess's eye. His secret smile buoyed her spirit. But she had no time to savor the feeling. More customers were coming up the front steps.

Ben sipped his coffee and watched Jess flit from table to table, taking orders, chatting with guests, serving meals and clearing away dishes. He couldn't have been more proud of her. She'd taken on this old house, and her alcoholic mother, and created something good.

Branding Iron Breakfast was a hit. True, some customers, like Silas's family and Hank, who'd wandered into the kitchen, had come here out of friendship. But there were plenty of strangers here too. Everybody seemed to be enjoying the cozy atmosphere and tasty food. Who would've guessed that Francine was such a terrific cook?

Ben's gaze followed Jess as she stacked dishes on a tray and carried them to the kitchen. She'd mentioned having worked as a waitress, and the lady was a pro. But as he watched her, he couldn't shake the feeling that something was wrong.

Some stress over the new business would be natural, but this was more. Her smile seemed forced, her beautiful eyes slightly averted, as if focused on some dark inner secret. Something was bothering her. If he could find out what it was, maybe he could help, or at least offer some understanding.

Shane Taggart had just come in with his family and taken a seat at one of the tables. Last year Ben's best friend had been ready to sell the family ranch and tour the country on his motorcycle. Then spunky, widowed Kylie, with her two children, had shown up, and Shane had fallen like a ton of bricks. Now, with Kylie expecting, Shane had never looked happier.

Was the same thing possible for him, Ben wondered. He'd met a wonderful woman, and he'd caught himself imagining what it would be like waking up to her sweet, sexy face every morning. But no, he wasn't Shane. He was still saddled with baggage from one unhappy marriage. Add the weight of concern for his mother and son, and he wouldn't have the time or energy to satisfy a wife. The last thing he wanted was another disaster like his first marriage.

Ben glanced at his watch. Today was a workday for him. Ethan and his mother had finished their plates. It was time he took them home and reported in. But first he needed to pay.

Catching Jess's eye, he flashed his credit card. She shook her head emphatically and mouthed the words, *Not on your life!*

Since arguing with her would create a scene, Ben let it go. Pocketing the card, he mouthed *Thanks*, then helped his mother up and got her coat. He would settle with Jess later. Maybe that would give him a chance to find out what was bothering her.

At the door, he turned to say good-bye and thank her again. But Jess had vanished into the kitchen.

It was 10:35 when Jess shooed the last customer out the door and sank onto the overstuffed couch she'd picked up at an estate sale. Her feet ached and her arms were sore from carrying heavy trays and plates, but the satisfaction she felt was worth the pain. Branding Iron Breakfast was off to a great start.

Francine walked out of the kitchen, drying her hands on her apron. She looked exhausted, but her face wore a grin. Arriving at the couch, she gave Jess a resounding high-five. "By glory, we did it, girl! We're in business!"

"Sit down," Jess said. "I'll get us some coffee if there's any left."

"There should be." Francine collapsed on a chair. "I made enough to fill a bathtub."

Jess filled two cups, added cream and brought them back to the coffee table, along with a saucer of leftover toast. "I'm glad I agreed to be on the Christmas Ball committee," she said. "The ladies supported me by showing up and bringing their families—all except Maybelle, that is. I wonder why she didn't come."

"Maybelle Ferguson?" Francine laughed. "Honey, Maybelle wouldn't be caught within a country mile of this place. She's never forgiven me for stealing her boyfriend."

Jess's hand splattered coffee on the table. She stared at her mother. "Her boyfriend? Are you talking about—?"

"About your father?" Francine grinned. "That's right. Maybelle was older than I was, and she was a looker in her day. She thought she had that handsome redheaded cowboy roped and tied. But she was wrong. If Maybelle had had her way, you wouldn't be here."

"And maybe you would've wed Hank." Jess spoke to mask a surge of emotion. She had Clara's story, but until now Francine had revealed next to nothing about the man she'd loved.

"Maybe," Francine said. "Maybe not. But Maybelle hung on to her anger for years. She let it turn her into a sour old maid."

"Poor Maybelle." Jess had believed the woman was just a natural snob. So much for snap judgments. In view of what she'd just learned, Maybelle's goodwill in inviting her to help with the tickets was an act of true generosity. And that night in the Christmas tree lot, when she'd caught Maybelle eyeing her—maybe she was just thinking of how her own daughter might have looked.

"I'm glad we decided not to open on Sundays," Jess said, changing the subject. "I'll be needing tomorrow just to recover."

"The weekdays are liable to be slower, with folks stopping by for a quick coffee," Francine said. "But next Saturday could be the biggest day yet. The Christmas parade starts at eleven. People will be in town for that, and for the Cowboy Christmas Ball that night. Too bad we don't have bedrooms ready."

"That was the plan. But now, looking at how much work we have left to do, we would never have made it."

"I've got an idea for Saturdays that could save us both," Francine said. "Why not get some warming pans and set up a buffet table. We could charge a flat price for one time through with a plate. No menu. No order taking. Just keeping the table stocked, refills on coffee and cleanup when folks are done."

"Great idea. The setup would take some work, but it would save everybody time. And speaking of cleanup—" Jess cast her gaze around the dining room. "This place isn't going to get spick-and-span by itself." She pushed to her feet and had begun to wipe the tables when a sudden question struck her.

"Francine, I never thought to ask you. Are you going to the Christmas Ball?"

Francine was headed for the kitchen. She paused in the doorway. "You bet I am," she said. "I go every year. My costume's packed away in one of those boxes we brought over from the trailer. Wait till you see me in it!"

While Francine cleaned up the kitchen, Jess polished the tables and swept the floor. Maybe by next weekend they could hire a teen to wash the dishes and help with the cleanup. That would make everything easier.

Where had the time gone? It seemed like only yesterday when her car had broken down on the way to Branding Iron. Now she had a business with her mother as a partner. She had friends, and she'd met a man who made her heart sing. Once a stranger, she was beginning to feel as if she belonged here.

The Cowboy Christmas Ball was just a week away. It was only a party, Jess told herself. But she couldn't help feeling as if the night would mark a turning point in her life, when everything would fall into place—or shatter into dust.

Chapter Sixteen

As usual, Saturday morning had kept Ben busy. He'd done follow-up interviews with the husband and wife on a domestic call, checked evidence on a break-in at the local convenience store, and pacified the farmer who'd caught a pair of teenage lovers in his barn last night—not exactly the stuff of TV crime drama, but it was all part of keeping this small community a safe place to live.

Every case required a written report, which Ben liked to fill in while his memory was fresh. By the time he found a moment to rest at his desk and have a fresh cup of coffee, it was almost two in the afternoon.

Jess had been on his mind all morning. Her nervous look had stayed with him since breakfast—especially after a sudden hunch had struck him like a thunderbolt. The more he thought about it, the more convinced he'd become that his hunch was right.

Now, alone in his quiet office, he finally had a chance to check it out.

Bringing up the NICS site on his computer, he found the link to the file on Gilbert McConnell. His jaw tightened as he read down the page to the most recent entry.

Ten days ago, McConnell had been granted early release and was on parole.

Ben swore under his breath. He would bet ten years of his life the bastard had already tracked down Jess, contacted her and was out to settle the score. His parole would require that he stay in Missouri. But if McConnell was obsessed with revenge, that might not be enough to keep him there.

The protective urge that rose in Ben was as overpowering as an earthquake. His woman was in danger, and there was nothing he wouldn't do to keep her from harm. Somehow, over the past weeks, she'd become precious to him—so precious that he could no longer imagine a future without her in it.

Damn it, he loved her!

It didn't matter that she had a dysfunctional mother, a criminal ex-husband and a scandalous past. It didn't matter that he was already burdened with as much responsibility as he could handle. He hadn't chosen to fall in love. But love had chosen him, and there it was.

Ben had never been one for relationship games. Now that he was sure of his feelings, the next step would be to make sure Jess felt the same way about him. If the answer was yes, he would do whatever it took to make her his, he hoped, with an engagement ring on her finger. Once they made it that far, they could figure out the complications of family and housing over the next few months.

There were bound to be some rough patches ahead. But with both of them trying, they just might be able to make this crazy thing work.

She would be at the Christmas Ball. So would he. That could be a good time to lay his heart on the line.

Right now, however, his first priority was keeping her safe.

Unless he'd misread her signals, Jess knew her husband

was out of prison. It troubled Ben that she hadn't told him. But she was a proud little thing. Maybe she didn't want him to worry. Maybe she thought she could handle McConnell herself. But she was wrong. Ben had seen people murdered for less than what she'd done to that man.

His call to her phone went immediately to voice mail. He was waiting to try her again when a call came in about a biker gang threatening folks at Rowdy's Roost. With Jess still on his mind, Ben grabbed a deputy and headed for his SUV. He was liable to be tied up most of the afternoon. But maybe Jess's problem would be best handled in person. After work, he would drop by the house, tell her what he'd learned and let her know he was looking out for her.

He could only guess how much she'd told her mother, but Francine needed to be kept in the loop. For Jess's protection, and for her own, she needed to know everything.

Toward the end of his shift, he called his mother to check on Ethan and see if they needed anything. Ethan, he learned, was at the neighbors' playing video games. Meanwhile, his mother had unpacked Ellie's Christmas Ball gown, pressed it and basted up the hem. If he wouldn't mind dropping it off to Jess, then she could try it on to make sure it would fit.

Welcoming the added excuse to see Jess, Ben picked up the dress after work and drove to her house. He found Jess in a paint-spattered sweatshirt and rubber gloves, polishing the table and chairs.

"Don't you ever relax?" he asked, laying the gown over the back of the couch.

"That'll have to wait till I'm rich," she said, giving him a smile.

"Where's Francine?"

"Taking it easy. Fixing all those breakfasts wore her out." She gave him a knowing look. "That was our deal.

She cooks, I do the grunge work. Now that you've tasted her cooking, you'll have to admit it was a good idea."

"Did I hear my name mentioned?" Francine appeared in the hallway, wearing black stretch pants, a baggy red sweater and a muzzy look, as if she'd been napping. Her gaze fell on the gown. "Oh, that's lovely! That deep green will be gorgeous with your red hair, honey."

"My mother sent me here with orders to have you try it on, Jess," Ben said. "She's already ironed it and taken up the hem. If it doesn't fit, she wants it back so she can alter it."

"Oh dear, I could've done all that and saved her the work." Leaving the polish and the rag on the table, Jess stripped off her gloves and crossed the room to the couch. Her fingertips brushed the soft cotton velveteen. "It really is beautiful—almost too beautiful to wear."

"Go put it on," Francine said. "I want to see you in it."

Jess hesitated, then, picking up the gown as if it were a priceless treasure, she carried it down the hall, leaving Ben alone with her mother.

"Sit down, Francine. We need to talk." Ben motioned her to the couch. "I didn't just come to bring the dress."

"What is it?" she asked as he joined her. "You look as gloomy as an undertaker's hound."

Ben got right to the point. "How much has Jess told you about her ex-husband?"

"Just that she had a lousy marriage. If I ever run into that jerk, I'll black both his eyes."

"So she didn't tell you he'd gone to prison—mostly on her testimony?"

Seeing Francine's surprised look, Ben gave her a quick recap. "He just got out on parole. And I'm afraid he may be contacting Jess. He may even be planning to show up here."

"But why wouldn't she have told me?"

"Probably because she didn't want to worry you, or involve you in her problems. But I'm telling you now because I need your help."

"You got it. I'd fight man-eating tigers barehanded for that girl."

"Not quite that." Ben suppressed a smile. This was serious business. "I need you to help me convince her she's in real danger. And I need you to keep your eyes open. If you notice somebody strange hanging around, or even a change in Jess's behavior, I want you to let me know."

"You're saying you want my mother to spy on me?" Jess stood in the entrance to the hallway, her eyes blazing.

Ben stifled a groan, knowing he was in trouble. "How long have you been there?"

"Long enough. I needed help with the zipper." She stood rigid as a poker, the dark green, lace-trimmed gown hanging off one shoulder. Francine had been right about the color. Even mad enough to spit lead, Jess looked ravishing.

"I'll get it." Francine rose and hurried to step behind her and pull up the zipper tab. "There, honey. Oh my, it fits like it was made for you."

Quivering with outrage, Jess flung her words at him. "I appreciate what you've done for me, Ben. But this time you've crossed the line. Checking up on me, managing me behind my back, asking my mother to report to you—I won't have it! I'm not a child! I can take care of my own problems—and that includes my ex-husband!"

Ben stood and took a step toward her. "All I want is to keep you safe, Jess. You think you know your ex, but you don't know how prison can change a man. He could hurt you. Damn it, he could kill you!"

She drew herself up. Her gaze was icy. "Please thank your mother for the dress. Tell her it's perfect, and that I'll have it cleaned before I give it back. Now please leave before I say something I'll regret."

Ben turned away and walked toward the door. He knew better than to hope Jess would crumble and call him back. She was a tough woman, scarred by past hurts. Trust didn't come easy to her. And once that trust was broken, she would be hard-pressed to forgive.

His intentions had been the best. But he tended to be overprotective of those he loved, and this time he'd gone too far. Now he could only walk away, give her time and hope to God he hadn't lost her for good.

The days of the week had crawled past—leaden days for Ben, without Jess in his life. Every day, he'd checked McConnell's parole record on line. So far, Jess's ex seemed to be behaving himself. He'd reported to his P.O. when required. He'd even applied for a sales job. Everything looked good. Too good. Ben could feel it in his bones—the bastard was up to something.

On Wednesday he'd stopped by Branding Iron Breakfast for a cup of coffee, hoping Jess would have something to say to him. She'd been outwardly pleasant, but he could feel the chill in her manner as she filled his cup and hurried away to serve other customers. Knowing better than to push her, he'd finished his coffee, laid a bill under the saucer and left.

At least she was all right, and her new business was doing well. Still, he worried about her safety. He could only hope Francine would warn him at the first sign of danger.

But Jess was far from the only worry on his mind. His time with Ethan was draining away like the sand in an hourglass. Boston and boarding school loomed closer every day, the prospect as ominous as a prison sentence. Ethan was doing his best to keep up a brave face, but he was so young, so scared of what lay ahead. Cheryl had already sent his airline ticket. Ben had bought himself a ticket for the same flight, so the boy wouldn't have to travel alone. Cheryl wouldn't be happy about his showing up and demanding to see the boarding school for himself, but it was the least he could do for his son.

Now it was Friday, the night before Branding Iron's Christmas celebration. Ben had taken Ethan to a movie, where they'd stuffed themselves with popcorn and hooted with laughter at the cartoon antics. Returning home, he'd shooed Ethan off to get ready for bed, then gone to his room to tuck him in.

"Sleep tight," he said. "Tomorrow's the parade and the Cowboy Christmas Ball. It'll be a big day."

"I know." Ethan lay back on the pillow, tousled and sleepy. "Dad, I'm still praying," he said.

"You do that." Ben rumpled his son's hair and left the room. Not that praying would do any good, he told himself. Boarding school in Boston was pretty much a done deal.

Ben rested fitfully that night, tossing and turning between the tangled sheets, his mind churning with unresolved worries. It was after midnight before he sank into a deep sleep—a sleep that was shattered a few hours later by the ringing of his cell phone.

His heart slammed. He was used to emergency calls at all hours, but what if this one was about Jess? What if her ex had shown up?

He grabbed the phone. "Hullo?"

"Ben . . . it's Cheryl." She sounded as if she'd been crying.

"What is it? Are you all right—you and the baby?"

There was a pause. "Yes. I'm—we're—fine. It's nothing like that."

"Then what's wrong?"

"Ethan—" The name ended in a sob.

"He's fine. He's asleep. What's the matter?"

"It's Nigel. . . . I overheard him, talking to his father on the phone. The things he said—"

"Slow down. Just tell me."

Ben could hear her anguished breaths as she tried to compose herself. "He said that raising his own child was one thing. But he didn't want anything to do with . . . with another man's brat. That's what he called Ethan—a *brat!*"

"Go on." Ben felt his pulse quicken.

"He said he didn't want Ethan around at all—that he planned to keep him in boarding school till he was old enough to be on his own. And he's already filed papers to make sure Ethan won't get a cent of the family money. Ben, it killed me. I had no idea Nigel could be so . . . so hard-hearted. And now I've married him. I'm having his baby!"

"Why are you calling me, Cheryl?" Ben's heart was racing. He knew what he wanted to hear, but the words had to come from her.

Her breath sounded drawn through tears. "I love my son too much to raise him here, with a stepfather who can't stand the sight of him. Ethan has begged me to let him stay with you and go to school. Could you keep him, for now at least? We can work out the details later."

Ben wanted to shout for joy, but he kept his voice calm, his words measured. "I guess I could do that. Do you want me to tell Ethan, or would you rather break the news yourself? It's early here. You might want to wait."

"Yes. I should be the one to tell him. I'll call him in an hour. Thank you, Ben." She ended the call.

Too elated to go back to sleep, Ben stretched out in the bed and watched the first rays of dawn steal through the curtains. The reality was still sinking in. He had his Christmas miracle. Against all odds, Cheryl had changed her mind. Maybe Ethan's prayers had been answered after all.

Jess carried a fresh pan of scrambled eggs to the table and scooped them into the warmer, then raced back to the kitchen for more flapjacks. The Saturday breakfast buffet had turned out to be a great idea. People were streaming in, anxious to eat and get a spot to watch the Christmas parade. Instead of waiting to be served, they could pay, help themselves to whatever they liked at the table, eat and head out for Main Street.

By now Jess was getting to know more people in the town. She welcomed each customer, making it a practice to remember their names. With a smile, she greeted Hank, who'd closed his hardware store for the day. The Taggarts—Kylie, Shane and their family—were here too, along with Kylie's aunt Muriel and her husband. But there was one person her searching eyes couldn't find.

She'd been racked with regret since Ben walked out last week. He'd given her a chance to apologize later, when he'd come in for coffee, but she'd been too busy—and maybe too proud—to say much more than hello. Now, days had passed since the last time he'd called her. What if her show of temper had driven him away for good?

At least Gil had left her alone. She hadn't heard from him since last week, when she'd hung up on him. Could her ex-husband have gotten the message that she wanted nothing to do with him?

But she'd be foolish to believe that. Gil was out there somewhere, and it wouldn't be like him to forgive and forget. He was playing mind games again, that was all—and his silence was every bit as unsettling as his phone calls. For now, short of running away, all she could do was carry on with her life and keep a sharp lookout over her shoulder.

She was refilling a customer's coffee cup when Ben walked in the door with his son. She glanced up. The coffee she was pouring sloshed onto the placemat. With a murmured apology she sponged it up with a paper napkin. Why now, when she wanted to say all the right things, had her mind suddenly gone blank?

She gave them a smile and a nod. Both of them were laughing, their faces flushed with cold.

"We're celebrating," Ethan said, as she came over to greet them. "Mom said I could stay here with Dad this year. No boarding school."

"That's wonderful!" Her gaze met Ben's. "What changed her mind?"

"A miracle," Ben said. "There's no other way I can explain it." He seemed so genuinely happy, so natural, that Jess felt the tension dissolving between them. Her hopes fluttered and took wing.

"Where's Clara this morning?" she asked. "Is she all right?"

"Mother's fine. She just wanted to save her energy for the Cowboy Christmas Ball tonight. You're still going, aren't you?"

"I promised to get there early and help with the tickets. You know, you never did teach me the Texas two-step."

His dimple deepened. "No time now, but if you'll save me a dance or two, I can teach you on the spot."

"I'll hold you to that." Her cheeks warmed as his gaze held hers.

"Dad, I'm starving!" Ethan said.

"Here, get in line." Jess guided them toward the buffet table. "Since you're celebrating, this breakfast is on me, and don't you dare argue!"

Other customers were demanding Jess's attention, but as she hurried away, her tired feet could barely feel the floor. Maybe things would actually work out between her and Ben. Maybe tonight's Cowboy Christmas Ball would mark a turning point in her life—a step into a world where she finally felt accepted, safe and cherished.

Was that even possible? Or was she just a loser, clinging to romantic dreams that would never come true?

"Oh my, just look at you!" Francine clapped her hands as Jess stepped out of her room and did a playful pirouette to show off her gown. The green velveteen 1890s-style dress fit her perfectly, with its tiny waist, flaring skirt and small bustle caught up in back. The sleeves and bodice were edged with ecru lace that matched the ribbon in Jess's hair, which Francine had curled and pinned up in an old-fashioned style. High-button shoes would have completed the look, but Jess had settled for her low-heeled boots. They wouldn't show much, and at least they'd be comfortable.

"You look pretty good yourself," Jess said. "No—forget I said that. You look spectacular!"

Francine's burgundy satin saloon girl costume, trimmed with black lace, was perfection. With her platinum curls piled high, violet eyeshadow and a star-shaped beauty spot on her rouged cheek, she could have stepped straight out of a classic western movie. The effect was a little startling, but as Francine had explained, she dressed this way every year. The townspeople, even the ones who gossiped about her, would be disappointed if she showed up in a more subdued outfit.

Jess glanced at the wall clock. "I'd better be going. I promised Maybelle I'd be at the ticket table by six-thirty. You're welcome to come with me."

"No, I'll be fine," Francine said. "Hank's picking me up a little later, after the fun starts. I'll see you there—but wait. I have something for you. Call it an early Christmas present."

She hurried back to her bedroom, and Jess heard the sound of rummaging. A few minutes later she came back with a little velvet box, the kind that might hold a ring. "I've had this since before you were born," she said, holding it out. "I think it's time I gave it to you."

With unsteady hands, Jess took the box and raised the lid. Inside was a heart-shaped gold locket, about the size of her thumbnail. On one side was a tiny hinge, on the other a catch. A thin gold chain ran through a ring at the top.

"Open it," Francine said.

Jess pressed the catch. The halves of the locket parted to reveal the small photo that had been cut to fit and glued inside—the photo of a man in his twenties with fiery hair. A lump rose in Jess's throat. He looked like a young Clint Eastwood, lean-faced and square-jawed with challenging eyes and a reckless grin. There could be no doubt. For the first time ever, she was seeing Denver Jackson, her father.

"That's the only picture I have of him," Francine said. "But I don't need it anymore. I've got you, honey."

Tears welled. Moved beyond words, Jess blinked them away.

"Now turn around." Francine took the locket from Jess's hand. "Let me put it on you so you can wear it tonight."

"Are you sure I should?" Jess protested as the chain settled around her throat. "I couldn't bear to have anything happen to it."

"It'll be fine." Francine fastened the clasp. "Wear it for me—and for him. He would be so proud of you."

"Thank you." Jess hugged her mother, her heart bursting. "I've got to go," she said, turning away before she could break down. Slipping on her coat and grabbing her purse, Jess dashed out the door and drove to the high school gym.

Even at this early hour, the parking lot was busy. Some people were dropping off food for the buffet. Others had arrived early to help set up the dining tables and folding chairs. At the parking lot's far end, behind the school lunchroom, the local volunteer fire crew was preparing to carve the pit-barbecued beef. The aroma of slow-roasted prime Angus floated on the cold winter air.

The dusty black tour bus that had brought the band from Nashville filled the space next to the gym's back door. Jess had never heard of the Badger Hollow Boys, but Francine had assured her that the band, which had played here before, was first-rate. They were already setting up when Jess walked into the gym and paused to look around.

Half the gym floor was taken up by the buffet and the dining tables. The other half was for dancing and the band. The decorating committee had done their job earlier. A nine-foot Christmas tree, aglow with ornaments, stood at one corner of the dance floor. Twinkling lights, hung with tinsel, were strung from the basketball hoops. The air smelled of pine and home cooking.

"There you are! I was getting worried!" Maybelle, dressed like a prim schoolmarm with her hair in a bun, bustled over and began giving Jess her orders. "The table's over here by the door. Most people will have tickets—you're to take them and stamp their hands as they come in. For the ones who're paying at the door, the price is fifteen dollars for adults, ten for students, five for children under ten, and babies under two are free. Any questions?"

"Don't worry, I know how to make change. I'll be fine." Jess took her seat behind the table as Maybelle hurried off.

Jess enjoyed a few relaxing minutes, watching the band warm up and taking in the festive atmosphere. Then people started arriving—trickling in at first, then flooding through the doors of the gym. Most of them had tickets, but everybody needed to be hand-stamped with a Texas star symbol.

After the first half hour, the crowd coming inside began to thin. Francine and Hank had arrived. So had Clara, with Ethan. Jess had yet to see Ben. But if he was on duty, he might not have to come through the ticket line.

By now the ball was well under way. People in old-fashioned western dress were lining up at the buffet and feasting at the tables. A few couples had ventured onto the dance floor. The Badger Hollow Boys knew their old-time music. Their playing was lively but mellow.

Jess was watching the dancers, wondering if she could ever learn those steps, when she heard a voice at her elbow.

"What's a beautiful lady like you doing all alone?"

She glanced up to find Ben grinning down at her. He was dressed as a cowboy, his sheriff's badge pinned to his leather vest.

"So, have you arrested any bad guys tonight?" she joked.

"Hey, keeping order in this place is serious business. No guns allowed, no alcohol, no drugs, no party crashers and no rough stuff. Just because all I have to do is walk around and look tough, that doesn't mean I'm not working. But I haven't forgotten that dance you promised me."

Jess glanced toward the dance floor. "Better make it a slow one. I don't want to make a fool of myself. Anyway, for now, I need to stay here. A few people are still coming in."

"Can I get you a plate?"

"Food can wait. But something to drink would be nice."

"I'll get you some cold apple cider. Be right back."

Ben crossed the gym to the buffet table, glancing back to make sure Jess was all right. He'd kept his eye on her all evening. He knew she wouldn't agree to being babysat, but his danger instincts were on high alert. If her ex was going to make a move against her, tonight in this noisy, crowded place would be ideal. The Cowboy Christmas Ball had been advertised on the town's web site. For anyone with computer access, finding the time and place would be no problem. All the bastard would have to do was put on cowboy gear and show up.

Ben had scanned the crowd repeatedly, looking for any stranger who resembled Gil McConnell's mug shot. So far, the coast looked clear. Maybe he was being overprotective.

Returning with the cider, he found that his mother had just joined Jess at the ticket table. "Why not let me spell you while you take a break, dear?" she was saying. "I've done this job before. You could relax, maybe get some food."

"Or give me that dance you promised." Ben stepped up to the table and held out his hand. "Come on. The tune just starting is a Texas two-step. I can give you your first lesson."

After setting her cup on the table, he swept her onto the crowded dance floor. Warm, soft and fragrant, she fit into his arms as if her shapely body had been made just for him. With his hand at the small of her back, he guided her through the simple steps. *Quick, quick, sloooow, sloooow . . . Quick, quick, sloooow, sloooow.* After a few tries, she began to move well with him, matching his steps as he held her close.

From the dance floor, he could see Francine sitting with Hank. She gave him a grin and a wink before he turned his full attention back to Jess.

"See, that's not so hard, is it?" he murmured in her ear.

Laughing, she shook her head. Reflected Christmas lights danced in her eyes. It was now or never, Ben told himself.

"Jess, I've been thinking," he began.

"About what?"

He cleared his throat, feeling as awkward as a school-boy. "About you and me. I know we're both carrying a lot of baggage, but I like to believe we've got the start of something good. If you feel the same—"

The ringing cell phone in his pocket cut off his words. Checking the caller ID, he saw it was the 911 dispatcher. Talk about bad timing. "Sorry," he apologized to Jess. "I've got to take this."

"What is it, Lois?" he asked, turning aside.

"Somebody just called in an armed robbery at Rowdy's Roost. One gunman inside and a driver outside in a beat-up green pickup."

"I'm on my way." Ben had no choice except to do his job. He could only hope Jess would be all right. "We'll finish our dance later," he told her. "Stay here. Don't go anywhere till I get back."

Grabbing a nearby deputy for backup, he headed out to his SUV. Siren blaring and lights flashing, he floored the gas pedal and roared out of the parking lot.

Rowdy's Roost was on the far edge of town. A fast ten minutes later, they swung off the main road and onto the graveled drive. A half-dozen vehicles were parked outside the bar. There was no green pickup in sight.

"The place looks pretty quiet," the deputy observed. "The robbers must've lit out and gone."

"Stay here. I'll check it out." Taking the 9mm Glock he'd left under the seat, Ben climbed out of the SUV and walked to the closed door. "County Sheriff," he called out. "I'm coming in."

Pistol at the ready, he opened the door. The interior of the bar was dim and smoky. The bartender was polishing glassware. A few regulars sat on stools, drinking beer. From the back, the *clickety-click* of pool balls told Ben there was a game going on.

The bartender turned and looked at him. "Somethin' wrong, sheriff?"

"I got a call about a robbery out here."

The bartender shook his head. "Never happened. Maybe you got the wrong place. Or maybe somebody's prankin' ya."

"Maybe." Ben walked back outside, closing the door behind him. Something wasn't right. Had the 911 call been a joke, a mistake or something more sinister? "What the hell . . ." he wondered out loud.

The answer slammed him like a lightning bolt.

Jess!

Chapter Seventeen

As Ben rushed outside, Jess composed herself, walked back to Clara at the ticket table and pulled up an extra chair. "So much for the Texas two-step," she said, forcing a smile. "I was just catching on. Does this sort of thing happen often?"

Ben's mother laid a gentle hand on her arm. "I'm afraid it does, dear. Charging off to help people is part of Ben's job—something you'll have to get used to if you stay with him."

If you stay with him.

Had Clara meant those words the way they'd sounded? Stunned into momentary silence, Jess felt the color warm her cheeks.

"I may be speaking out of turn," Clara continued, "but I've seen how much Ben cares for you. It's as if, for the first time since his divorce, he's come to life again." She gave a nervous little laugh. "I just want you to know that, if things work out between the two of you, it would make me very happy."

Jess was caught off-guard but then found her voice. "Thank you. You can't imagine how much that means." She hesitated, still struggling for the right words. "You've probably guessed that I feel the same way about him. Ben's the most wonderful man I've ever known. But there are so many complications . . ."

"Dear, there will always be complications," Clara said. "If you love each other, you'll find ways to work them out."

Jess lowered her gaze. Her hand crept up to finger the gold locket at her throat. For years she'd dreamed of being part of a real family, surrounded by warmth and love and acceptance. Now that the dream was almost close enough to touch, she found herself gripped by fear. Ben had never said he loved her, but before being called away, he'd come close. And now his gracious, respected mother had given the relationship her seal of approval. Did she know who Jess really was? Had Ben told her? Or would she be shocked to learn the truth?

Tonight, happiness was like a bubble, beautiful and shining but so frail that it could be shattered by a breath.

Glancing up, she could see Ethan making his way toward them. He'd spent most of the night playing games with his friends. Now it was getting late, and he'd had a long day.

"Hi, Jess." He stifled a yawn. "Have you seen my dad? He said he'd take me home when I got tired of playing."

"Your dad's off chasing some bad guys," Clara said. "I'm getting tired too. But I guess we'll have to wait till he gets back."

"I can drive you both home," Jess offered. "It'll only take a few minutes."

"That would be lovely," Clara said. "But you can't just go and leave the tickets and money here on the table."

"No problem," Jess said. "Maybelle is here somewhere. I'm sure she'll be glad to watch the table while I take you home. Hang on while I look for her."

Jess rose, scanning the gym for Maybelle in her dark,

matronly gown. But Maybelle was nowhere in sight. What she saw instead was a tall, burly stranger pushing straight through the crowd toward her.

For an instant her heart dropped. But the stranger wasn't Gil. This was a big-bellied man, dark-haired, with a mustache that skimmed his upper lip. He was wearing what appeared to be a state trooper's khaki uniform, complete with a holstered gun and a badge 'on the front pocket. But he wasn't local, and he hadn't come through the ticket line. Jess had never seen him before in her life.

However, he seemed to know who she was. The man had zeroed in on her like a missile on a target. She froze in place as he strode closer, one hand resting lightly on the butt of his pistol. Fear crawled up her throat. Had something happened? Was he here to warn her about Gil?

He stopped in front of her, looming so close that it made her skin crawl. With her eyes at the level of his chest, she could see his badge—a number and the insignia of the Missouri State Police. Jess willed herself to stay calm and stand her ground.

"Are you Jessica Ramsey?" His voice was loud and penetrating. His breath reeked of beer and garlic pizza. Sweat rings glued his shirt to his torso.

"What is it you want?" Jess demanded, aware that a hush had fallen over the dance floor. People were turning, listening.

"Jessica Ramsey," he boomed, "you're wanted in St. Louis for fraud and perjury. Turn around and don't cause any trouble. You're under arrest."

Unclipping a set of steel cuffs from his hand-tooled leather belt, he jerked Jess's arms behind her back and snapped the cuffs around her wrists. "You have the right to remain silent . . ." he began.

"Now, hold on a minute, officer!" Clara had shot to her feet. "You can't come in here and take someone without a warrant. My son is the sheriff. I demand that you wait until he gets here before you arrest this woman."

He shoved her out of the way. "Shut up and sit down, Grandma, before somebody gets hurt."

Yanking Jess's arms, he propelled her toward the nearest door. A startled hush had fallen over the crowd. Even the band had stopped playing.

Numb with shock and terror, Jess stumbled ahead of him. Back in St. Louis, she'd been absolved of any wrongdoing. Had Gil lied to the police to get her in trouble? And what about the people here who'd heard the charges—the people whose trust she'd tried so hard to earn? What were they thinking? Even if she got out of this mess, would they ever trust her again?

Ben knew the truth. Why did this have to happen when he wasn't here to help her?

Suddenly everything fell into place. There was no robbery. Ben had been lured away by a fake emergency so this could happen. And this crude, unkempt excuse for a police officer was no lawman. She wasn't being arrested. She was being kidnapped.

The crowd parted as he shoved her across the dance floor toward the front door. Even now that she understood the danger, Jess didn't dare to struggle or call for help. The man had a gun, and the gym was filled with innocent families. She couldn't risk any of them coming to harm.

They burst outside. Wind whipped Jess's skirt and tore at her carefully pinned hair. Her captor shoved her down the front steps, yanking her up just before she would have fallen. "I know you're not a real cop," she said as he dragged her toward a rusting Chevy sedan. "Let me go now and I'll give you a chance to escape. Otherwise you'll do time for aggravated kidnapping."

"Shut yer trap, lady," he snarled. "I might not be a real cop, but I got a real gun."

As they reached the Chevy, she started to struggle in earnest, trying to pull away from him. But with her hands cuffed behind her back, there was little she could do. He opened the car's rear door, pushed her head down and shoved her into the dark interior that smelled of sweat, cigarette smoke and stale tacos.

She caught herself on her knees. Even before her eyes adjusted to the dark, she knew she wasn't alone.

"Hi, baby." Gil's hand reached out and cupped her face, squeezing her cheeks until they hurt. "Hey, you're lookin' good."

She wrenched herself away from him. "You're crazy to come here!" she hissed. "Let me go and get out of here while you still can!"

His laugh was a humorless cackle, his face leaner and harder than she remembered. "You mean you aren't glad to see us? I thought that little stunt we pulled to get you out here was pretty clever. Ollie made a great cop, didn't he? Too bad that gun didn't have any bullets in it. He could've put the fear of God into those country rubes."

So the gun was empty. If she'd known that before Gil's friend got her in the car, she would've screamed and fought for all she was worth. But it might not have done any good—especially if the people who'd witnessed her "arrest" believed she was really a criminal.

Ollie had climbed into the driver's seat. The big man was visibly nervous, anxious to get away. With her wrists cuffed and two strong men in the car, Jess realized that her only chance was to try to stall them until Ben could get back here.

"Can't you at least take these cuffs off?" she pleaded. "They're hurting my wrists."

"Maybe later, baby." Gil slung an arm around her

shoulder. "But not till we hit the highway. We got a long way to go, and we want to keep you around awhile."

"Where are we going?" she asked, feeling sick inside.

"We're thinking Florida, maybe the Bahamas or the Caymans from there. Keep us happy and we might let you tag along. Otherwise—" He chuckled, letting the implication hang.

"Shut up, Gil!" Ollie, who was trying to start the car, was losing his temper. He cranked the starter again, then again. Jess prayed silently. If Ben was on his way back here, every second of delay could make a difference.

"Maybe it's the carburetor," Jess suggested, hoping he'd have to get out and raise the hood.

"Shut up, bitch!" Ollie gave the starter one last, furious crank, and the engine roared to life. "Let's get the hell out of here!"

He slammed the gears into reverse and floored the gas pedal. As the car shot backward, there was a sudden explosion of popping sounds. The Chevy lurched, shuddered and sagged toward the right, grinding along the asphalt as it came to a halt. Looking in the rearview mirror, Ollie swore.

"What the hell just happened?" Gil demanded.

"You're never gonna believe this," Ollie groaned. "Dolly Parton just shot out two of our tires!"

Jess twisted far enough to look out the side window. Standing a dozen yards from the car, in all her burgundy satin, platinum-curled, stiletto-heeled magnificence, was her mother, gripping a pistol in her lace-gloved hand.

What happened next was almost as amazing. People came pouring out of the gym and into the parking lot. They raced to their vehicles, started them up and drove, headlights bright and horns blaring, to surround the beat-up Chevy, cutting off all escape. Even if Ollie had been able to fire his gun, the lights would have blinded his aim.

"Now what?" Gil had slid down in the back seat, his head below the window.

"I have a suggestion," Jess said. "Unlock these cuffs and let me out of the car. No promises, but with luck I might be able to talk these good folks out of stringing you up."

She was just climbing out of the car when the shrill of an approaching police siren rose above the clamor. Lights flashing, the sheriff's SUV rocketed into the parking lot and screeched to a stop outside the circle of cars and trucks.

Tears sprang to Jess's eyes. Not only had these good-hearted people seen through the fake arrest—they'd trusted in her innocence and cared enough to rush to her rescue.

Within minutes the crisis was over. Ollie and Gil had been arrested, handcuffed and herded into the back of the SUV. The vehicles surrounding the Chevy were backing away, and Ben had Jess in his arms.

For a long moment they just held each other, both of them shaking. Then Ben turned to Francine, who was standing nearby, a broad grin on her face.

"What were you doing with that pistol, Francine?" he scolded her in mock seriousness. "You know guns aren't allowed at the Christmas ball."

She gave him a naughty wink. "Why, Sheriff, I hid it where no *gentleman* would think to look. Something told me it might come in handy."

"Hell, I didn't even know you owned a gun."

"That's because I don't have a permit." She laughed. "You wouldn't throw your future mother-in-law in jail for that, would you, now?"

Francine handed Ben the pistol and sashayed off toward the steps, where Hank waited for her. At the last moment, she turned back toward Jess.

"About that bet you wouldn't make with me, honey. Something tells me you would've lost."

"What bet was that?" Ben asked as Francine disappeared through the double doors of the gym.

"I'll tell you later. Right now, you need to get your prisoners to jail. You'll know where to find me."

As Jess stood on tiptoe to kiss him, a lacy white flake drifted down to melt on her cheek. Another flake fell, then more. It was snowing!

They were going to have a white Christmas!

Christmas night, one week later

Snow lay soft on the ground, glittering diamond white in the light of the risen moon. The sky was a glory of stars, the wind no more than a gentle whisper. It was the perfect ending to what had been a perfect Christmas.

In the Marsden house, Jess and Ben snuggled on the sofa, bathed in the light of the tree they'd decorated weeks ago. Clara and Ethan had gone to bed. Francine was off celebrating the holiday with Hank. At last the house was quiet.

Jess rested her head on Ben's shoulder. "Thank you for today," she said. "I'd forgotten what a real Christmas could be like."

He brushed a kiss along her hairline. "For me, it's a real Christmas because you're here."

"And because Ethan won't be packing to go to Boston." Her eyes rested on the shiny blue bicycle that stood against the wall. Ethan wouldn't be taking his bike outside until the snow melted. But when the walks and streets were clear, he would still be here in Branding Iron, racing around with his friends. That, as the boy had said, was the Christmas present he'd wanted most.

Ben's arm tightened around Jess's shoulders. "I have a question," he said. "What was that bet Francine mentioned, the one you refused to make? You said you'd tell me later."

"I did, and I'm still not ready."

"Why not?"

"Because I still don't know which of us would have won."

"Then I guess I'll just have to settle it myself." He shifted, reached under the edge of the couch and came up with a very small velvet box. "This is for you if you'll have it," he said, and raised the lid.

The diamond ring was rose gold and had the look of a family treasure. The stone was small but exquisite in its old-fashioned setting. "This is the ring my father gave my mother when he asked her to marry him," Ben said. "Now I'm asking you, Jess. I'm aware that we have a mountain of complications to work out between us, but I want to know you'll be there when it's all settled—and I want you to know that I'll be there for you." He slipped off the couch and dropped to one knee. "I love you, Jess. I think I've loved you ever since I saw you trying to push that car off the road. Will you be my wife and Ethan's mother?"

"Yes!" She flung her arms around him, pulling him up beside her. "A thousand times yes!"

He slipped the ring on her finger. It fit perfectly.

"Well then," he said, his eyes twinkling. "It looks like you would've lost your bet."

She stared at him. "My mother told you!"

He grinned. "She did. She said you wouldn't bet against my proposing before the end of the year."

"That's not how it was. I said I wouldn't bet at all!" Jess protested.

"Feisty little thing, aren't you?" he teased. "Are you going to be this contrary all the time?"

"Probably. If you want meek and submissive, you've got the wrong woman."

"I've got the only woman I want." Taking her in his arms, he captured her mouth in a kiss that went on and on, a kiss filled with passion, promise and hope for the future.

For both of them, it was the best Christmas ever.

Epilogue

Six months later

Dressed in Clara's ivory lace wedding gown, Jess stood in the hallway, waiting for the music to begin. At last the day had come. She was about to marry the love of her life.

She and Ben had agreed on a simple wedding. Branding Iron Bed and Breakfast may not have been the most elegant place for such an event; but today the old refurbished house overflowed with joy. With its freshly painted siding, green lawn, blossoming flower beds, and long-neglected pink floribunda roses climbing over the porch, it welcomed everyone who came to celebrate.

From where she stood, Jess could see into the dining room where the guests were waiting. The mothers had been seated in the front row. Clara wore soft, tasteful blue, Francine was spectacular in red, from her perky hat and flashing nails to her four-inch stilettos. Somehow the contrast seemed perfect.

Jess had phoned Ben's sister Ellie and asked her to be matron of honor. Ellie, tall, dark and even more beautiful than her photographs, had come just for the weekend, without her husband. Her polite but subdued manner suggested that her marriage troubles were far from over. Jess had known better than to ask personal questions. She could only hope that later, as they got to know one another, they might become close.

Ethan, a little superstar in a boy-sized tux, was greeting the guests and showing them to their seats. When the ceremony began, he would take his place beside his father as best man. After the wedding he'd be flying to Boston to spend a few weeks with his mother and new baby sister. But he'd be back here in plenty of time for summer fun before school started.

Now Ellie, her designer gown a slim mauve column, slipped in front of Jess to enter first. Glancing back over her shoulder, she gave a flicker of a smile. "Ready?"

Jess nodded, smiling back. Getting to this day had taken time and patience. The issue of Ben's mother had been settled when the smaller home next to Clara's went up for sale. Now it would be theirs—private but close by in case Clara needed anything. Jess's growing business was another complication. But Francine, now six months sober, had agreed to run the bed and breakfast from night to morning, with Jess taking over during the day. So far it was working out fine.

The music, a solo guitar arrangement of The Beatles' "Long and Winding Road," brought the guests to their feet. With Ellie gliding ahead of her, each of them carrying a single white rose, Jess walked out of the hallway and up the makeshift aisle to where Ben waited for her. The love in his eyes warmed her, as it had warmed her on that magical Christmas night when he'd asked her to marry him. How would their family change in the years ahead? How would they celebrate the Christmases to come? Only time would tell. But whatever the future held, they would face it together.